MURDER, BY GEORGE

A VERONICA WALSH MYSTERY

MURDER, BY GEORGE

JEANNE QUIGLEY

FIVE STAR

A part of Gale, Cengage Learning

GALE
CENGAGE Learning·

Farmington Hills, Mich • San Francisco • New York • Waterville, Maine
Meriden, Conn • Mason, Ohio • Chicago

GALE
CENGAGE Learning®

LIBRARY OF CONGRESS CATALOGING-IN-PUBLICATION DATA

Names: Quigley, Jeanne, author.
Title: Murder, by George : a Veronica Walsh mystery / Jeanne Quigley.
Description: First edition. | Waterville, Maine : Five Star Publishing, a part of Cengage Learning, Inc. 2016.
Identifiers: LCCN 2015050625 (print) | LCCN 2016005995 (ebook) | ISBN 9781432831431 (hardcover) | ISBN 1432831437 (hardcover) | ISBN 9781432831516 (ebook) | ISBN 1432831518 (ebook)
Subjects: LCSH: Women detectives—Fiction. | Murder—Investigation—Fiction. | Adirondack Mountains Region (N.Y.)—Fiction. | BISAC: FICTION / Mystery & Detective / Women Sleuths. | FICTION / Mystery & Detective / General. | GSAFD: Mystery fiction.
Classification: LCC PS3617.U5353 M87 2016 (print) | LCC PS3617.U5353 (ebook) | DDC 813/.6—dc23
LC record available at http://lccn.loc.gov/2015050625

Find us on Facebook– https://www.facebook.com/FiveStarCengage
Visit our website– http://www.gale.cengage.com/fivestar/
Contact Five Star™ Publishing at FiveStar@cengage.com

Printed in Mexico
3 4 5 6 7 20 19 18 17 16

For my sister, Patti, and my brothers, Bob and John.

ACKNOWLEDGMENTS

I am grateful to Tiffany Schofield, Gordon Aalborg, Deni Dietz, Alice Duncan, Nivette Jackaway, Tracey Matthews, and everyone at the terrific Five Star Publishing. Thank you for helping me realize my dream.

Thank you to my mother, Oona; my siblings, Bob, Patti, and John; their spouses, Marilyn, Jim, and Pam; my nephew, Kevin; and my nieces, Meaghan, Kelly, Shannon, and Colette. I must also thank the many members of my Quigley and Murphy family, all of whom eagerly and enthusiastically promoted *All Things Murder*. To my cousin Eileen Habacker and friends Charles Fortier and Laura Devlin, I am grateful for your insight and helpful recommendations on *Murder, by George*. I am also thankful for the friendship of Yvonne Kobayashi, Sandy Ferguson, Hannah Fenton, Maureen Ferrari, Joann Appleton, Melissa Reilly, Phil Antoine, Owen Mitchell, Mike Kuzma, Marianne Fairclough, Peter Brex, Erol Gureli, Brandon Baker, Maria Cruz, Michele Bunting, Pat Ix, Jackie Paez, Amanda Schiffmacher, and Renga Narayanan. And a warm thank-you to fellow Domer Laurine Megna-Davis for her gracious support.

When Five Star accepted *All Things Murder*, I joined a community of book lovers, among them Nancy Moskowitz, Sue Melnyk, Sandy Welsh, Lori Caswell, Lisa Haselton, Yvonne Hering, Kathy Kaminski, and Dru Ann Love. I thank you all for your kindness and generosity.

Acknowledgments

Finally, I deeply appreciate all the readers who welcomed Veronica Walsh, the residents of Barton, and me into the cozy world. Thank you!

CHAPTER ONE

"What are the odds we'll find something really valuable today, like a Picasso?"

"I'm a historian, not a mathematician," Mark said, "but my best guess is the odds in your favor are not very good."

"Well, a girl can dream."

Mark put his arm around my shoulder and pulled me close. "You never know. I can be completely wrong."

I kissed his cool cheek. "I haven't known you to be wrong yet."

We continued our stroll around the high school parking lot, casually surveying the goods available for sale at Barton's annual fall flea market. Many residents rented tables and sold possessions they no longer wanted, hoping the items would be things someone else just had to have. Mark and I had promised each other we would only look; neither of us needed more stuff. But, as Mark just said, you never know.

I pulled the collar of my jacket against my neck as the intermittent chilly breeze stirred again. Despite its briskness, the Saturday afternoon was gorgeous thanks to the radiant sunshine and the crimson and gold foliage on the trees bordering the lot. This was my first "full-time" autumn in Barton in more than three decades and I was enjoying it immensely. With the cancellation of *Days and Nights*, the soap opera I had acted in for thirty-plus years, I had returned to my hometown four months earlier for a respite while in search of a new role and ended up deciding to permanently stay in the village.

I spotted elderly sisters Ella and Madeline Griffin up ahead. Standing with them were their grandniece, Regina Quinn, and their friend Dotsie Beattie. Regina, a chef at The Barton Hearth, had recently moved to the village and into the Griffins' home. She held several cookbooks.

Madeline, forever cheerful, greeted us with an exuberant "Hello!"

Her older, more subdued, sister, Ella, said, "Hello, Veronica. Professor Burke."

"Good afternoon, ladies," Mark said.

"Are you making each other miserable yet?" Dotsie asked, chortling.

"At least three times a day," Mark replied with a wink.

"You love to stir things up, Dotsie," I playfully scolded.

"It keeps me young and others on their toes."

"That's a lot of cookbooks." I pointed at Regina's armload.

"Too many," Ella huffed. "Her room is so jam-packed with things the floor is going to collapse."

Regina smiled at her great-aunt. "Don't worry, Aunt Ella. I'll find a place to live soon and will get myself and my stuff out of your hair. But, you know, a chef can never have too many cookbooks. I found some great ones from the fifties."

"Does that mean we can expect a menu change at The Hearth?" Mark asked.

"Perhaps," Regina said with an arch of her eyebrow.

"We'll be the taste testers!" Madeline said. "We've been eating very well since Regina came to live with us."

"You're lucky to have a personal chef," I said.

Madeline glanced at a nearby table and exclaimed, "Mother's old letter box!" She walked to the table manned by Food Mart manager, Ned Fleming, and his wife, Irene.

"Hi, Miss Griffin," Irene said. She pursed her lips as her eyes nervously darted from Madeline to the wooden box. "I hope you don't mind we're selling it."

"Of course not, dear. It's a simple box. I remember giving it to your Amanda a few years ago when Ella and I were in spring-cleaning mode."

"Amanda still talks about how sweet you are," Irene said, "and how you were a great piano teacher."

"Amanda was a gifted student."

"The girls simply outgrew the box," Ned said. "But they did make great use of it. When they were younger, they stored their crayons and finger paints in it. Now that they've moved on to makeup and nail polish, they insist they need fancy, expensive bags to hold it all."

Ella, who was standing next to me, took in a sharp breath. "That was my mother's and it was used to store *crayons*?" She checked the price sticker on the box. Another affront. "Ten dollars?"

I held my breath, waiting to see if the octogenarian would snatch the box and dash off to an antique restorer. When Ella didn't, I exhaled and moved to the table to get a closer look at the box.

The box was about the size of a shoebox. Made of cedar, it had a lift lid and a drawer at the bottom with a well-worn knob. A lock above the knob required a very small key. A lovely swirl design etched on the cover was the sole decoration.

"Professor Burke!"

I turned to check out the caller and spotted two men and a woman, all in their early thirties, walking toward us. The woman and one of the young men held hands.

Mark greeted the group and turned to me.

"Veronica. I want you to meet two of my former students, Jack Sweeney and Scott Culverson. Guys, this is Veronica Walsh."

A bland introduction, yes. After four months of dating, Mark and I still hadn't figured out the proper terminology for introducing each other. We agreed that "boyfriend" and "girlfriend" didn't fit people in their fifties. Not to mention it seemed a ridiculous way for Mark to introduce me to his academic friends and colleagues at Arden College. Lady friend just didn't sound right. Leading man was too corny given my acting career. "Companion" sounded like a live-in health aide or a person who accompanied one to family functions. And labels didn't seem to matter much anyway, since we had many mutual friends and acquaintances before we got together and they all knew when we became a couple without any announcement or fanfare.

"Nice to meet you," I said as I shook hands with Jack, the tall one, and Scott.

A brown-haired, stocky fellow, Scott had an easy grin and an engaging flash in his dark eyes. "It's a pleasure to meet you. This is my girlfriend, Isabel."

"Hello." Isabel's tawny hair was pulled into a loose bun, showing off her wonderfully perfect complexion and brown eyes. She wore an oatmeal-colored, bulky sweater over stone-washed jeans. The overall effect was a picture of a young woman without a care in the world.

"So what kind of dirt can you give me on Mark as a teacher?" I cracked to the two guys.

"He was such a bad influence on me, I became a history teacher," Jack replied.

"How horrible. Where do you teach?"

"Albert Academy," Jack matter-of-factly answered.

I admired Jack's modesty. Albert is a very prestigious private academy about fifteen miles west of Barton. It's known as the Exeter of the Adirondacks. It was just as difficult to gain employment at the academy as an instructor as it was to gain admission as a student.

"I'm very impressed."

"Thanks."

"If I recall correctly, Scott took just one of my classes," Mark said.

"That's right. I minored in history. I studied architecture. I'm at SRB Architects now. And Isabel is a lawyer at Franklin and Associates."

Scott glanced at the Flemings' table, where Madeline still chatted with the couple as Ella stood silent, listening as Dotsie rambled to Regina about the marvelous cuisine of the 1950s.

"That's a nice piece," Scott said, pointing at the wood box.

"It belonged to my great-grandmother," Regina said with pride.

"An antique, then."

"We of a certain age prefer the term vintage," Dotsie said.

"I stand corrected." Scott made a bow toward Dotsie. "It's a very nice *vintage* box."

"And it is an excellent container for crayons and finger paints," Ella said.

There was no way anyone could miss the well-structured sarcasm in her delivery, especially not a man trained in architectural design. Scott smiled, I'm sure with the assumption he could charm Ella. Ella, however, is not the type of elderly woman flattered by such attention. She does not humor people, nor does she take prisoners.

Scott lifted the box's lid and peeked inside. He then lowered the lid and pulled on the knob, tugging a bit harder when the drawer did not open.

"Key?" he asked.

Ned shook his head as Madeline said, "It was lost decades ago."

"Not a big deal." Scott glided his fingers across the smooth cover. "I like to give my clients something at the end of a project. With some refurbishing, this would be a fine piece to display in the addition I'm planning for a client. I'll take it."

Ned gave Scott a thumbs-up and said, "Sold!"

"I hope your client loves it as much as our three girls did," Irene said as Scott handed Ned a ten-dollar bill.

Jack turned to Mark as Scott tucked the box in the crook of his arm. "It was great to see you, Professor. We're having dinner at The Hearth later. Why don't you and Ms. Walsh join us?"

"Great idea," Scott said. "I'd love to talk with you about a project I'm working on right now."

"We're dining at The Hearth, too. We're meeting friends. How about we join you for after-dinner drinks?"

"Sounds good," Jack said. "We'll see you there."

Poor guy, I thought. Unless he had a date for dinner, he'd be the third wheel. Or the fifth table leg.

As he started to follow Scott and Isabel, Jack turned to me and said, "It was nice to meet you, Ms. Walsh."

"Please, call me Veronica," I said.

Mark and I said good-bye to Dotsie, Regina, the Flemings, and the Griffins. We continued our perusing, casually glancing over the sale items as we passed the packed tables. We trailed several feet behind Scott, Isabel, and Jack.

The trio stopped at a coffee cart. As Scott was pulling his wallet from his back pocket, a man knocked into him, roughly jostling Scott's other arm and knocking the box from his grip. The impact with the blacktopped ground cracked the bottom of the box. The impact must have broken the lock on the drawer, for it now jutted out from the cracked box.

In the following instant I noticed Scott's stunned expression and the man's challenging scowl.

"I'm sorry." The bully didn't appear regretful at all. He was an unshaven, muscular man, broad-shouldered and with a bit of a gut. I knew him by sight as the contractor who had recently started work on a building across the street from my boutique.

"That was intentional," Isabel said. Her pretty face took on an angry glower.

"It was not!" said the guy's wife. She was Debbie Bradley, a hairdresser at the salon where I have my hair cut. A feisty, flashy type who always wore her artificially cherry-red hair in a high ponytail and favored blingy jewelry, Debbie often displayed a long line of bracelets on her arm as she cut and styled hair. I sometimes wondered what the client in the chair thought of the clatter of the bangles as Debbie fluttered around her with a sharp pair of scissors. Debbie's language was as colorful as her fingernails. She lobbed some of that spicy language at Isabel.

"Don't worry about it," Scott said. "How are you, Vin?"

Vin ignored Scott's polite question. "You stopped short."

"He did not, *Mr.* Bradley," Isabel said. "You hit Scott on purpose."

"Don't go accusing my husband," Debbie said. "Let's go, Vin, before these people have you arrested." Debbie tugged on her husband's arm. Vin warily eyed Scott as they started away.

Dotsie, Regina, Madeline, and Ella reached us. "What a shame," Madeline said when she saw the damaged box on the ground. Ella shook her head.

Jack leaned over and tugged on the drawer's knob. It gave easily. In a moment, he pulled something from it. He handed Scott a scarlet-colored velvet bag.

"What's in it?" Isabel asked.

The Bradleys moved toward us as Scott tugged open the bag's drawstring and pulled out a square-shaped board. "A painting." His jaw dropped. "Look at this!"

He turned the board around to show us a small painting. I guessed it was about seven-by-seven inches.

Ella and Madeline gasped. "Goodness gracious," Madeline

said with delight. "It's Orchard Street!"

"What in the world?" Ella murmured.

I squinted and moved closer. The watercolor was indeed a view of Barton's main street, with *Orchard Street* written in script across the center bottom of the canvas. A Model-T stood in the foreground, giving us a good estimate of the era of the painting.

"Is that the inn?" Regina leaned forward, pointing at the canvas. "There's a woman standing on the front porch steps!" She pointed at the figure of a dark-haired woman wearing a light-blue dress, standing on the bottom step, her hand resting on the porch railing.

Regina's reference was to the Barton Inn, which the Griffin family founded in the village in 1770 and operated until Ella and Madeline closed it in the 1990s. The sisters continued to live in the large Victorian that graced the real Orchard Street.

Jack said, "Check the signature."

Scott turned the painting over and located the artist's scrawl in the bottom corner. His eyes widened as he said, "George Bradshaw."

Like everyone around me, I caught my breath and moved closer. A few passersby stopped.

"George Bradshaw?" Mark asked.

"Yes," Scott said.

"What?" Vin exclaimed.

"Are you kidding?" Debbie's anger and disbelief were tangible.

George Bradshaw, who hailed from Barton's neighbor community, Bear Lake, was a prominent artist in the mid-twentieth century. Now deceased, Bradshaw beautifully rendered Adirondack landscapes, towns, and inhabitants. A very kind gentleman, he was also well-known for his philanthropy on behalf of local causes. He would welcome elementary school classes several times a year, giving a tour of the art studio he had built behind his house and happily discussing his work with the students. I fondly remembered my own class trip. I couldn't sleep the night before, so excited was I about meeting him. And then I was so nervous I might break something in the studio, I kept my arms folded across my chest for the entire visit.

Isabel pulled a sheet of paper from the velvet bag. She glanced at it and then held it out to her boyfriend.

Scott took the sheaf and spent a moment studying it. "Wow." His voice barely reached a whisper.

"What is it?" Jack asked.

"A love letter."

"Read it," Isabel said.

"It's dated November sixth, nineteen twenty-five."

"The day before our parents wed." Madeline's voice was soft, her expression a blend of anticipation and apprehension.

"Please, go on," Ella said.

The two sisters stood with their shoulders touching. Their strained looks caused me concern.

With a respectful nod, Scott began reading. " 'My dearest *Eloise. My heart is broken over what you are to do tomorrow and I am certain it will never mend. My only consolation is that you are doing it for love, not money or social position. How I wish that your love were still for me! I cannot count how many times I have regretted leaving Bear Lake to attend Princeton. My absence made my heart fonder for you, but made yours fonder of Richard Griffin.'* "

"How romantic!" Regina said. "George Bradshaw carried a torch for great-grandma!"

"It's not romantic," Ella said. "The romance was between my mother and father."

Scott glanced at the Griffin sisters. "Maybe I shouldn't continue." He extended his arm, as if offering the letter to Ella.

Isabel swiped the letter from his hand. "I'll read it." Her eyes scanned the paper for a moment before she began to read. " *'I know you do not act out of cruelty, for you have not one malicious tendency in your soul. I can see it in your eyes. You look at Richard in a way you never looked at me. And so there is nothing for me to forgive, nothing for you to regret. My threat Wednesday evening was an act of desperation, a final attempt to win back your heart. I will not interfere in your marriage ceremony, for I believe what the priest will declare. What God hath joined together, let no man put asunder.*

" *'I send with this letter my last gift to you, Eloise. Your beloved Orchard Street, with your new home warmly drawn. I hope you recognize yourself on the porch steps. I did my best to capture your beauty. With you as the inn's mistress, the Barton Inn will be the village's crown jewel.'* "

"Mother is in the picture?" Ella asked.

"Yes, ma'am," Scott said. He held the painting for Ella and Madeline to see the famous artist's tribute to their mother. A tear dropped from Madeline's cheek.

"Is there anything else in the letter?" Charlotte Farrell, a reporter for the local newspaper, stepped from the crowd. She held a small notepad and pen.

"Just a few more words," Isabel said. " *'My love will always be with you, dear Eloise. Always. George.'* "

Our group, which had grown as word of *Orchard Street*'s discovery traveled through the crowd, stood in awed silence. We were all too stunned to say anything. Charlotte Farrell, a reporter for the local newspaper, furiously scrawled on a small notepad.

Someone in the crowd broke the silence, saying, "That's got to be worth a million. At least!"

Debbie loudly uttered a popular four-letter word. Vin added another expletive to the record.

"I'll say," said Dotsie.

"That painting belongs to my family!" Regina shrieked.

"It belongs to the Flemings!" Ned bellowed from behind me. As he pushed past me, I took a glance at his face. It was purple with fury.

"Finders-keepers," someone from the crowd shouted.

Another said, "Possession is nine-tenths of the law!"

"Not always," Regina said.

"Are you going to give us a lesson in the law now?" Isabel gave Regina a challenging smile.

"Our mother is the subject of the painting. And it was given to her as a gift. Therefore, it rightfully belongs to her heirs." Ella was calm and controlled.

"But one of her heirs *gave* it to me," Ned said.

"I gave it to your daughter," Madeline clarified.

"Did you expect us to return it when they had outgrown it?" Ned's snark had a terrible edge.

What a difference a million-dollar discovery makes. Pleasantries between friends changed into sarcastic retorts within minutes.

I wanted the confrontation to end before a long-time friendship was destroyed. "Stop!"

Only Mark acknowledged my plea. "Nice try." He put his hand in the small of my back and guided me away from Ned.

Regina answered Ned with sass. "You were given the box, not the painting. Aunt Madeline obviously didn't know the painting was in the drawer."

Ned said, "It doesn't matter."

"Well, you just sold the box to Scott," Isabel said. "So you have no claim to the painting."

"Had I known the painting was in the box, I certainly would not have sold it."

"That's the argument I just made," Regina said with a derisive snort.

Isabel ignored Regina. "You didn't know, so it doesn't matter, Mr. Fleming." Her tone could have cut through granite. Regina said to Isabel, "You have no say in this matter."

"Excuse me." Isabel took a step toward Regina. "*You* are the one who has no say."

Jack stepped between the women. "Let's just all take a deep breath and relax."

"The painting belongs to the Griffin family," Ella insisted again. "And we will take this matter to court if we must."

"As will I!" Ned declared.

Irene, a kindergarten teacher expert at soothing children, stroked her husband's back in an effort to calm him. "Ned, it doesn't matter. We don't need it."

"It's worth a million, Irene!"

"And a lawyer would take half of it after a years'-long court battle. Come on, honey, we don't need it."

Isabel took the painting from Scott and put it back in the velvet bag. "Let's go."

"We are not done!" Regina lunged toward the couple. Mark grabbed her by the arm before she could land a punch.

"What lungs!" Dotsie said. I think she was the only one enjoying the scene.

"Yes, we are," Isabel said. "The painting belongs to Scott. End of discussion."

Isabel possessively linked her arm through Scott's and pulled him through the crowd, past the Bradleys, and out of sight. I spied Charlotte scurrying behind them, calling to Scott for an interview. Vin, his expression fixed in a wrathful stare, watched.

Debbie shook her head. "Some people have all the luck."

"Someone needs to tell that young lady this is none of her concern," Ella said. With her eyes on me, it was obvious to whom she was assigning the task. She had never been a mother, nor a Catholic nun, but boy could she hurl the disapproving look both mothers and nuns excelled at casting.

"I just met Isabel," I said.

"We'll see you later at The Hearth, Professor," Jack said over his shoulder. After giving us all what I interpreted as an apologetic glance, he hurried to catch up with Scott and Isabel.

"I'm calling my lawyer," Ned huffed as he stomped back to his table. Irene, helpless, followed.

"He has no claim," Ella said before she also left.

"What are the odds everyone will sleep on it and decide the fight's not worth it?" I asked.

"About the same as me winning the Miss America pageant," Dotsie said.

The heat of the argument dissipated and the afternoon chill intensified. "Ready to leave?" I rubbed my hands along my arms to warm myself. A cloud rolled in front of the sun, marring the day just as the bitter argument had spoiled the magnificent discovery.

"The fun's certainly over." Mark put his arm around me. As we started through the dispersing crowd, I heard a young woman say into her cell phone, "Nat, you won't believe this."

"Well, you were almost right," Mark said to me when we were clear of the crowd. "It's a Bradshaw, not a Picasso. But you were close."

"I'm glad I wasn't the one to find it," I said, still reeling from the vitriol of the argument.

"Smart woman."

CHAPTER TWO

"I can't get over it," my best friend, Carol, said as a waiter served our salads at The Barton Hearth that evening.

"So the key that Madeline Griffin said was lost was *lost* by her mother," Carol's husband, Patrick, said, twitching his fingers as he did to make air quotes.

"Did Richard Griffin know about Eloise's relationship with Bradshaw?" I asked.

Mark shrugged. "That's a question that will never be answered." He glanced across the dining room, where Scott, Isabel, and Jack sat. A woman I did not recognize was also at their table.

My eyes followed his gaze. Isabel sat close to Scott, practically in his lap, with her hand pressed against his on the table. She held a jumbo shrimp to his lips and beamed as he bit it.

"He's a lucky man," Patrick said. "A pretty lady on his arm and a George Bradshaw painting that cost him just ten dollars."

"I'd like to know the history between Scott and Vin Bradley," Mark said. "There's something nasty there."

"Isabel's part of it," I said. "Maybe she'll dish during drinks."

Mark gave my knee a squeeze. "You can be in charge of asking her."

"I wonder how far the Griffins will really take their fight," Patrick said.

"And Ned Fleming, as well," Carol added.

"I believe Ella's vow to take it to court. She'll take it all the way to the Supreme Court if she has to," I said.

"It's a shame Ned and Irene didn't find the painting in all the years they had that box," Patrick said. "With three daughters to send through college, he and Irene could really use the money."

I swallowed a sip of my Seven and Seven. "You know who we haven't mentioned: the Bradshaw family."

Mark nodded. "Another party who will make a claim."

"This will get interesting," Carol said.

"Perhaps Scott will give the painting back to the Griffins the way that guy gave Derek Jeter his three thousandth-hit ball. That fan knew it was the right thing to do."

I liked Patrick's suggestion, but doubted the generosity would be repeated in Barton.

We all reflected on the matter as we dug into our salads. I took another glance across the room and saw Jamie Chang, owner of Barton's art gallery, standing beside Scott. She was smiling brightly and gesturing with her hands as she spoke to him.

After a moment Carol said, "George Bradshaw did find love again. It took him a few years, but he did marry. Wasn't he almost fifty when he did?"

Patrick shrugged. "I remember meeting his wife when our class went to his studio."

"I do, too," Mark said. "Wasn't she a good twenty years younger?"

Carol nodded. "I remember her. Her name was Olivia."

"He named their house for her," I said. "Oli Hill."

"So what did she know about her husband's love for Eloise?" Carol asked.

"I bet she never knew," Patrick said.

We all nodded in agreement of Patrick's guess as Isabel's giddy laughter floated across the room.

"Are you set with your costumes for the Halloween party Friday night?" Carol asked Mark and me.

"We certainly are," I answered.

The Halloween party, to be held at The Hearth, was an annual Barton benefit held to raise money for the local chapter of the Red Cross.

"So who, or what, will you be?" Patrick asked.

"I'm going to be a flapper. I have a costume from one of the soap's Halloween Balls that unbelievably still fits. Plus a bob-styled black wig."

"And you, Mark?"

"I'm wearing a dark suit and bow tie and pretending to be F. Scott Fitzgerald. How about you two?"

"I'm going to be Rita Skeeter." In response to the quizzical tilt of Mark's head, Carol explained, "I'm still stuck in Harry Potter world years after my daughter and I finished reading the books. Rita's a yellow journalist who can transform into a beetle. I'm going for irony. Everyone would expect me to be Professor Sprout, the Herbology teacher."

"Good choice," Mark said.

"It would be nice if we were coordinating our costumes like you two are." Carol frowned at her husband. "Someone I know always goes as a Yankee player."

"As long as the uniform continues to fit."

"But don't you think it's a little too on the nose, seeing as you are a baseball coach?" Carol pinched her husband's cheek as a tease.

"Going as a science teacher would be on the nose." Patrick turned to Mark. "I feel abandoned. You're really giving up your standard Halloween get-up?"

"I'll always be Arden's number one fan, even when I don't wear the sweatshirt," Mark said.

"Change is good," I said.

"It is." Mark leaned toward me and lightly kissed my cheek. Life was good, too.

Carol and Patrick left after dessert while Mark and I crossed the dining room for the promised after-dinner drink.

"This is my colleague Hillary Simmons," Isabel said, introducing us to the willowy blonde who had made the group a foursome.

"Pleasure to meet you," Hillary, who was a few years older than the others, said as she shook my hand and Mark's.

"Where's the painting?" Mark asked, pulling a chair away from the table for me to sit.

"Home," Scott said. He didn't elaborate as to whether it was in a safe, under his mattress, or hidden in a cupboard behind cereal boxes. Or in a cereal box.

"You must be overwhelmed," I said.

"I am," Scott said. "It's amazing how ten bucks turned me from a pauper into a millionaire. Plus I met a soap star today!"

"I don't think my fame will endure as George Bradshaw's has. Have you had any time to think about what you are going to do with the painting?"

"All the possibilities have been going through my mind. And Isabel's."

"He can buy me something that fits in a small box from Tiffany." Isabel stroked Scott's arm and gave him a suggestive grin.

"First, I'm going to pay off my student loans. It will be a relief to clear that debt. I'll be left with a good chunk for the dream house I've been designing for the last ten years. I saw a gorgeous piece of land for sale on Ridge Road that would be perfect for it."

I tried to put myself in their shoes to understand their "bean counting." Young people with huge student loans, dream homes to build, finer things to acquire. I couldn't help, however, feeling dismayed that they didn't seem to appreciate the masterpiece, for art's sake.

"I'm going to put *Orchard Street* up for auction at one of the New York houses. But before I do that, I'm going to loan it to the Daley Gallery at Arden for a month or two. The public deserves to see the painting. I hope it will give a nice financial boost to the gallery."

"It will. That's an excellent idea," Mark said.

"There will be a private showing at Jamie Chang's gallery Monday night. She's inviting all the local dignitaries. I hope you two can come." Scott looked from me to Mark. "You should be there since you witnessed the discovery."

"We'd love to," Mark said. "Thank you."

"I have a question for the lawyers," I said, looking across the table to Isabel and Hillary. "Is Scott definitely the legal owner of the painting?"

"I don't believe the sale can be rescinded," Isabel answered. "There was no fraud involved. Obviously, Scott didn't know what was in the locked drawer. And he accepted the price set by Mr. Fleming."

"Can't Ned argue that he sold the box, not the painting?"

Hillary answered. "I'm sure he will. But because of the setting, a flea market, all sales are considered as-is and final. One person may buy a blender that will break the next day and have no recourse; another may buy an item worth more than the set price and the seller is out of luck."

Jack spoke up. "I feel sorry for the Griffins. All those decades and they had no idea the painting was in the box."

"I have sympathy for them, too," said Scott, "but I can't get caught up in emotions. I am now the painting's owner, and I can do with it what I want."

"If the Griffins are wise, they won't get involved in a lawsuit.

It will only break them financially and ruin the few years they have left." Isabel's expression was sour. "I've been involved in lawsuits over money, and this is what this is really all about, and they're never pretty."

I wanted to attribute Isabel's coolness to professional reasoning, but, darn it, couldn't the young lawyer show a shred of compassion for Ella and Madeline?

"It was a bit weird, reading that love letter Bradshaw wrote to their mother," Scott said. "I felt like I was going through her underwear drawer. What Bradshaw wrote is so intimate. I don't think it would be appropriate to sell it. He expressed very private thoughts and feelings. I don't feel I own it like I own the painting. It should probably go back to the Griffins."

"Scott, remember it has a monetary value." Isabel tapped her finger against his wrist.

"Not much, I would think. I don't think some stranger should have it," Scott replied.

"Let's stop all the money and legal talk," Jack said.

I obliged by asking Isabel, "How long have you two been dating?"

"Five months," Isabel said. She grinned like the feline that nabbed the canary.

"How did you meet?"

"Not exactly cute," Scott said. "Funny you should ask."

"I guess we can thank Mr. Bradley," Isabel said.

"What about me?" Hillary's lower lip extended into an exaggerated pout.

"And Hillary," Isabel said. "Scott caught Bradley overcharging a client for materials."

"Yeah. Vin was supposed to use specific materials listed in the contract. He bought cheaper materials, but charged the client the price of the more expensive required materials. I found out when I visited the site one day and saw what his crew was using."

"Wow." In my mind I finished with, "No wonder Bradley was ticked off this afternoon." A quickly traded glance with Mark told me he was thinking the same.

"So Scott's client, who is also one of my clients, sued Vin," Hillary said.

"Isabel and I *bumped* into each other in the hall," Scott said. He moved his hand under the table. A moment later, Isabel's hand went missing, too.

"So that's how we met," Isabel said.

"And since then, I have to go to work to see you," Hillary said.

"I've been a stranger, too," Jack said. "Scott had to give me another tour of his house last week because I hadn't been there in weeks. I forgot where the bathroom was."

"Sorry about that," Scott said, acting abashed. "I haven't seen much of my house, either, lately."

"He's been in a corner, hanging over his drafting board." Isabel dampened the playful exchange with the sarcastic remark.

"How was the case resolved?" Mark asked.

"The matter was settled through mediation," Hillary said. "Vin said it was an honest mistake."

"Well, it cost him," Isabel said.

"That's why Vin was less than friendly today," said Scott.

"Got it," Mark said.

"I suppose you know he's working on the renovation of the building across from All Things."

"I hope someone keeps an eye on Bradley," Isabel said. "I can't believe he's still getting business."

"I hope I don't have to deal with him again. But Barton's a small town. Unless one of us moves, Vin and I will have to do business together in the future. I'd certainly keep a sharp eye on him, and the licensing board's number on speed dial."

From the corner of my eye I saw a beacon of white crossing the dining room. I turned and saw that it was Regina, dressed in a chef's smock. Her hair was tucked under a red bandana. Oh dear, I thought, as she headed for our table, her scowl a clear indication she hadn't calmed down in the few hours since the painting's discovery. Isabel fixed her pretty face into a frown as Regina approached the table.

"Not her again."

"Hi," Jack said. "Dinner was delicious." It was a nice attempt to defuse the impending confrontation.

It didn't work. "Thank you," Regina said tersely. "I would have come out here sooner, but Aunt Madeline told me to take a chill pill and let you enjoy your meal."

Isabel snorted and mumbled, "Should have taken two pills."

Regina ignored her. Addressing Scott, she said, "I do want to apologize for my outburst this afternoon at the flea market. I tend to get a little crazy in heated moments."

"Apology accepted." Scott surprised Regina by extending his hand across the table. She clasped it and the pair sealed the apology. Isabel put her hands in her lap.

"The Griffin family's position remains firm. *Orchard Street* belongs to us and we would like it returned immediately."

Another guffaw from Isabel. "As I stated during your earlier outburst, your family has no claim to the painting. If you would like to make an offer for it, we would happily consider it."

"An offer?" Regina blurted.

"There they are!"

We turned at the sound. Led by a regal blonde, two young women and a man in his early thirties marched across the room.

"Here they come," Mark muttered and I knew who "they" were. George Bradshaw's family.

"That's the guy who has the painting," one of the young

women said, pointing at Scott. I recognized her voice from the flea market; she was the gal who made the phone call as Mark and I left the sale.

The older woman lifted her chin and said, "Young man, I am Leona Bradshaw Kendall. I understand you are in possession of one of my father's paintings?"

Scott slid his chair back and stood, as did Mark and Jack.

"I'm Scott Culverson, Mrs. Kendall. It is a pleasure to meet you."

The two shook hands. While Scott maintained a pleasant demeanor, Leona remained stiff and distant.

"Well, do you have my father's painting?"

"Yes. I purchased an antique box at the flea market this afternoon and the painting was discovered in a drawer."

"We've heard the story," the second young woman said. Most certainly Leona's daughter, she had the same haughty tone and expression as the elder woman. "Where's my grandfather's painting?"

"It's in a safe place," Isabel said.

"And you are?" Leona's daughter asked.

"Isabel Fischer. And you are?"

"Natalie Kendall." She self-reverentially uttered her name, as if she expected the whole room to drop their forks and bow before her.

Natalie would make a terrific soap villainess. She was definitely her mother's daughter. Not only did she have Leona's frosty, blue-blood attitude, she also had her mother's heart-shaped face and piercing blue eyes. Natalie's blonde hair was fixed in a ballerina topknot.

"Mr. Culverson, I would like to see the painting," Leona said.

"Scott will loan the painting to the Daley gallery at Arden College on Tuesday morning. You can see it along with the general public once it's on display."

Leona recoiled at Isabel's announcement. It was a bit harsh, telling the artist's daughter she'd have to pay to view her father's work for the first time while elbow-to-elbow with sweatshirt-wearing college students or tourists visiting for a long weekend. Though Leona was surely acquainted with the gallery's curator and would get a free pass and private viewing.

"And then it will be auctioned off. You're most welcome to place a bid." Even I, a neutral observer, felt the twist of that knife.

"Is this true, Mr. Culverson? You are going to auction off my father's work?"

"Yes."

"Theo, do something," Natalie demanded of the young man who had been silently observing the heated debate.

I glanced at Theo. His lips remained firmly pressed together. I couldn't tell if he was embarrassed by Natalie's posturing or was just getting ready to let loose his fury. He was a handsome young man. His brown hair was trimmed and combed in a side part. His dark eyes did not wander the room; they remained fixed on the group, his attention shifting along with the conversation.

"Natalie, quiet."

Natalie recoiled a bit and looked abashed by her mother's admonition. Her eyes swept over our little group until resting on Mark.

"Good evening, Professor Burke."

That gave Mark an opening to quell the fury. "Hi, Natalie. Folks, this really isn't the place for this—"

Theo finally spoke, interrupting Mark with, "It is in your best interest to hand the painting over to us, Mr. Culverson."

"It belongs to my great-aunts, Ella and Madeline Griffin. And my grandmother." Regina lifted her chin with pride.

"Oh," Natalie said with scornful condescension. "The daughters of my grandfather's *supposed* lover!"

"She's the one I told you about, Nat," snapped the young woman with Natalie.

That was it. I liked neither Natalie nor her friend. They reeked of entitled childhoods and arrogant, indulgent adulthoods, of cliquey school days and postgraduate years where you weren't anyone if you didn't know the right people and travel in the proper circles. A swap of glances with Hillary told me she had the same impression.

"Natalie. Bianca. Enough," Leona said.

"Supposed!" Regina yelped as she took a step toward Natalie. Jack scrambled to get between the two, the second time that day he had to separate the two bickering women.

"George Bradshaw loved my great-grandmother. He gave her that painting as a wedding present."

"My grandmother is the only woman George Bradshaw ever loved! *My grandfather* named their home in her honor! Your grandmother probably stole the painting and forged the *love* letter!"

Regina sputtered and shook her fist at Natalie. Jack grabbed her forearms, saying, "Relax."

I loved this type of scene when I was acting on a soap opera. In real life, I don't care for them as much.

Just as I had the flash of my former career, Natalie looked at me. "And who are you? What is your role in this?"

"I'm Veronica Walsh."

Leona fixed her glance on me. "Oh, yes. The former actress. You are the new owner of All Things."

Dan Miller, The Hearth's owner, hurried to the table. "Good evening, everyone. I'm going to have to ask you to take this conversation to my office. Regina, please get back to the kitchen."

"Kitchen staff," Natalie sniffed.

I wanted to punch the princess in the face and wipe the ugly smugness off it, but five people and a table of desserts and hot coffee stood between us.

"Head chef," Regina corrected her.

"Go." Dan's stern look worried me; I hoped he would not fire Regina for her passionate defense of her family.

"We are *not* done." Regina gave Natalie and Isabel one last glare of contempt and walked from the dining room.

"I apologize for the commotion," Leona said to Dan. "We will be leaving, too."

"We will discuss this with our lawyer first thing in the morning," Theo said to Scott.

"As Scott's lawyer, I know you have no legal claim to the painting," Isabel said.

Natalie narrowed her eyes and glared at Isabel, but said nothing. Her friend tugged on her arm and the pair led Leona and Theo to the hallway.

"I'm very sorry for the disturbance," Scott said to Dan.

"You didn't cause it," Isabel said, seething as she watched the Kendalls' exit.

"It's all right." Dan shook Scott's hand and left.

"Whew." Scott's eyes widened as he let out an exaggerated exhalation. "The sooner I sell *Orchard Street*, the better. I don't think these people will leave me alone until then."

"I can get restraining orders against them all," Isabel said.

Scott kissed her. "I don't think that's necessary, honey."

"We should all call it a night," Mark said.

"Good idea," Jack agreed. Hillary nodded.

Isabel picked up her purse. "I'm going to the powder room."

Jack turned to Mark and me as Isabel left the dining room. "I'll walk out with you."

We said good night to Scott, who sat down and signaled for a refill on his drink.

"Looks like we might be heading for another round of mediation," Hillary murmured as the four of us walked into the hall.

"I hope they have security at the art gallery Monday night so there isn't another scene," I said.

"A bouncer at the door is a good idea," Jack said with a chuckle.

Mark and I discussed the confrontation on the short walk to my house.

"So how do you know Natalie Kendall?"

"She works at the college in the Development office. I don't have much contact with her, but I hear she's a very forceful fund-raiser."

"I don't doubt that. I'd like to see Natalie and Isabel go a few rounds. Those two have sharp claws."

"Trying to start a catfight?"

I grinned, thinking of the many slugfests I had participated in during my time on *Days and Nights*.

"Just reminiscing about the good old days."

CHAPTER THREE

"I wonder how many people walked right past that box without giving it a second glance," Claire Camden said as we prepared to open the shop Monday morning. Claire, the manager of my newly-acquired business, All Things, counted the money for the cash register as I did my usual walk around the floor, checking that everything was in order for the day's business.

"I bet people kicked themselves when they saw the newspaper headline," Haley Anderson called down from the second floor. " 'Should have bought that box,' they said."

Orchard Street was the front-page story in the Sunday edition of the *Chronicle*. A color picture of Scott holding the painting accompanied the above-the-fold article.

"Yeah, but without the well-timed shove, they wouldn't know what they had sitting on their family-room shelf," I said.

"True," Claire said as she closed the register drawer.

"Maybe they would have picked the lock," Haley countered. "Ned Fleming is certainly wishing he did."

"I wonder if Vin Bradley thinks he should get a finder's fee," Tina Torrelli said. She emerged from the stock room carrying a cardboard box. "That was a big assist to Scott."

"Speak of the devil," Claire said. "He just pulled up."

She nodded to the side window at the pickup truck parked on the opposite side of Sycamore. Vin got out of the truck, grabbed a toolbox from the bed, and walked to the back of the building on the corner. In the 1960s, Doctor Rosen had converted the private home into an office for his pediatric practice. Now Bradley and his crew were fixing it up for a bridal business new to Barton.

"I'm going to see the painting as soon as Arden hangs it on the wall," Molly McDonald said. Scott's decision to loan *Orchard Street* to the campus gallery was also mentioned in the newspaper article written by Charlotte Farrell.

"We should have a staff field trip!" Tina suggested.

"I'll need permission notices from your parents," I said.

We went about our work in silence. I stopped for a moment and glanced around the shop, which I had the opportunity to purchase after the death of its owner, my neighbor Anna Langdon. Still in the honeymoon phase of business ownership, I was thrilled by every detail and unbothered by even the fussiest customer. I knew I was very fortunate in my situation; the elegant boutique was a huge success when I assumed its ownership. I just had to stay out of the way of Claire, Molly, Haley, Tina, and the weekend crew.

I walked to the front door and unlocked it. "Showtime!" I said with flair. I did it every morning, to the staff's amusement. The ladies enjoyed working for a former soap-opera actress. I guess it gave them some cachet with their friends.

"Break a leg, everyone!" Claire said.

Around nine thirty, Claire, Molly, and I were standing outside the shop's front window, discussing ideas for our Thanksgiving window, when the front door opened and Tina leaned out.

"Veronica, you have a call from Leona Kendall."

Claire and Molly turned to me, their eyes wide.

I shrugged. "Thanks." I followed Tina into the store. I jogged up the staircase to my office, shut the door, sat behind my desk, and took one deep breath before picking up the phone.

"Mrs. Kendall, hello."

"Ms. Walsh," Leona began in her over-enunciating tone. "I want to apologize for the spectacle you witnessed Saturday evening."

"Please, call me Veronica. It wasn't exactly a spectacle," I said.

"It was very embarrassing. I would have preferred to deal with the matter in private, but Natalie was determined to pursue the matter at that very moment."

"I see," I said, biting my tongue to keep from further commenting on her spoiled daughter. "She has spirit. It's sweet how protective of her grandfather she is."

"Thank you for those kind words. There is a second reason for my call. I am mortified that I have not contacted you earlier to congratulate you on your acquisition of All Things. It is an important business in our community."

"Thank you, Mrs. Kendall."

"Leona, please." She sounded as if she was bestowing on me a high honor, not given to many of the unwashed.

"Thank you, Leona."

"I would like to have you to a luncheon I am having at my home Wednesday. I apologize for the late invitation."

"Well, I . . ." I stammered. I had no plans for lunch on Wednesday, other than the typical tuna on white or turkey on pumpernickel I usually grabbed from the deli when I didn't run home for a quick meal. "That would be lovely."

"Wonderful."

After she told me the time I asked, "And what is your address?"

"I reside in my father's house. Oli Hill."

"Oh." I felt like a dumbo for not knowing Leona's domicile. "My friends and I recently reminisced about a wonderful class trip we took to the studio when we were students at Saint Augustine's."

"Father always enjoyed having school children visit."

The warm, gleeful tone of Leona's voice caught me off guard. "We enjoyed it as well."

"I'm pleased you remember, Veronica. I work hard to maintain Father's legacy. I look forward to seeing you on Wednesday."

"I'll be there. Thank you for inviting me, Leona."

Claire was lingering in the hall when I emerged from my office.

"And . . . ?" she asked.

"I'm invited to lunch at Leona's house on Wednesday. Or I should say a luncheon."

"Wow. Why?"

It was as if I had been asked to perform brain surgery. I regarded Claire's startled expression.

"What do you mean *why*?"

"Well, you're not Meryl Streep. I mean, I love soap operas, but Leona Kendall is more high-brow."

"You mean artsy fartsy? She's art and my acting career was commerce?"

"Uh-huh."

I sighed. A few months earlier, I had suspected Claire of Anna's murder after learning Claire was upset with Anna's plan to sell All Things to me. Claire was a cool, closed-mouth gal then and we treated each other with kid gloves. "I liked you better when you were monosyllabic and hiding things from me."

"I liked you better when you thought I was a murderer."

"Touché."

"What else did Mrs. Kendall say?"

We walked toward the stairs. "First she apologized for the scene at The Hearth Saturday night. And then she apologized for not calling me when I bought All Things. She says we're an important part of the community."

"We are," Claire said with emphasis. "It will be good for you to get in with Leona Kendall and her friends. They have a lot of influence. And money. We support the community, but we need its support as well."

"I just don't know if I would really fit in with Leona and her *people*. What if I spill something? Or knock something over?"

"Take small bites and only drink water. And keep your elbows to your sides at all times. You do tend to lean on the table."

CHAPTER FOUR

A visit from Scott brightened the early afternoon. The moment I spoke his name, all the gals stopped what they were doing and gave him the once-over with interested looks.

Scott complimented the boutique and laughed when I quipped that everything in the shop was for sale, but not the shop itself. "In case you're thinking of using your newfound fortune to become a retail mogul."

"I wouldn't dream of stepping on your kingdom. I hear you have an excellent selection of candy. I thought I'd buy Jamie Chang a box of your best chocolates in thanks for hosting the party tonight."

I led Scott to the rear of the shop where we kept our large stash of locally-made candy. I pointed out our bestsellers and after a few minutes' deliberation, Scott gave me his order for a generous deluxe box.

"How about a box for Isabel, too?" The first lesson Claire gave me when I bought All Things was this: Boost sales by encouraging impulse purchases.

"Sure. Make it three boxes. I'll bring one to the office." Scott was at a nearby display of ceramic bowls crafted by a Barton resident. "I learned the other day the original name of your store was All Things Adirondack. That's cool."

I arranged a few truffles along the side of the box. "Yeah." I explained how the shop's founder opened the store to support local artists. For years, Mr. Frazer only sold handcrafted items.

When his wife, Anna, took over after his death, she dropped *Adirondack* from the name, stopped selling the work of our artisans, and started selling high-priced "lifestyle" items. With Claire's help, I was returning the shop to its roots by striking a balance between one-of-a-kind and mass-produced stock.

Scott wandered back to the counter. He crossed his arms over the counter and leaned his chin against them. "I'm starting to understand how some lottery winners wish they hadn't won the jackpot."

The admission caught me off guard. Scott seemed very pleased with his "jackpot" on Saturday night. "What do you mean?"

"A lot of open hands have suddenly appeared before me."

"You can ignore all of them, if you want."

Scott chuckled. "I hope that I'm not cursed like some mega-winners have been."

"Don't even think that."

"I'd like to run away and hide until all this blows over."

"As long as you come back. We like having you here." I handed Scott a caramel. "Free sample."

"I'm glad, because I really feel like I'm a part of a community. I like Barton very much."

"I've always been happy here."

"I've been thinking about what kind of contribution I can make to the village."

"You're making a fine contribution with your architectural designs."

"Yeah, but I'm thinking of something more personal. Giving something from me the person, not me the architect."

"Take your time. There's no rush. You'll find the right place to make your mark." I closed the box and tied a wide, gold ribbon around it. We continued our chat about Barton while I put together two more boxes of chocolates.

A few minutes later, Scott walked out with the chocolates in a shopping bag and a satisfied grin on his face.

Hours later, I'd wish that the people who held him dear had seen that look.

CHAPTER FIVE

Several people had gathered at Jamie Chang's art gallery when Mark and I arrived that evening. Jamie welcomed us at the door, a broad smile on her face as she took our coats.

"Welcome!" she said. "Isn't this exciting? I just can't believe how this Bradshaw painting was discovered. And you were there!"

Jamie pressed her hands against my cheeks, the way my grandmother used to do when she wanted a kiss from me. Jamie's no grandmother; she's ten years younger than I. She has a taste for big jewelry; for the Bradshaw showing she wore chunky, jade beads around her neck, bracelets jangling on both arms, something that resembled strings of pebbles dangling from her ears, and three rings on each hand. Cold rings that chilled my already cool face.

"I was!" I said, not knowing what else to say.

Jamie released my face and gave Mark a quick kiss on his cheek. She got us out of our jackets like an impatient mother getting her kids out of their coats and handed them off to her assistant. She then put one hand on my arm, the other on Mark's shoulder and pushed us against each other.

"It's so good to see you two together! You give me hope that someday I'll find Mr. Right." Jamie turned to the man she had been talking with when we entered. "Do you know Charlie?"

Charlie said, "I don't believe we've met." He had thick, gray hair and a bushy mustache that partially hid his cheerful grin.

"I'm Charlie Gannon."

Jamie introduced us. "Charlie is an artist. He does portraits and art reproduction. He's quite talented. You should see his reproductions of the masterpieces."

"Is that legal?" I blurted out without thinking.

Charlie chuckled. "Oh, yes. I never try to pass off my Mona Lisa as the real girl."

Jamie fluttered her hands and said, "Now come in you two, get a glass of wine, some nibbles, and mingle. Scott should be here soon with the painting. I cannot wait to see it. And take a look around. Maybe you'll see something you like." Her soft sales pitch done, Jamie hustled over to two couples studying a painting on the back wall.

"I'm going to grab a coffee. It's nice meeting you." Charlie nodded and wandered over to the coffee urn.

I linked my arm through Mark's. "Mr. Right. Maybe that's how I should introduce you."

"No, thank you. Though it's encouraging to know that you've already decided that I am."

We stepped over to the refreshment table and helped ourselves to glasses of red wine. Just as we were about to wander over to a group of abstract paintings, Isabel glided over and greeted us with exuberance that matched Jamie's. She wore a sleeveless black sheath matched with a pearl choker. Her hair was gathered in an elegant chignon and fixed with a sparkly gold clip.

"I'm so excited about all this." Isabel pressed her cheek against mine.

"As well you should be," I said.

"It will be a nice distraction through the long winter months. There's Jack." Isabel rushed off to have a word with Jack, who was by the coat rack, slipping his jacket onto a hanger.

A slim, attractive woman in her mid-fifties soon joined us.

"Hello, Mark."

"Brenda; it's been a while. Veronica, this is Brenda Donovan, Executive Director of the Historical Society. Brenda, this is Veronica Walsh."

Before Mark could add any further identification of me, Brenda said, "I know who you are!" She grasped my hand and gave it a soft squeeze as the bob of her golden-blonde hair bounced. "It's a pleasure to meet you."

"Likewise."

"I've been meaning to call you for a while, Veronica, but I've been so busy," Brenda said.

"I understand." I kept my expression free of surprise as I wondered why the head of the historical society would call me.

"I'd love to have lunch with you. You know, I'm free on Thursday. How about we meet at the Farley Inn?"

"All right." I thought of Leona's lunch on Wednesday. My once bare social calendar was suddenly packed with appointments.

"I'll make the reservation for twelve thirty. Is that good?"

"Fine."

"Wonderful," Brenda said. "I'll see you then." She went back to the refreshment table to refill her glass and then headed to the back wall of paintings.

"Why does she want to have lunch with me?" I asked Mark.

He gave me a wry look. "She'll probably hit you up for a donation, I'm afraid. She's given you some time to establish yourself back in Barton; now it's time to make a move."

"Great." I spotted Barton's mayor, Jason Quisenberry, entering the gallery. "I'm going to go say hi to my accountant. See if I can even afford to make a donation." I knew fifty dollars would not be a sufficient donation if Brenda was springing for lunch at the Farley Inn.

I strolled over to Jason. Since Barton's mayoral position is a part-time job, Jason earns his living as an accountant. In his late twenties, he is a very capable man as both mayor and numbers keeper and I was very happy to hire him when I bought All Things.

"Hi, Veronica," Jason said as he pulled off his jacket. "I didn't expect to see you here."

"You don't think I'm one of Barton's luminaries?" A blush raced from Jason's cheeks to his earlobes. "Just joking. Mark and I were on the scene when the painting was found."

"Ella Griffin called me at nine a.m. sharp demanding that I do something."

"What could you do?"

Jason shrugged. "I have no idea. Maybe she thought I had the power of confiscation."

"Better you than me." Jason went off to see Jamie and I joined Mark, Isabel, and Jack. A few more people entered; I recognized members of the Village Council and our County Executive. Jamie was very savvy in her invitations—bring people in to see an unaffordable painting by a famous artist and nudge them toward canvases they could purchase with just a small pinch to their wallets. Jamie walked over and put her hand on Isabel's arm. "Isabel, do you know where Scott is? He should be here by now. People are anxious to see the Bradshaw."

"He's probably hanging over his drafting board again, lost in some blueprint. He does that all the time."

"Maybe he's trying to remember the combination to that safe you made him buy yesterday," Jack quipped. "The dope was going to hide it in his attic."

Isabel punched a number into her iPhone and held it to her ear. She did nothing to conceal the impatient pout on her face. After a few moments she sighed and said, "Scott, it's me. Where the hell are you? A group of very important people is here at the gallery waiting for you. Get your butt here." Isabel dropped her hand, saying, "Voicemail. He didn't answer. Maybe I should go to his house and drag him back here."

"Be gentle with the painting," Jamie said. She wasn't joking.

"I'll go with you," Jack said. "Make sure Scott doesn't show up here with a black eye," he added, smirking.

"Ha ha," Isabel said. "Let's get going."

"I offered to keep the painting in my safe," Jamie said when Isabel was out of earshot. "But Isabel insisted on Scott keeping it at his home. She was like a mother of a newborn about that painting."

"A million-dollar baby, I'd say," I said before leaving to join Hillary at the refreshment table. Like Isabel, she wore a black cocktail dress accessorized with a gold belt.

"It's good to see you again, Veronica," she said.

"How was the law today?" I asked, grabbing a slice of cheddar and a cracker.

"Very well-behaved."

A tall, lanky man in his mid-fifties joined us. His graying, black hair was arranged in that familiar comb-over used to hide male-pattern baldness. After introducing himself as Isabel's boss, Aaron Franklin, he asked, "May I refresh your drink?"

"Please. Just a half glass."

"Charlie Gannon is going to make a killing on this painting." Aaron made no effort to keep his observation private.

"Can you be any louder, Aaron?" Hillary scolded her boss and then laughed.

"I'm praising, not criticizing. I encourage mixing business and social whenever possible. Charlie may be here as an art lover, but we all know he's going to be taking notes on every detail of this Bradshaw painting. Probably already has a dozen orders to reproduce it. He'll be busy through Christmas. Want to wager on whether he tries to take photos of the painting?"

"If he does, he'll be escorted out of the gallery by Isabel.

She's become a docent at the Louvre over this painting."

"Isabel will want a royalty on every reproduction."

"Will you be placing an order?" I asked Aaron. "One for your home and one for your office?"

"Bradshaw isn't abstract enough for me. I'm not one for sentimental portraits of small-town life. But my wife may have other ideas. But enough about the painting. How are you adjusting to your full-time life in Barton, Veronica?"

"The transition has been very smooth."

"And you're happy with your legal team?" Aaron eyed me over the rim of his glass as he took a healthy sip of wine.

"Good grief!" Hillary griped. "Talk about mixing business with social."

"My legal team of one is excellent. But thank you for asking." I took a sip of wine and tipped my glass to the pair. "It was nice chatting with you."

"Scared another one off," Hillary cracked as I walked away.

I returned to Mark, who was chatting with an African-American couple. He introduced them to me as Sabrina and Rob Burton, Scott's employers.

Sabrina, a petite woman, smiled. "I keep meaning to pop in your store, but between work and kids, I just haven't found a moment." Her warm demeanor won me over at once.

"We'll be there when you do. We have a wonderful children's section. Christmas is coming, hint hint."

Sabrina laughed. "I was saying to Mark and Rob, you never know what you'll find at a flea market, huh?"

"We're hoping he doesn't take the bundle of money he'll get from selling the painting and run off to open his own firm," Rob said. He had a wonderful baritone voice. "Scott's a very talented architect. He'd take all his business with him."

"He's too nice of a guy to do that," I said.

We all bided our time for another twenty minutes, studying

the paintings and drinking wine. Jamie, Mark, and I were discussing a lovely spring depiction of Lake George when Jason pulled her aside. His expression was somber. Moments after the two stepped into Jamie's office, Mark's cell phone rang. He walked halfway down the hall that led to the office to take the call in relative quiet. I watched as he listened more than spoke, and as his expression changed from calm to shock. He looked up and met my gaze.

After a couple of minutes, he tucked the phone into his pocket just as Jason emerged from the office. The two exchanged a few words before returning to the gallery. Jason brushed past me as Mark returned to my side.

"What's wrong?" I asked.

"Scott is dead."

CHAPTER SIX

"What?"

"Scott is dead. That was Jack. He said that when he and Isabel got to Scott's, they found him dead in his kitchen. He was stabbed in the throat." Mark gave my arm a squeeze. "I'll be right back."

I stood, numb, watching as he walked over and said something to Rob. My attention drifted to Jason, who was speaking to Hillary. The two retrieved their coats from the rack and left the gallery.

"Oh, Veronica." The doleful words pulled my attention to Jamie, who stood beside me.

"You've heard about—"

Jamie answered my question with a nod. "Excuse me. I have to make an announcement."

"About Scott's murder?"

"No. The mayor asked me simply to announce that there has been an unexpected delay. That will be hard enough to do."

Mark returned as Jamie went to the refreshment table.

"Who would kill Scott?"

"Someone who wanted *Orchard Street*. The window in Scott's kitchen was broken. The painting is gone."

He nodded at Jamie, who was preparing to address the gathering, and guided me toward the small crowd.

Jamie lightly tapped a pen against a wine glass to get everyone's attention. "I hate to say this, but unfortunately, we won't be able to have a showing of George Bradshaw's *Orchard Street* tonight. Scott has been delayed and won't be able to join us."

"Is everything okay?" Brenda asked.

"I really can't comment right now." Jamie forced a smile and continued, "I'm sorry that we're not able to show you the painting. I hope we can reschedule a showing soon. I am as eager as you to see George Bradshaw's work. Thank you so much for coming and have a good evening."

Aaron handed me his business card. "In case you have second thoughts about your legal team."

"Thanks. Good night, Aaron." I gave a polite nod to his wife, who trailed behind Aaron.

Brenda followed the Franklins. "I'll see you Thursday."

"I'm looking forward to it," I said.

Soon all who remained in the gallery were Jamie, the Burtons, Mark, and I.

"So what's the unexpected delay?" Rob asked.

"Someone broke into Scott's house to steal the painting," Mark said.

"Oh, no," Sabrina said.

"And Scott apparently walked in while the intruder was still there. Scott was killed."

"Scott's dead?" Rob asked, his face softening into a pained grimace.

"No!" Sabrina cried.

Mark nodded. "I'm sorry."

"How?" Rob asked.

"He was stabbed."

Tears clung to Sabrina's eyelashes. "Isabel. She went over there with Jack. Did she see—"

Mark's nod silenced her. Sabrina reached for her husband's hand.

"Let's go home. I know the kids are okay, but I want to see them."

Rob nodded. "I'll drop you off. Then I'm going to Scott's. I don't know what I can do, but I think I should be there in his parents' stead."

"That's right, sweetie. You should go."

Mark said, "Please call me if there is anything I can do."

Mark and Rob exchanged contact information and then the four of us said good-bye to Jamie.

The Burtons headed up Orchard to their car while Mark and I started our walk to my house. Mark's car was parked there since we ate dinner at my house before going to the gallery. I live just two short blocks from Barton's main street, so we typically walk to Orchard to minimize our carbon footprint and get a bit of exercise. It is usually a quick, enjoyable walk. With Scott's death, however, it was a frightfully dark, chilly stroll home.

"I don't want to point any fingers," I began as we jaywalked across Orchard. "But I can't help but wonder if any of the aggrieved parties are involved."

Mark put his arm around my shoulder and gave it a squeeze. "Don't wonder, Veronica," he said. "Leave this one to the police."

Mark's words were a veiled caution not to become involved in the murder investigation. When we (or mainly I) got involved in the investigation into my neighbor's murder, the two of us almost ended up dead in a cornfield after we discovered the killer's identity during dessert at an Italian restaurant.

"Of course." I glanced over my shoulder to cast a long look down the quiet Orchard Street.

I meant my words. Truly.

CHAPTER SEVEN

"That poor boy. He makes this amazing find and then forty-eight hours later he's killed for it." My mother said this as she squeezed the last drop from a wet teabag. She plunked the bag on the edge of her plate and stirred a half teaspoonful of sugar into the tea.

"It's terrible." I ate a forkful of scrambled eggs. The day's *Chronicle* sat folded next to my plate. I glanced at the headline—*Bradshaw Painting's New Owner Murdered*. What a shame, I thought. Scott would now be remembered as the guy who found *Orchard Street* and not for his own character and accomplishments.

Mom and I sat in a window booth at Herman's, our family's longtime favorite diner. After I bought All Things, Mom and I took up the weekly habit of having breakfast there. Though we saw each other every day—Mom is just a few doors up from All Things in the bookstore she and my father opened decades ago—and had dinner together once or twice a week, breakfast at the diner was a treat. That was our family's place for celebrations when I was a child, for everything from ice cream for a good report card to dinner for a particularly good month of sales at the bookstore.

"Veronica Anne, you are not thinking of getting *involved* in the murder investigation, correct?" Mom asked.

"Of course not. It's the police's job to find who did it."

"Because you're the only child I have. And, at my age, if my heart stops again like it did the last time you got *involved*, it might not start up again."

"Sorry about that." I reached across the table to pat her hand. "Anyway, I'm too busy to get *involved*. I'm having lunch at Leona Kendall's on Wednesday and Brenda Donovan invited me to lunch at the inn Thursday."

"My daughter, the socialite. Well, the H.S. wants your money, obviously. But I wonder what Leona wants. You don't exactly move in her social circles, dear."

"Claire basically said the same thing. I guess I should be flattered I'm considered a regular gal and not a swell." I took a sip of my coffee and said, "Leona said she was mortified by the scene at The Hearth Saturday night. Maybe she just can't bear for anyone to have a negative opinion of her."

"Whatever the reason, it's good for you to expand your network. Now that you own All Things, you need to raise your profile in the community as a businesswoman. It won't hurt to meet Leona's people. Or be a patron of the historical society."

"And I thought I was coming home for a quiet retirement."

"You can't retire before your mother does. And I have no plans to leave the family business."

"Yes, Mother."

A police car pulled up to the curb outside our window. In a moment, Officer Tracey Brody emerged and walked into the diner. She walked to the register and commenced a conversation with the waitress. They chatted for a few minutes before the waitress headed into the kitchen. Tracey sat down on a stool by the counter, swiveling to sweep her gaze over the room. She nodded when we locked eyes.

"Don't even think about it," Mom warned.

"What? I can't greet my friend?" I ate my last bite of toast and chased it with a gulp of orange juice.

Before we could really get going on one of our mother-daughter staring contests, Tracey came over to our table.

"Good morning, ladies."

"Good morning, Officer Brody," my mother said.

I slid across the vinyl-covered bench to make room for the officer.

"Thanks," Tracey said.

"You must have had a long night," I said.

"I wasn't the only one. I understand you were at the flea market when Mr. Culverson found the painting?"

"Yes."

"And you were at the art gallery last night?"

"I was."

"I hope you are not thinking of trying to solve this case, Veronica," Tracey said.

"She's already been warned," my mother said.

"Good. So if you don't listen to me, you will listen to your mother and not get involved in this investigation. Correct, Veronica?"

"Of course," I said. "Was anything taken besides the painting? What about the letter Bradshaw wrote to Eloise Griffin?"

"Veronica!" Mom gave me the same pointed look she had given me when I was a child and attempting to sneak my hand into the cookie jar ten minutes before dinner.

"I can be curious, can't I?"

"Don't say that phrase about curiosity and feline mortality," Mom said to Tracey.

"Yes, ma'am. The letter is gone, too. Isabel Fischer didn't notice anything else missing."

"What about the velvet bag the painting was in?"

"That was in the house."

"Hmm."

"When you arrived at the art gallery, were Isabel and Jack there?"

"Isabel was there. Jack came in a few minutes after Mark and I got there. You don't think that one of them—"

"I'm just asking," Tracey said.

"What about fingerprints? And the time of death?"

"Enough with the questions, Veronica," Mom said.

The waitress came over to our table, a Styrofoam food carrier in one hand and a tall coffee cup in the other.

"Saved by breakfast," Tracey said. "Thanks."

"My pleasure. Nancy, can I get you anything else? Veronica, should I top off your coffee?"

"No, thank you, dear," Mom said.

"Just the check, please," I said.

Gripping her food container, Tracey slid from the booth. "It was good talking with you Veronica. Mrs. Walsh."

"The new Tom Wolfe is in," Mom said.

"Great. I'll stop by when I have a chance and pick it up. And remember, Veronica," Tracey said, fixing a warning stare on me, "no snooping."

With that final word, Tracey turned on her heels and left the diner. Mom and I watched through the window as she got into her patrol car and pulled away from the curb.

"You better listen to her," Mom said.

"Should you really be announcing what she reads?" I teased. "Isn't there some type of bookseller slash customer confidentiality?"

"Veronica."

"I mean, what if she reads romances? A cop may not want people knowing that."

"Finish your eggs, Veronica."

"Yes, Mother."

"I didn't do it," Claire declared when I entered All Things.

"Do what?" I asked. "Is there money missing from the

register? Did something break?"

"No. I'm talking about Scott Culverson."

"Oh. Why would I think you were involved?"

"Because I was on your suspect list the last time someone was murdered in this village." Claire sighed. "I'm being flip. I'm sorry. I'm making light of a horrible situation."

I cupped my hand around her shoulder. "No worries. I promise you are not on the suspect list, because I'm not making one. I'm leaving this case to the police."

"Thank goodness," Claire said. "We're going into the holiday season and the shop needs your full attention."

"You've been reminding me of that for a month."

"Oh," Haley said. "Does this mean I don't have to hang all these ornaments?"

My attention moved to the door of the stock room, where Haley stood holding a large box of Christmas decorations.

"No," Molly said. "We promised. It's better to be safe than sorry."

"What did you promise?"

"Carol called a few minutes ago and asked us to keep you busy so you'd stay out of the investigation," Claire explained. "She's worried about you, too."

"We figured it would take you some time to trim a tree," Tina said. She pointed to our Christmas corner, where we kept three small, decorated trees and other holiday items year-round for visitors to the Adirondacks who wanted to display, or give as a gift, a keepsake of their vacation. "We've already pulled out a box with one of the extra trees and lights."

"It's a little early to put a tree in the window, but when duty calls . . ." Molly said.

"It is too early." I'm against the retail habit of selling Christmas stuff in October and November, All Things' little Christmas corner notwithstanding. "Now put the boxes back until the Thanksgiving dishes are washed and put away."

"Yes, boss," Haley said. She turned around and disappeared back into the stock room.

Tina sighed and put the box of stringed lights on top of the tree box. "All right."

"So we move to Plan B, then," Claire said. "Locking you in your office."

"You're all hilarious. Not one of you is to come within ten feet of my office today, except to get to the restroom."

I glanced out the window and spied Vin Bradley's pickup parked on the opposite side of Sycamore. Vin was walking to the back of his work site. He carried his toolbox in one hand and held a cell phone to his ear with the other hand.

"Did anyone happen to notice when Bradley and his crew finished work yesterday?"

"They usually leave around five," Tina said. "Why?"

"Just wondering."

"Veronica, you just promised there would be no suspect list," Claire said, punctuating her warning tone with an arched brow.

"Just wondering out loud," I said. I took out my cell phone and dialed Carol's number as I started up the stairs to the second floor.

"Thank you for your concern, pal," I said when she answered.

"Just fulfilling my best-friend duties."

I unlocked my office door and stepped inside, throwing my jacket across one of the visitor chairs and my purse into the bottom file cabinet before plopping myself on the chair behind the desk. I pulled my laptop from my briefcase and set it on the desk.

"Thank you. There's no reason to worry. I just said to the ladies here, I won't be involving myself in this investigation."

"Good. Because you almost bit the dust when you did involve yourself. I'm used to you being around here permanently. I like it," Carol said.

"Me, too."

"Good. I have to go. Talk to you later."

When I went back downstairs, Tina said, "We all think Natalie Kendall did it."

"Natalie Kendall? Why?"

"She's a stuck up, phony, entitled snob," Molly retorted.

"Well, if that's your evidence, lock her up and throw away the key."

"Maybe it was her brother," Haley said.

"Or Regina Quinn," Tina said. "She made a big stink about the painting, too. Plus she's new in town. And why did she move here anyway? We don't know anything about her."

"Her great-aunts live here," Claire said.

"Why would a woman in her twenties want to live with two old ladies?" Tina asked.

"No rent," Molly said.

"She got the head chef job at The Hearth and she's only staying with her aunts temporarily. Now no more finger pointing! Boss's order."

I was able to keep my nose out of the investigation until my phone rang at nine forty-five. I was in my office, going over the payroll. A glance at my cell phone told me my caller was Madeline Griffin.

"Madeline, good morning."

"It's a terrible, sad morning."

"It is."

"That poor young man. How horrible. And it just makes me sick that it's all because of that painting. I should have thrown that box in the garbage."

"That's not guilt you're feeling, is it?"

"No, dear, but I do have a part in this. I suppose you could say I put the wheels in motion when I gave the box to Amanda Fleming."

"Madeline, that is ridiculous. It's no one's fault except the awful person who killed Scott."

"I certainly hope they find the devil soon."

"Me, too."

There was a long pause before Madeline said, "That is why I'm calling."

"Oh?"

"Would you be able to come by this morning? Ella and I would like to speak with you about a certain matter."

Now it was my turn for a long pause to wonder why the two elderly sisters wanted to speak with me. "Sure."

"Can you be here in fifteen minutes?"

Make that certain matter an urgent one.

"Of course."

"Wonderful. We'll see you in fifteen minutes."

"Huh," I muttered as I shoved the phone into my purse. I wondered if Regina would be at the meeting. And then I wondered if she was the subject of the meeting.

CHAPTER EIGHT

I arrived at the Griffins' house promptly at ten, stopping for a moment on the sidewalk in front of the grand house to imagine the three-story Victorian back in 1925, when George Bradshaw rendered it on canvas for posterity. Gazing at the home while recalling *Orchard Street* from the brief glance I had of it, I decided the artist had done a masterful job.

I hurried up the porch steps and rang the doorbell. In a moment, the door swung open and Madeline stood before me. The atypical expression of anxiety on her face worried me.

"Thank you for coming, Veronica."

"It's no problem," I said as I stepped into the hall.

Madeline offered me a cup of coffee as she led me into the living room, or parlor as the Griffins referred to it.

"No, thank you," I said. "I've already had three cups."

"Then you're wired, as they say."

"Yeah." I appreciated the moment of humor.

"Please sit. I'll go tell Ella you're here."

I settled on the sofa and glanced around the room. The Griffin home had become one of my regular haunts. Due to the death of a friend, Madeline had invited me to become the sixth member of their canasta club, a group that meets weekly to play the card game. Since I had nothing else going on, I joined the ladies and grew to enjoy the gatherings, which are hosted on a rotating basis by each member.

My gaze fell on the painting over the piano. Richard and

Eloise Griffin posed on the front porch with their daughters, Ella, Madeline, and Amelia, Regina's grandmother. I had looked at the painting many times, but now my curiosity was sparked—who was the painting's artist?

I got up and moved across the room for a closer look at the family portrait. Everyone, including Ella, wore a smile. Their shoulders were turned in, as if they were protecting and nurturing each other. Leaning forward, my hands cupped around the top edge of the piano, I squinted to decipher the artist's signature.

"Harvey Yount."

My hand thumped down on the piano keys and a discordant tone echoed as I turned to find Ella standing in the entry to the parlor, Madeline close behind her.

"Good morning, Ella."

"That's not how I taught you to play the piano," Madeline teased.

"Harvey Yount is the artist," Ella gruffly said.

I scurried back to the sofa, saying, "It's lovely." I massaged the heel of my hand to stop the numbness moving up my palm.

"It is, isn't it?" Madeline said. "I remember that day like it was yesterday. We had so much fun."

Ella's memory of the day wasn't so cheery. "I fell off the step and sprained my ankle."

The sisters walked into the room. Ella sat in one of the wingback chairs while Madeline took a seat on the second sofa.

We stared at each other for an awkward moment of silence before Madeline spoke. "We have a request, Veronica."

"Yes?"

"Officer Brody was just here," Ella said.

"She was?"

"Yes. She had a few questions for Regina."

"She did?"

Ella gave me an exasperated frown. "Must you parrot our every statement?"

I shrank back against the couch. "No, ma'am."

"Officer Brody inquired as to Regina's whereabouts yesterday evening," Madeline said.

I kept my mouth shut.

"Regina told her she was out of town on business during the day," Ella said. "She paid a visit to a food supplier in Saratoga Springs. After she left Saratoga, Regina said she stopped at the Lake George outlet stores."

"She arrived home around five thirty and drove us to Dotsie's for dinner and a movie," Madeline said. "We watched *The Best Exotic Marigold Hotel*. Judi Dench is marvelous."

"I suppose Regina didn't join you?"

Madeline shook her head as Ella said, "No. Regina said she took a short nap when she got home, had dinner, and then went to The Hearth around eight thirty. She picked us up at Dotsie's at ten o'clock."

"We are concerned about those three hours when no one saw her," Madeline said. Her fingers played at a button on her pink cardigan.

Thinking Regina might be right outside the room, listening to our conversation, I said in a hushed voice, "You certainly don't think she killed Scott?"

"We certainly do not," Madeline said with a proud rise of her chin. "But her behavior, we fear, will raise others' suspicions."

"And we understand you witnessed her argument with Mr. Culverson at The Hearth," Ella said.

"It was more of an argument with Scott's girlfriend. Leona Kendall and her children argued with Isabel, too. Is Regina here now?" I whispered.

"No, she's at The Hearth," said Madeline.

We sat in silence for a few moments.

"And why did you ask me here?" I finally asked.

Both Ella and Madeline shifted in their places before Madeline answered. "We need you to find out who murdered Mr. Culverson."

"The police will do that. Soon, I'm sure."

"We are concerned the investigation won't be thorough," Ella said.

"Why wouldn't it be? The Barton police are top-notch professionals."

"Yes, but the Kendall family has a great deal of influence in this county. And money to pay people to overlook evidence, if necessary. Or create evidence, as the case may be."

"So you think one of the Kendalls murdered Scott?"

Ella shrugged. "I wouldn't be surprised. Leona's children have been spoiled rotten. They think they can get away with anything. But I think it more likely they hired someone to handle the matter."

"And you think they may try to frame Regina?"

"Oh, yes."

"Regina is new in town," Madeline said. "People don't know how sweet and kind she is. After Saturday's display, she has the reputation of being a hothead. She'll be railroaded!"

"And you want *me* to find the murderer?"

"Yes. You can do it!" Madeline declared, as if solving a murder case was as easy as snapping a finger.

"You really think so?"

"You solved Anna Langdon's murder."

"By accident."

"In the end, yes," Ella said. "But you did snoop around and no one knew you were doing so. You did learn a good deal of information."

"Remember, you told us everything at canasta," Madeline said. She smiled; she sounded like a mother boasting about her genius child.

"Just to make conversation. Not for future reference. Why don't you hire a private investigator?" I asked.

Ella made a face as if she were simultaneously sucking a lemon, stepping in dog poop, and smelling said poop.

"Sleazy," she pronounced.

"And expensive," said Madeline.

"We think you can do this *quietly*. Or at least Madeline does."

"People like to get close to you, because of your fame."

"And we hear you are having lunch at Leona's home tomorrow," Ella said.

The two alternated like tag-team wrestlers. "How do you know that?"

"Sandy."

As in Sandy Jenkins, my canasta partner and the Griffins' housekeeper. The woman knew everything that happened between the forty-second and forty-fourth parallels. Madeline and Ella should be asking her to find the murderer, I griped to myself.

"Oh. Do you expect me to do a search of her home while I'm there?"

Ella groaned at my flippant inquiry. "Of course not. Get creative. Keep your eyes and ears open. You seem to have a knack for being in the right place at the right time. Or the wrong place at the right time."

"You can give us an update at the canasta game," Madeline said.

I looked from Madeline to Ella and sighed.

I had promised my mother, Mark, a police officer, my employees, and my best friend that I would not involve myself in the murder investigation.

"All right. I'll see what I can find out."

CHAPTER NINE

Being just two blocks from the Food Mart, I decided to start my sleuthing by paying a visit to the market to surreptitiously inquire about Ned Fleming's activities from the previous night.

I walked by the checkout lanes, hoping to see one particular cashier. The store wasn't too busy, so there were only two registers open. Neither was manned by Desiree, the Food Mart's resident chatterbox.

I grabbed a carry basket and began a slow march past each aisle, pretending to be a shopper. I glanced up to the manager's office, which was above the female, baby, and pet supply aisles. A long flight of stairs led up to the office, which had tall fiberglass windows that allowed the manager a view of the entire store. My glance caught no one observing the below commerce.

The dental and medicine aisle reminded me I needed toothpaste, so I hurried down the aisle and grabbed two boxes. I then found Desiree two aisles over, stocking cans of vegetables. I swiped a box of spaghetti as I passed the pasta shelves and tossed it in my basket before breezing along to where she stood next to a cart holding two large cardboard boxes.

"Morning, Veronica," she said, taking two cans of sweet peas from one of the boxes and placing them on a shelf.

"Hi, Desiree," I said.

"That's some news about the guy who found the painting."

"It's terrible."

"It's interesting that since you came back to town, two people have been murdered. And you were associated with both."

"I didn't know Scott. I just met him at the flea market."

"Still. You knew both victims."

"Somewhat."

"But still."

"I'm not a jinx, Desiree."

She laughed and stacked two more cans of peas. "Of course not." She lowered her voice. "It's so bizarre that Ned's the one who sold him that box."

"How is Ned?"

"I don't know. I haven't talked with him today. He's been in his office all morning," Desiree said. "Officer Nicholstone was here about fifteen minutes ago."

"Hmm." I handed her two cans from the open box. "Did you work yesterday?"

"Yep."

"And Ned?"

"Are you asking if he has an alibi, Veronica?" Desiree asked with a wink.

I nodded.

"I followed him out the door around a quarter to six. He said he and Irene and two of the girls were going to have a quick dinner at The Hearth and then go to the other kid's volleyball game." She held up her hands for more cans. "Keep up, if you're going to help."

I handed her two more cans. An easy enough alibi to check, I noted. Already I could eliminate one suspect.

Desiree leaned toward me and spoke in a low, conspiratorial whisper. "I would have suspected him, too, if I didn't know he had such a solid alibi."

"Oh, yeah?"

She nodded and went back to stocking the shelf. "He was really testy yesterday. A lot of people asked him about that painting and how it really stunk that he had it in his house all those years. Right under his nose. He got real tired of hearing about it."

"I don't blame him." I handed her the last two cans from the box. "Thanks, Desiree."

"What are you doing here? Why aren't you at your shop?" Carol asked as she eyed me with suspicion.

"I have a confession." I stopped in the middle of Carol's flower shop and theatrically beat my hand against my chest.

"I don't want to hear it. Tell me. And don't trip on that bucket of carnations."

I scooted past the bucket as I stepped up to the counter. Carol sat on a stool on the other side.

"Hi, Veronica," Amy Reynolds, Carol's floral designer, called from the workroom.

"Good morning, Amy." I waved to Amy and Casey, who was one of Carol's delivery guys. Casey was headed out the back door, two large floral arrangements firmly in his grasp.

I turned back to Carol. "The Griffins have asked me to investigate Scott's murder."

"Investigate? You're suddenly in law enforcement?"

I ignored her snark. "They're afraid Regina is going to be unjustly accused."

"And so they went to you?"

"I'm one-for-one on murder solving."

Carol shook her head. "Those odds won't last."

"You never know." I turned at the sound of the bell jingling over the door.

"Good morning," Hillary said. She came over to the counter and set down her leather tote. "I need to order a very large bouquet of flowers. To be delivered to an Albany address. Today."

"How is Isabel?" I asked.

68

"I talked with her a half-hour ago. She's a total mess."

"I can only imagine," Carol said.

"She's beating herself up. She thinks if she had been with Scott, if she had him to her place for dinner, or set the gallery showing for a half-hour earlier, or done something, he would still be alive. Instead, we were at her house, discussing a case we start next week. We ordered dinner from Yau's."

"Can we do anything?" I asked.

Hillary managed a faint smile. "No, but thank you, Veronica."

"You'll tell Isabel we're thinking of her?"

"I will."

I wandered around the small shop as Carol helped Hillary with her order. When Hillary left, with a pink rose Carol had given her as a gesture of solace, Carol said to me, "I hate to see young people in such anguish."

"Isabel will carry this grief in some corner of her heart forever."

Carol, perched on the stool behind the counter, leaned her elbow on the register, and rested her cheek on the palm of her hand. "Perhaps you should do something," she said with care, "to help Regina avoid her own anguish."

I took my best friend's blessing and hightailed it from the shop before she changed her mind.

I stopped at the art gallery on my way back to All Things. No one was in the main room when I entered. "Jamie?"

Jamie dashed from her office. She hurried over and gave me a hug. The long strand of jade beads around her neck thudded against my chest. "How are you this morning? I'm still reeling."

"I'm all right." I removed myself from the embrace.

"I've been kicking myself all morning for not insisting Scott keep the painting in my safe."

"Only one person is to blame, and it's not you. So stop. I

69

have a question about the letter that was found with *Orchard Street*."

Jamie pressed her hand against her heart as she took a step back. "Wasn't that so romantic?"

"Yes. What would be its monetary value, since it was written by George Bradshaw and bears his signature?"

Jamie fingered the beads. "Not much, compared to the painting. I'd say a few hundred. Why?"

"It was stolen, too. I'm wondering, did the killer take it for the money, or because it had another value."

"A sentimental value," Jamie said, nodding. "Or perhaps he, or she, just grabbed it because it's a companion piece to the painting."

"What are the odds *Orchard Street* will be recovered?"

Jamie dropped the beads and crossed her arms. "Not good. The recovery rate for stolen artwork is very low. About five percent."

"Yipes."

"Yeah."

We talked for a few more minutes and then I left. My friend Glen Weber was passing the gallery as I walked out.

"Hi, Glen. How are you?"

"Same old same old." That was an accurate statement; his clothes were as rumpled as ever.

"Any interest yet on Anna's house?" Glen, a Realtor, was the listing agent for my late neighbor's home.

"Not yet. Lots of looks, but not offers."

"You'll get one soon. How's Pauline?"

"She's great. She misses everyone on Orchard, but she's so much happier now. And less stressed."

"We miss her. But I'm happy she's doing well."

Pauline, Glen's wife, had two months earlier closed her family's stationery store. The business had been struggling for a while and Pauline was stretching herself thin trying to keep it afloat while also being a good wife and mother.

"So she's enjoying her job at Arden?"

"Pauline loves it. She's thinking about taking a class next semester."

"That's wonderful. Good for her."

"I'll let her know you were asking for her. I gotta go, Veronica. I have a meeting with a client in twenty minutes."

I watched as Glen hurried across the street and up the other side to the bakery. I stood for a moment, savoring the sight of the storefronts along Orchard Street. Everyone was in the Halloween and autumn spirit with their shop windows decked out with jack-o'-lanterns, strands of orange lights, and props like doll-size coffins, skeletons bobbing for apples, and a steaming cauldron filled with green goo. I love how everyone's inner kid comes out to play at this time of year.

I looked over to the All Things windows. Molly had decorated the two displays with artificial trees, adorned with silk leaves in shades of green, gold, and red. Beneath the trees she had arranged more fake foliage and pieces of blown glass, candles, and ceramic cornucopias. My staff stood behind the appealing tableau, their eyes fixed on me.

"Hey, you!"

I turned toward the sound of the voice. My mother's, from across the street. She stood in front of the bookstore, which had a window display of horror books arranged around hay bales, pumpkins, and a stuffed raven reading the tales of Edgar Allan Poe. Holding the shop door open with one foot, she stood in a schoolmarm pose—one hand on a hip and the other hand in the air, index finger pointed right at me. I waved and in return got a glower and a finger waved so vigorously it was as if she were casting a spell on me.

"Go to your business, right now!"

"Yes, Mother."

She gave me one last scowl and head shake and went into her shop as passing pedestrians cast me sideways glances.

I crossed Orchard, marveling that no matter how old I am, I'll never be too old to be scolded by my mother.

"What were you doing at the gallery?" Molly asked.

"Saying hi to Jamie."

"Glen didn't ask you to help him sell Anna's house, did he?" Tina asked.

"No. Of course not."

Claire's unblinking gaze unsettled me. "They pulled you back in, didn't they?"

"Ella and Madeline just want the support of their friends. An arrest will be made well before we're in the swing of holiday sales."

"You'd be safer helping Glen."

The gals returned to business while I stood by the window, contemplating my nascent investigation. And then my memory clicked and I remembered where Pauline worked at Arden College. And with whom.

CHAPTER TEN

That afternoon I found myself by the window, staring across Sycamore to the soon-to-be bridal shop. As I was wishing for an opportunity to approach Vin for a friendly chat and circumspect interrogation, the contractor pulled his truck up to the opposite curb. Vin and an assistant emerged from the pickup and began unloading lumber from its bed.

"I'll be outside, getting some air." I hustled to the stock room, grabbed a mug from the counter of our small pantry, sloshed some cold coffee into it, and dashed into the alley behind All Things.

I slowed my pace when I reached Sycamore and crossed the street. "Hi there," I said, nearing the truck.

"Hey," the young man said in a friendly manner. Vin simply nodded.

"I'm Veronica Walsh. I own All Things. So we're neighbors. Temporarily, at least."

"I'm Evan Collins."

I shook his rough, slightly dirty hand. I turned to Vin.

"Vin Bradley." His palm was coarse against mine.

"I'm excited about this renovation you're doing. I can't wait to see it finished. My store manager is ready to start a bridal registry and snare all the women coming in for their dresses."

"Good business move," Evan said.

"It'll be a while." Vin pulled several two-by-fours from the truck.

"Of course."

Vin eyed me for a few seconds and then turned away as he balanced the beams on his shoulder. "You were with Scott Culverson at the flea market. I'm sorry about what happened."

Did he mean what happened at the flea market, or Scott's death?

"I had just met Scott," I said. "Literally, just a few minutes before he bought the box. I guess you knew him, though, being in the building business."

"He was a good guy," Evan said.

"Yeah," Vin said. "He had talent. I enjoyed working with him."

I noticed a slight rise in Evan's eyebrows as he slid a few planks from the truck.

Vin jerked his head. "We gotta get moving."

"I'm glad we've officially met."

"Yeah." Vin turned and started for the building. I backed up to avoid being knocked out by a two-by-four.

I crossed the street and went into All Things. Were Vin's words about Scott sincere? Since his behavior on Saturday indicated he still had bad feelings about Scott, was he now truly remorseful and saddened by Scott's death, or just speaking kindly of the dead so he didn't look like a bad guy? Evan's reaction indicated the latter.

I walked over to the counter, where Tina was assisting a customer. "I see you've met our new neighbors," Tina said after the woman had left.

"Yes." I reached under the counter for the telephone book. "They're not very chatty."

"Evan is," Tina said. "He's very nice."

I caught her shy grin as she straightened the stack of shopping bags on the shelf under the counter.

"So you've already met the *new neighbors*?"

"Our coffee breaks have coincided once or twice."

"Well, Evan does seem like a very nice guy. It's his boss who's the gruff one." I walked around the counter and headed for the stairs.

"Evan says Vin's pretty easy to work with," Tina called to me.

"That's good to hear."

I went up to my office and closed the door. I sat down, thumbed through the phone book, found the listing for SRB Architects, and dialed the number. I waited a minute while the receptionist transferred me to Sabrina's line.

"Veronica. This is a nice surprise."

"You sound weary."

"It's been a long day. We've received a number of calls from Scott's clients. Rob and I have been in reassuring mode all day."

"Better than having to do damage control."

"True. So how are you?"

I paused a moment, then told her of my conversation with Vin and what Scott had told me about his history with the contractor. "How well do you know Mr. Bradley? Do you think his words about Scott were sincere?" I grabbed a pen and a scrap of paper, ready to take notes.

"I've dealt with Vin on a few projects, but not since Scott caught him overcharging our client. He's not the warmest man, but his crew does excellent work."

"So was it just a matter of overcharging? He doesn't do shoddy work because of the cheaper materials?"

"Oh, no. What's your interest in this?"

"Well, Madeline and Ella Griffin are dear friends."

"They are so sweet. They gave me a tour of their house a

couple of years ago after I begged and groveled to see it. Ella is a walking encyclopedia of Barton history and her family's place in it."

"They do have a beautiful home." So that's how you bring out Ella's sweetness, I thought. Stroke her ego with questions about her house and kin. "Ella and Madeline are worried their niece, Regina, will be dragged into the investigation. In a negative way."

"Scott told us about her behavior at The Hearth."

"She's very protective of her aunts." I paused for a beat. "Is there anyone else with whom Scott had issues, like he did with Vin?"

"No. Scott's clients loved him. He had trouble with no one."

"What time did he leave the office on Monday?"

"I think he left around four thirty."

"Have the police interviewed you? Are they aware of Scott's history with Vin?"

"Yes. Officer Nicholstone interviewed us this morning. Rob did mention the matter with Vin, since Vin was the catalyst in a way for this whole situation. But Rob did say that Vin never threatened Scott, or had any contact with him after the overcharging matter was settled."

"Until they met at the flea market."

"Right."

"How much money did Vin lose in that settlement?"

"Twenty-five thousand dollars."

"Ouch."

"Plus the dent in his reputation. Veronica, I have to go. But thanks for calling. Let's get together for coffee or lunch soon and talk about something more pleasant."

"I'd like that. I'll call you next week. Thanks for the talk, Sabrina."

After we exchanged cell phone numbers, I hung up and stared at the dollar signs I had scribbled on the paper. They told me Vin Bradley had a motive.

CHAPTER ELEVEN

"So what does Ella Griffin have on you that she was able to pull you into the investigation?" Mark asked over our dinner of cheese ravioli. "Compromising pictures of you taken before you became famous? How much do I have to pay to see them?"

"She has nothing on me." I set my fork on my plate. "The Griffins are my friends. I want to help them."

Mark crumpled his napkin and tossed it on his empty plate. "So you're going to defy a police officer's request not to get involved? And, more importantly, your mother's?"

"Yes, I am. You should have seen the worry on Madeline's face. And Ella never asks anyone for help. To ask me means she's very concerned about Regina. I can't ignore that."

"You should leave it to the police. They will conduct a fair investigation."

"What if there's pressure put on them from the district attorney to ignore evidence, or pursue only certain leads? Leona might not hobnob with Chief Price, but I bet she's cozy with the D.A. She could be a big donor to his campaigns for the very reason she might need a legal break someday."

"The Griffins should not have put you in this position."

"But you'll help, right? You are the man of mystery."

"That's an even worse sobriquet than Mr. Right. But of course I'll help. Just to make sure you stay out of trouble."

"You're the best."

"And I'll start by accompanying you to The Hearth. While

you're talking with Pauline, I'll sit at the bar and watch game one of the World Series."

"So we've reached that stage in our relationship, where we show up together and spend the night in separate rooms?"

"Just tonight. Let's not make it a habit."

"It's so good to see you, Veronica!" Pauline reached across the table to give my hand a quick grasp. She had given me a breathtaking hug and a peck on both cheeks when she arrived and a second hug before she sat. We were in The Hearth's dining room, seated at a corner table for two. Our waitress had just delivered our cheesecake and tea.

"You're busy with your new job. And I'm busy with my new business. We're busy people."

"We're so fabulous." Pauline raised her teacup to mine.

Pauline shook her head. "That's terrible what happened to that architect. Sounds like he had everything going for him. He was an Arden grad. It made the front page of the student newspaper this morning."

"I met him at the flea market. He was a former student of Mark's."

"What a shame."

I took a sip of my tea. "Are you enjoying the job? Glen said you're less stressed now."

"I love it. I like being out of the sales world, even though Development is fund-raising and selling the college. I answer the phones, make the appointments, and do the filing and let the others hustle for money."

"Glen said you might take a class next semester."

"Maybe. History or English. I can take one course per semester and Arden will cover ninety percent of the tuition."

"Take that deal!"

"Well, if you insist."

"But no flirting with the professor if you take one of Mark's classes."

"Absolutely not!"

"You work with Natalie Kendall, don't you?"

Pauline nodded and wiped her mouth with a napkin. "Yeah," she said and then rolled her eyes. "She's not my favorite co-worker."

"She has a reputation, I hear."

"She thinks she owns everything."

"Did she talk about the painting yesterday? I saw her here Saturday night and, boy, was she mad. She wanted Scott to turn over *Orchard Street* immediately."

"She talked about it incessantly. Natalie didn't close her office door, so I heard everything. She called her mother a few times to whine. And she called her brother five or six times to demand that he do something."

"She started that on Saturday night."

"You'd think she would have gotten it out of her system by Monday," Pauline said.

"You'd think. Though maybe Theo avoided her on Sunday."

"I wouldn't blame the guy at all." Pauline let out a snort that said a lot about her opinion of Natalie.

"How was Natalie today?"

"She wasn't in the office. She worked from home. I guess she's in mourning." Pauline shook her head as her sarcastic words lingered.

"What time did Natalie leave the office last night?"

"Just a few minutes before I left at five."

"Any idea what her plans were for the evening?"

"I heard her tell her mother she would 'see her later.' I think they were having dinner together."

"Have you met Theo Kendall?"

Pauline shook her head. "No. She's a real pest to him, though.

She expects him to solve every problem she has."

"Sounds like she needs to grow up. Does she have a boy-friend?"

"Her romantic history is a string of first dates. There's no one in the picture right now. It's a good thing. She'd nag the poor guy." Pauline ate two forkfuls of cheesecake. "Why all the questions about Natalie?" She paused, mid-chew. "Oh! You're trying to solve the case!"

"Shh!"

"You are!"

"Ella and Madeline Griffin asked—"

"Is their niece a suspect? She's so nice!"

"She's been questioned. Ella and Madeline asked me to help her."

"Super Sleuth Veronica is on the case!"

"I don't think I deserve the superlative just yet."

"You do. You should focus on the Kendalls. That family will do whatever they have to to shift the blame off them. But I doubt Natalie killed the man. She doesn't do anything that will get her hands dirty. Wouldn't want to break a nail."

"Thanks for the info."

"If Natalie slips and divulges anything of interest, I'll let you know."

Pauline and I talked for a while longer before she left to get home to Glen and the kids. I finished the remaining drops of my tea and set the cup on the table, to the notice of our waitress.

"May I get you another, Veronica?" she asked, taking the cup and my empty cake plate.

"No, thanks."

Her eyes suddenly welled. "Mr. Culverson gave me a very generous tip Saturday night."

"You deserved it."

"Thank you. You just never know, do you?"

"No, you don't. Did you work last night?"

"Yep."

"Did you notice if Ned Fleming from the Food Mart was here for dinner?"

"Sure. They're regulars. He was with his wife and two of their daughters. I waited on them. They skipped dessert to get to a volleyball game."

"They're a nice family, aren't they?" I said, trying to pay my penance for suspecting Ned.

"They are. Are you sure I can't get you anything?"

"I'm sure. Thanks."

I went into the bar, where Mark sat watching the baseball game on the television above the bar. Jack sat next to him. His shoulders slumped over the bar. He didn't seem too interested in the game.

"Look who showed up," Mark said.

I pressed my palm against Jack's back, holding it there for a moment. "I'm sorry about your friend, Jack."

"Thank you."

I hoisted myself on a bar stool and watched a Detroit Tiger player stroke a base hit. "Who's winning?"

"The Giants," Mark answered.

Regina pushed through the swinging door that separated the bar from the kitchen. She handed the bartender a plate of french fries and said hello to us. She surveyed Jack with a wary glance.

"I'm sorry. I've forgotten your name."

"Regina, this is Jack Sweeney," Mark said.

"My aunts and I are very sad about the death of your friend. Could you give me his parents' address so we can properly express our condolences?"

"How sincere would that be?" Jack said, scowling. "You were at his throat on Saturday."

"I didn't want to hurt him!" Regina's voice faltered. She gave me a doleful, beseeching look. Her hazel eyes filled with tears.

I slid from my stool and waved her around the bar. "Let's talk."

We went into the dining room and sat at the table I had shared with Pauline. Regina pulled the blue bandana off her head and ran her fingers through her hair.

"I can't wait for this day to be over. It started with a visit from the cops and has been downhill since. I've been so distracted, I've come close to cutting a finger off four times."

"You should have taken the day off."

"And sit at home with Aunt Ella? I need to work."

"Then keep your mind on it."

"I didn't kill Scott, Veronica."

"I don't think you did, Regina."

"But I can't prove it. I was down in Saratoga and then I went to the outlets in Lake George. I drove Aunt Madeline and Aunt Ella to Dotsie's at five thirty. I took a nap, ate something, and then came here to hang at the bar for a while. There are three hours when no one saw me."

I nodded, not giving away that I already knew all that. "It will all sort out. Hang in there. The police will make an arrest soon."

"Until then, I'll have to dodge the pitchforks." She tilted her head toward the bar.

"Jack's still in shock. He's releasing his anger and you're an easy target. It will pass."

Her disconsolate sigh pierced my heart. "I just hope I don't lose another job. I thought Barton would be a nice change of pace after Hartford. A small town and a job in a restaurant that's been around for forty years."

I nodded, remembering that she came to Barton after the Hartford restaurant where she worked closed after two years in business.

Regina stood. "I better get back to the kitchen. Thanks for listening, Veronica."

"You know where to find me whenever you need to talk."

I followed her back to the bar and took my seat next to Mark while Regina disappeared beyond the swinging door.

We three were quiet for a minute. Jack leaned forward and looked past Mark. "Veronica, does she have an alibi?"

"Regina was home."

"Were her aunts there?"

I couldn't lie. "No."

Jack leaned back, shaking his head. "So no one can back her up. I hope the police are keeping an eye on her that she doesn't slip out of town and head for the border."

"Jack, there are others who want the painting just as much as the Griffins. Regina is my friend. I believe her."

"Veronica, Scott was my friend and he's dead. I don't trust anyone who can't say exactly where they were Monday afternoon between the time Scott's boss last saw him and Isabel and I found him."

I said nothing; Jack's anger was understandable. He was right to trust no one.

The bartender stood in the corner by the beer tap, watching us as he dried a glass with a white towel.

Jack got off his stool and slapped Mark on the back. "It's time I head home, Professor."

"Are you okay to drive?"

"I am. I only drank half my beer." He gave me a curt nod as he passed me.

"Take care, Jack."

Once Jack was in the hall, the bartender came over to us. "Can I get you anything, Veronica?"

"No, thanks."

After Mark refused a fresh beer, the bartender threw the

towel over his shoulder and leaned his elbows against the bar. "I believe in Regina, too. Everyone in the restaurant does."

"That's good to hear. Regina is worried about losing her job. Were you on duty last night?" I asked.

He nodded. "And Regina came in and hung out with me for a while. She seemed just fine to me. She was in a good mood. We watched the Knicks game and talked about who would win the World Series."

"Did she say anything about the painting?"

"No. We talked about that Saturday night, after that brouhaha, and then she briefly mentioned it Sunday."

"What did she say?"

"That the family would be discussing their options with their lawyer."

A couple sitting in a booth signaled to him. The bartender excused himself and went to take their order.

Mark and I didn't talk for a minute or two. Then I said, "I wonder how the killer knew where Scott lived. Maybe Vin Bradley would know from working with Scott. Or do you think someone followed him home from work? Or from here Saturday night?"

"Scott's address can be found with a simple Internet search. Our personal information is out there and we don't even know it. Jack told me the window in the kitchen door was smashed in. If someone had followed Scott home, he would have forced himself in when Scott entered the house, not gone around to the back door and broken the window."

"The killer could have broken the window to make it look like a random break-in."

"That's an excellent point. What did Pauline have to say?"

"Natalie talked about the painting a lot yesterday and worked from home today. She overheard Natalie demanding that her brother do something about the painting. Pauline doesn't think

Natalie would actually commit murder. She's too attached to her manicure. Maybe Natalie put the plan together and Theo carried it out."

"Or maybe she's just a nuisance of a little sister."

"Or a criminal mastermind."

Mark chuckled at my exaggeration. "And I doubt Leona Kendall would handle it herself. So that leaves Vin Bradley and Theo. And a village full of people curious about a newly-discovered million-dollar painting."

"Don't forget it was all over the regional news yesterday. And there was a small blurb in the *New York Times* Monday morning."

"So the police have a large radar screen and the means to investigate. Maybe you can leave it to them."

"I promised Ella and Madeline."

"You'll need an expense account if there are suspects up and down the state."

"I'll keep it local."

"You should at least charge Ella an hourly rate for your service." Mark checked his watch. "Are you ready to go?"

"Yep. I have to get my beauty rest to look good for Leona and her gang tomorrow."

"See what you can find out about where she and her kids were yesterday evening."

"So *now* you want me poking around the investigation? Am I supposed to excuse myself to go to the powder room and run upstairs to look under all the beds?"

"Just keep your ears open. Ladies who lunch like to chat."

CHAPTER TWELVE

My phone barked as I parked along Leona's tree-lined driveway.

"Good morning, Alex."

"Ronnie!" Alex Shelby, my former leading man, sang from Los Angeles. "How are you this fine morning?" Alex often called me from the set of the soap *Passion for Life*.

"Just swell. I'm on my way to a luncheon at George Bradshaw's house."

"*The* George Bradshaw?"

"The very one."

"Wow! How did you snag that invite?"

I told Alex the saga of *Orchard Street*, Scott's murder, and the Griffins' request for my help.

"Another murder? How awful. Do you need me to help investigate?"

"I'm fine, thanks."

"Because I can get on a plane this afternoon."

"Whatever you do, don't do that!" I pleaded.

"Keep in mind it may not be what you think. The assumed motive may not be the motive at all."

"Those are some pearls of wisdom, Alex. Or should I call you Monsieur Poirot?"

"Just tuck them away. I suppose the professor is helping you?"

"He is."

"We've been texting. I'm happy that he's finished the Van Buren bio."

Mark had recently finished writing a biography of Martin Van Buren, a nineteenth-century governor of New York and the eighth president of the United States.

"So are we. It's going to be published next October."

"I've already requested a signed copy."

"Will you read it? Or just put it on your coffee table to impress the babes?"

"I may option it and play Van Buren myself," Alex shot back.

"I can't wait to see that. How's it going on *Passion*? Have you settled in?"

"It's not the same without you."

"I see your character is paired with a considerably younger woman."

"Who doesn't have half your talent. Like I said, it's not the same."

"I'm blushing."

"Good! And Carol? And the lovely Claire? And Connie? And your delightful mother?" Alex was breathless by the time he finished naming all the women he had charmed during his summer visit to Barton.

I said they were all fine and that I'd have to get off the phone so as not to make the faux pas of being late for the luncheon.

"Good luck!" he shouted before I shut the phone and tossed it in my purse.

I got out of the car and took a few tentative steps. I stopped and took in the house that loomed ahead.

In my youth we called it The Castle. Designed by George Bradshaw and built in the 1940s, the Gothic-style stone mansion stirred the imagination of every school kid visiting on one of those famous class trips. The two turrets had more ivy than I remembered, but the steep roofs, wide arches of the veranda, and wide-paned windows were as imposing as my memory recalled. My gaze moved from the first floor slowly up to the third. I focused on a small window and remembered my girl-hood fantasy that crazy Bertha from *Jane Eyre* lived in that room. The overcast sky fit the looming sense of foreboding the house always stirred in me.

I stiffened my posture and continued to the front door, hoping I was suitably attired in my gray pantsuit and pale pink blouse. It was one of the suits I'd bought when I became a professional businesswoman.

I rang the doorbell and stood frozen in front of the oak door, as if I were being watched or filmed by a surveillance camera. My heart began to punch against my chest and I thought I would break into a sweat. Many would think I would be comfortable going into the home of obvious wealth, thanks to my years in show business. And I was, to the extent that the show biz folks were also friends and colleagues. But now I was going into the home of a legendary artist's imperious daughter. Leona and her friends might not be impressed that my daytime television experience was on a soap opera, not on the educational and intellectual public television station.

"Check your attitude at the door, Veronica," I whispered just as the door swung open.

A young woman, I guessed she was twenty-four or -five, greeted me. "Welcome to Oli Hill!" she said in a thick Slavic accent.

The exuberant welcome startled me. "Thank you."

The woman stared at me for a moment. She was tall and athletically built. Her braided, honey-colored hair fell midway down her back. Her gray eyes flashed with recognition.

"Miss Wesley, what an honor," she said, her enthusiasm turning to reverence.

I hate to admit it, but the reference to my soap character's name (maiden; she was married six times) gave me a thrill.

"I'm Veronica Walsh."

"Oh, yes." The woman bowed. "I'm so excited to meet you. I am Dusanka Moravek." She seemed to grow taller as she proudly said her name, pronounced Du-*sahn*-ka. I wondered how many Americans confused her name with the popular instant coffee brand. "It's very nice to meet you, Dusanka."

"Dusanka." The clipped utterance came from inside the house.

Dusanka's face and back stiffened. "Please, come in, Miss Walsh," she said with a formal demeanor.

Crossing the threshold, I spotted Leona's back as she moved into an adjoining room.

I stepped into a broad foyer and marveled at the gleam of the hardwood floor. A wide staircase opened before me, with a grand piano standing in the corner beside it. I imagined a tuxedo-clad pianist sitting behind the keys, playing Mozart and Gershwin for Leona's evening soirees. If Oli Hill did not have a ballroom, dancers could twirl around the foyer and never bump into each other. Yeah, the house inspired Gatsby-esque, as well as Jane Eyre-ish, fantasies.

To my left, a door led to what looked like a rival to the New York Public Library. I caught a glimpse of a floor-to-ceiling bookcase. On the wall facing the doorway hung a formal portrait of a man and woman standing behind a chair in which a young girl was seated. I didn't need a closer look to know the subjects were George, Olivia, and Leona. Their stiff poses did not give me a warm and fuzzy feeling.

To the right was a room simply furnished with two chairs flanking a fireplace. I didn't need to see the signature on it to know the painting over the mantel was a George Bradshaw. A Persian rug with a medallion design added ivory, red, black, and gold hues to the room's palette. I guessed this was the designated reception area, for Leona stood there greeting two women.

Dusanka strode to the entry to this room. "Mrs. Kendall, Miss Veronica Walsh has arrived."

I felt like I was in a reception line, waiting my turn to meet the president or queen. Leona, dressed in an elegant camel-colored, wool pantsuit, turned to me. I stuck out my hand and successfully kept my knees from bending into a curtsey.

"I am so happy you could come, Veronica." Leona clasped my hand and leaned in to press her cheek against mine.

"Thank you for including me." Leona stepped back, giving me an excellent view of the painting—a young girl wearing a straw hat watching a lone swan glide across a serene lake.

Leona waved her arm toward a corner doorway as the doorbell rang. "Please join the others in the living room for some refreshment before lunch. I will be in shortly."

"Thank you."

I tiptoed across the Persian rug and through the arched portal into a room of beautiful dentil crown molding, ivory walls, and a luxurious carpet of a deep scarlet shade stretched from wall to wall. There was another fireplace, with another Bradshaw painting above it, and two Queen Anne chairs positioned in front of the hearth. A sofa and a table completed the furniture set.

The six women gathered in the living room turned as one as I entered the room. "Hello." I searched for one identifiable face I could cling to for the rest of the afternoon.

"Veronica!"

I turned to the voice as Ginnie Pinkerly, one of my high school classmates, stepped forward. She gave me a quick kiss and squeeze as I exhaled with relief and inhaled a whiff of Chanel No. 5. Thank goodness I would have an ally at the lunch, as well as someone to cling to if necessary.

"It's so good to see you," Ginnie said.

"You, too. It's been a while."

"Let me introduce you to everyone."

Ginnie introduced me to the women. Not one was named Bitsy or Mimsie, but they all had that cultured air about them. They politely took turns addressing me.

"I love your boutique," one said.

"I think it's wonderful you've returned part of it to its original purpose of promoting the work of local artists," said another.

"Is an Emmy heavy? They look heavy."

"It is, but it's weight I don't mind bearing."

Naomi said, "All those love scenes must have been fabulous. All those men." Her mouth, heavily glossed with a deep red lipstick, curled into a mischievous smile.

So much for my worry that the women would look down on my acting resume. "As fabulous as they could be with all the crew watching."

"That makes it even better," Naomi returned.

A woman wearing a mandarin-style, lavender-colored blouse with *D'Amato Catering* scrawled on the collar approached with a tray of mini-quiches. I thanked the woman and took a cocktail napkin and a quiche.

My friend Sandy stepped forward with a tray bearing several crystal glasses filled with a pink, foamy punch. Sandy's eyes sparkled with mirth as she gave me a slight bow. She wore a D'Amato Catering blouse over black pants.

"Would you like a glass of punch, Miss Walsh?"

I took a glass and thanked her. Sandy winked and disappeared into the next room.

"Sandy gets around, doesn't she? So, how have you been?" Ginnie asked as the other women broke up into conversation groups. I couldn't eavesdrop like Mark suggested, for Ginnie took my arm and led me to the window that overlooked the grounds behind the house.

I lowered my voice and said, "I'm glad you're here. I didn't think I'd know anyone. I guess you know Leona from the D.A.R.?"

Ginnie is the head of the local chapter of the Daughters of the American Revolution. I assumed that was how she wound up in Leona's social orbit.

"No. Leona's not a member. She and I serve on the Botanical Society's board." Ginnie gave my arm a light squeeze. "How are you and Mark? I'm so thrilled you two got together!"

"We're doing very well, though we don't know what to call each other. Boyfriend and girlfriend? Significant other? Nothing sounds right."

"It doesn't matter."

I took a sip of the punch—a combination pineapple, orange, and lime flavor with a bit of a lemon zinger—and studied the outside scene. George Bradshaw's studio stood about thirty yards down the lawn. A one-story building, it was constructed of the same stone as the main house.

"Do school kids still come here on class trips? Carol, Patrick, Mark, and I discussed ours the other night."

"Yes," Ginnie said. "And it's open to the general public one weekend a month."

I glanced over Ginnie's shoulder and saw into the dining room. Barton-based caterer Connie D'Amato and Sandy stood by the table, their heads close as they engaged in conversation. Connie spotted me and wiggled her fingers in greeting.

"Would it be a social no-no if I said hello to the caterer? She's a friend."

"I'll cover for you. I'll say you're getting her business card."

I dashed into the dining room and to Connie's side. "It looks like your business is a huge success."

"Thanks." Connie grinned and "knocked wood" by lightly rapping her knuckle against the white tablecloth. "I'd love to chat, but I'm on duty. I have to check things in the kitchen."

"Alex says hello."

Connie giggled and her cheeks flushed. "Tell him I say hi back."

"I didn't know you worked with Connie," I said to Sandy as Connie left through an entry at the far side of the room.

"Once in a while. She doesn't have permanent staff yet."

Dusanka came through the doorway Connie had just used. She beamed when she saw me and headed straight to us.

"Rachel Wesley taught me English," she said as she took my hand. She almost broke my fingers with her strong grip. "I grew up in Czechoslovakia watching your show with my grandmother."

I have met many fans over the years who told me stories of how the soap affected their lives. A few, like Dusanka, had learned English by watching the show.

"I'm delighted to hear that, Dusanka. Do you work for Connie, too?"

"Oh, no, Miss Walsh. I work for Mrs. Kendall."

"Wonderful."

"Yes," Dusanka said through a clenched smile.

"Dusanka," I heard Leona call from the living room.

Dusanka gave Sandy and me a deep bow and hustled into the next room.

Sandy clutched my arm. "Madeline and Ella are in a panic over Regina. They told me they've asked you to track down Scott Culverson's killer. Who do you think did it? Who's on your radar?"

"I have no idea." I lowered my voice and said, "I'm hoping to learn a thing or two while I'm here."

"I'll be on the lookout, too. I have to get back to work. I'll see you at canasta tonight."

I had forgotten that our weekly canasta game was at Dotsie's that evening. Madeline and Ella would expect an update. Ugh, I thought as I went back to the living room.

The women were gathered around Leona and a newcomer, a frosted brunette in her early sixties. She was dressed in a powder-pink skirt and jacket set. She gave off a definite "Doyenne of Society" vibe.

Leona guided the woman to where I stood. "Veronica, I want you to meet my friend Frances Wells. Frances, this is Veronica Walsh. She is now the owner of Anna Langdon's boutique."

"It's a pleasure," Frances said as we shook hands.

"Excuse me while I check with the caterer." As Leona went into the dining room, one of the women came over to talk with Frances.

"How are you, dear?"

Frances's mouth twisted into a dramatic grimace. "I've had it up to my eyeballs with this damn will."

I excused myself—the two women didn't even notice me leave—and went back to the window. Ginnie soon joined me.

"What's her story?" I whispered.

"Frances's father was Judge Damon Sorensen. He passed away two months ago."

So, I was right about Leona having friends in the corridors of justice. "I remember reading that in the newspaper."

Ginnie nodded and took a fast glance over to Frances. "His death is not what everyone's concerned about." She took another sweep of the room and stepped closer, turning me to face the window. "Frances is in a snit over a codicil to the judge's will."

"Did he leave money to his dog?" I asked.

"No!" Ginnie laughed. "The judge left three hundred thousand to the historical society."

"Frances isn't happy about that?"

"She's not happy because she doesn't have control over the money. She claims he meant to set up a charitable trust, with her as the sole trustee."

"That's a nice sum of money he gave."

"It is for the restoration of the parsonage." In response to my blank look, Ginnie explained, "You weren't back home yet. Judge Sorensen bought the old parsonage in Barton and donated it to the H.S. last December."

I gripped my glass of punch. "Very generous. Is Frances going to contest the will?"

"Yes. The case is going to probate in a week or two. Judge Sorensen had dementia that worsened the last weeks of his life. Frances is going to argue diminished mental capacity."

"Surely his lawyer wouldn't have proceeded with the codicil knowing the judge was confused."

"I agree. Aaron Franklin is his lawyer. He has an excellent reputation."

"I met Aaron at Jamie Chang's gallery the other night. Funny man."

"Frances is just doing her typical control-freak thing," Naomi said from behind me.

I twitched with surprise. I had not realized Naomi was standing so close to Ginnie and me.

"Shh, Naomi," Ginnie said.

Naomi grinned and continued. "Frances just wants a legacy to watch over, like Leona. She doesn't have the brains to understand his legal work, so she's grabbing the building. Brenda worked her tail off making that parsonage deal happen and put up with a lot of garbage from Frances. In my humble opinion, Judge Sorensen showed mercy by giving the money outright to the H.S. He knew his daughter would be a pit bull about how the money was spent, so he spared Brenda the agony."

Leona returned. She twice shook a small crystal bell and said, "Ladies, please join me for lunch."

I marveled over the theatrical staging of the affair as we filed into the dining room and stood around the table eyeing the name cards placed at each plate setting. I was assigned the seat next to Naomi. Ginnie was on the other side of Naomi, at the foot of the table. As I settled at my place, the women chattered about the beautiful china, the shine of the crystal, the exquisite colors of the floral centerpiece.

I understood my minor role in this production. Shameless flatterer. "This is quite lovely, Leona."

"Thank you, Veronica," Leona said from the head of the table. "I am so pleased that you could join our group."

The women muttered similar thanksgivings for my presence and gave me a smattering of applause. Leona tinkled the bell again and Sandy, Dusanka, the quiche-serving woman, a young man, and Connie stepped in from the kitchen, each carrying two plates of salad.

"This is simply divine," the woman on my right said.

"Indeed," Frances confirmed.

I followed the lead of the others, keeping my hands clasped in my lap until the servers had left the room. Once Leona picked up her salad fork, each woman picked up her own fork and delicately dipped it into the food. A few minutes of requisite compliments and silent chewing followed. I took a sip of my water, careful not to let the floating slice of lemon bump my nose.

"Ruth, how is your granddaughter at Yale?"

I politely listened as Ruth launched into a proud monologue of her granddaughter's life in the Ivy League. I attentively ate my salad, more carefully than I had ever eaten a salad in my life, taking just one leaf of greens at a time and chewing it exactly twelve times. I smiled throughout as I listened to Ruth. As she went on about how her little darling desperately wanted to get into Yale Drama, my eyes drifted to the Bradshaw painting on the wall behind her.

Leona noticed. "My father painted that in nineteen fifty-seven," she said of the depiction of Bear Lake's Main Street.

"It's stunning," I said.

"Thank you." Leona paused for a moment. "Father was always quite taken by a village's main street. He knew it was the heart of the community. He loved the life, the bustle that he saw there."

All the women nodded in agreement of these sage words, so I did the same.

"I am not surprised he painted Barton's Orchard Street," Leona continued. "My heart aches that I did not have the opportunity to see it before it was stolen."

A few forks clattered against the good china at the mention of the controversial painting. Frances grabbed the opportunity and ran with it.

"What a dastardly deed was done," she said.

"Shocking," said the woman sitting across from me. "It's just awful that the painting was taken. Leona, it should have been given to you immediately. I'm heartbroken that your father's work has been kept from you."

"Sycophantic drama queen," Naomi whispered.

I turned slightly to regard her; Naomi winked and blithely put a forkful of salad greens in her mouth as a curtain of her soft, gray hair fell and hid her face.

She turned serious. "The young man is the real loss."

"Yes," Ginnie fervently agreed.

The other women murmured similar sentiments and conversation stopped for a minute or two.

One-track mind Leona broke the silence. "I am sure the painting will be recovered soon and returned to its rightful home." Leona did not need to state the location of that "rightful home." Perhaps it was this dining room, or the living room.

Or maybe the reception room.

"I am envious of Veronica, though. She was present when *Orchard Street* was found."

"You were?" several women said as every head turned toward me.

I nodded. "Yes. I was nearby when Scott found the painting in the antique box."

"I understand you were also with Mr. Culverson at The Hearth Saturday evening," Frances said.

Frances sat at the end of the table, next to Leona. I leaned in to make eye contact as I answered. "Yes, I was. My companion and I had an after-dinner drink with Scott and his friends." Did I just refer to Mark as my *companion*? I didn't much like it, but it was the appropriate label for this lunch crowd.

"Then you met my daughter, Bianca," Frances said.

"Yes, I did." I paused for a beat and added, "She's a lovely young woman." I flashed a warm smile, waited a moment, and then sat back.

"Thank you."

"How is Bianca?" Ginnie asked.

I relaxed as Frances took over the conversation with an update of her dear Bianca.

"You *are* an excellent actress. That girl's a viper," Naomi said, her words again barely audible. Ginnie lifted her napkin and gently pressed it against her lips to cover the evidence of a smirk.

"Thanks," I whispered.

"Bianca attended the flea market, too. She has a dreadful fascination for previously-worn clothing."

"My cousin's daughter owns a pair of Audrey Hepburn's pants," the woman next to Leona said. "She does not wear them, however."

"Veronica, are any of your pants currently being worn by

anyone else?" Naomi asked.

Tongues clucked and I said, "I suppose. I have donated my real-life pants to clothing drives. And some of my costumes have been auctioned off for charity."

"How wonderful," Frances cooed.

Leona rang her bell. Within seconds, Dusanka and the quiche woman swept in from the kitchen, took our salad plates, and breezed back into the kitchen. They returned in a moment, along with Sandy, Connie, and the young man, to serve our entrée. Salmon cakes and asparagus on a bed of wild rice. At least I was getting an excellent meal as a lady who lunched.

CHAPTER THIRTEEN

The conversation during the meal was innocuous—charity events, grandchildren, the arts. What I thought would be an arduous, fish-out-of-water experience turned out to be rather enjoyable. When the ladies began to depart after dessert, Leona looped her arm through mine and patted my hand.

"Before you go, Veronica, would you like to see my father's studio? I believe it has been a while since your last visit."

"I would like that very much." I watched as Ginnie and Naomi walked down the driveway.

We talked about the lovely autumn weather as Leona guided me to a stone path that led to her father's studio. After unlocking the door, Leona moved aside so I could enter first.

"I was very lucky that Father was not one of those temperamental artists who must work in perfect peace and solitude. I spent many hours of my childhood here, watching him create his masterpieces. Of course, I was quiet as a mouse."

"A great privilege. I can relate in a way. I spent hours in my parents' bookstore as a child, watching them work and helping out as I could."

"We two were very blessed to spend time with our parents in their work."

"Agreed. Do you paint, Leona?"

"I attempt to paint. I may be proof that artistic talent is not genetic."

Her humility surprised me. "I bet your father would think

differently."

Leona gave a shy nod of thanks and we stood quietly for a moment. I studied the room, amazed at how unchanged it was from my class visit. An easel, with a rocking chair nearby, stood by a window that faced the dense woods behind the house. There was a sofa along one wall and a chair pushed into a corner. A long table cut the room in two and had the tools of an artist spread across it. Paints, brushes, sketch pads, blank canvases, sponges, and rags. I wondered how many of the objects were embellishments, never used by George Bradshaw, but added over time to accentuate the tableau.

Leona pointed to another easel a few feet away from the first. A half-completed canvas rested on it.

"My father was working on this when he died."

I moved closer. George Bradshaw had painted the trees in a vivid green, with a black Labrador retriever emerging from the forest. The detail was so refined I could see the dog's tongue hanging from its mouth.

"Father was going to paint himself, too," Leona said quietly. "It would be his one self-portrait. Him and his dog, Harry."

"A very unassuming portrait. I'm sorry he didn't finish it."

"I am, too. My son, Theo, actually mourns for it."

A bit dramatic, but I didn't react. "Mark mentioned your daughter works at Arden. What does Theo do?"

"He oversees the Bradshaw House. I finally relinquished the reins last year and let Theo assume the director's chair."

I nodded. I knew the Bradshaw House; it was the second stop on our long-ago class trip. It was George's childhood home, converted into a museum of his paintings and photographs of his life.

Leona gestured at the unfinished painting. "Theo would love to display this at the museum, but I like to keep it here. I believe as long as it is here, in Father's studio, so is Father's spirit.

Perhaps that's a bit silly."

"Not at all." I meant my words. "I haven't been to the museum in years. I should go one day."

"You should. I think Theo would love to give you a tour. He is mortified by how we all behaved Saturday evening. As am I."

"I can understand the emotion of learning of a long-lost work of your father's."

"Thank you." Leona moved to the window, inviting me to join her with a flick of her hand. "So many days I would find my father staring out this window, contemplating his next brush stroke."

Leona was laying on the paint with a steamroller, I thought, but all I said was, "He had a beautiful view to inspire him." Trees, that's what he had, trees.

"That he did." Leona regarded me for a moment and then went back to staring at the trees. "I had an ulterior motive for inviting you to lunch."

"Oh?" I assumed an air of naïveté.

"Yes. Though events have changed my plan. I know you are close with the Griffins. When I saw you with Scott Culverson at The Hearth, I assumed you knew him well, too. I had planned on asking you to help broker a deal to return *Orchard Street* to my family. I thought you could convince everyone to give up their fight. You could persuade them that the Bradshaw House is the proper home for the painting."

Now Leona was the naïve one, thinking I had the influence to arrange such a deal. "You overestimate my power to influence."

"Perhaps. I thought it would be best to have an intermediary help us all arrive at the best outcome. I thought I'd ask your help first before calling in my lawyer. It would be wonderful if we could resolve this without a bitter court contest. And given the uproar at The Hearth, I decided it would not be wise to approach Mr. Culverson again about the painting. I know my children and I came on like a sledgehammer Saturday evening. I felt a velvet touch might be better."

"I don't think Scott would have been swayed by anything I said, assuming I took your position on the matter."

"Well, we will never know. The matter has changed with Mr. Culverson's horrific death. I certainly hope, once *Orchard Street* is recovered, that the Griffins do not pursue it through the courts. That would be unseemly."

I spoke up for the Culversons. "I would think the painting would be considered a part of Scott's estate and therefore pass to his beneficiaries. Probably his parents, since Scott wasn't married."

Leona gave me a sharp look. "Their son is dead because he possessed that painting. I doubt they would want to keep it. I think they would be amenable to making a deal with me. A memorial in his name at Arden, or perhaps a donation to his favorite charity."

Despite the delicious lunch, a sour taste rose to my mouth. All I could say was, "Perhaps."

Leona turned her face back to the landscape beyond the window. "I am sure I can also dissuade Mr. Fleming from pursuing the matter. A grocery store manager certainly does not have the funds to see a case through the courts. Certainly not against us. Yes," she said with a nod, "I could certainly dissuade him. That leaves the Griffins. Ella is a very stubborn woman. I think Madeline could be persuaded to give up the fight. She is the more compliant of the two."

"She can be tough when necessary."

Leona flashed a patronizing smile. "I defer to your opinion. But I hope you will use your influence to convince them that it would be in their best interests to avoid a battle over the painting. The sisters would not want to spend whatever time they have left in a bitter dispute with me. The stress would certainly be harmful to their health. They can have the letter. I certainly do not want it. It is a slap in the face to my mother."

"Leona, I value my friendship with Ella and Madeline. I'm not going to risk it by involving myself in their personal business. Even if I did, I believe *Orchard Street* belongs with them. Your father gave it to their mother as a wedding present. I support their position."

Her eyes creased into slits. "Of course, this is all contingent upon the outcome of the murder investigation. You may be supporting a killer."

I caught my breath. "I don't believe for a moment—"

"I know Ella and Madeline's niece does not have an alibi."

"I don't believe Regina had anything to do with Scott's death."

"I think you may be the only one. I understand Mr. Fleming has an alibi. As do my children and I. If you will not help me retrieve my father's work, you should help your friends salvage their good family name and convince Miss Quinn to be fully forthcoming about her whereabouts Monday evening. It will be better for her to be honest."

A soft "ahem" ended our conversation. Leona and I turned toward the door, where Dusanka stood.

"You have a phone call, Mrs. Kendall."

"I will be there in a moment, Dusanka."

I started toward the door. "Thank you for the invitation to lunch, Leona. You have a beautiful home and a lovely group of friends."

"Please consider my request, Veronica. You will come to realize it is the best outcome for all concerned parties."

I merely nodded and stepped outside. Dusanka hurried ahead of me as I climbed the stone path. She slowed as she neared the house and turned slightly as I drew even with her. In a low voice she blurted two Czech words to me.

"Excuse me?"

Dusanka's eyes shifted to Leona, who was fast approaching us. "It was a pleasure to meet you, Ms. Walsh." She dipped her head in deference and dashed into the house.

I rounded the house and trotted down the driveway to my car. I slammed the door after I got in and took a few moments to calm myself before starting the engine. Leona's gall didn't surprise me, for the same sleazy behavior of the rich had been portrayed on *Days and Nights*. I just had never encountered it to this extent in real life. It took my breath away.

My worry for Regina deepened on the drive down Leona's pretentiously long driveway. I turned onto the road, eager to get back to my crowd in Barton and anxious to get the glare of Leona's accusation off my friend.

CHAPTER FOURTEEN

Before returning to All Things, I stopped at home for a fast wardrobe change before heading to Scott's house.

When I arrived, I found a quiet neighborhood; there were no cars parked on the street, no dog walkers out with their buddies, and no police activity at the crime scene. Scott's home was the last on the dead-end street. A belt of trees stretched from the end of his driveway and around the back curve of a gravel-covered cul-de-sac to the driveway of the house on the opposite side of the street. A row of fir trees separated Scott's property from his next-door neighbor. Great walls of privacy. Drats.

I turned around in the cul-de-sac and parked in front of the house. A car was in the driveway; from the Arden sticker on the rear window I guessed it was Scott's vehicle.

I let my eyes drift over the white, two-story house. The drapes were drawn across the windows that faced the street, concealing what I guessed to be the living room. I walked along a slate path leading from the garage to the backyard. Several azalea bushes planted in a thick carpet of pachysandra bordered the house. I swept my gaze over the ground, looking for something that might be a clue. In the backyard, a few yards of grass opened to a forest of trees that stretched well beyond the border of Scott's property.

I turned to the deck. A short length of police tape dangled from the railing leading up the deck steps.

"I guess the crime scene is officially closed," I said as I ascended the stairs. I breezed by the domed barbecue and glass-top picnic table to the kitchen door. A smudge-free pane had replaced the broken window.

I peered in the window and saw a tidy kitchen. Of course. The crime-scene cleaner had been through and done a thorough job of scrubbing away all signs of violence.

"Oh, well."

I regarded the door. To avoid marking the scene with my fingerprints, I pulled my jacket over my hand, pulled back the storm door, and gently twisted the doorknob. Locked, of course. But I had to be sure of it.

My eyes scanned the deck for any small thing that might be evidence. Nothing.

I left the deck and crossed the backyard to the tree line. Thirty feet of tree-covered land separated the rear of Scott's property from Hill Road. The killer could have parked on Hill and dashed back and forth through the woods.

I returned to the front yard. At the house across from Scott's, a teenager was striding up the driveway. He had a backpack slung over his shoulder. I saw a white cord extending from each of his ears, leading to a device in his hand.

"Hello!"

The boy did not react. Blasted loud music. The kid would be deaf in ten years.

I scampered across the gravel, slowing my pace when I reached his driveway. "Hello!"

The teen, now at a side door that opened into the garage, turned. He pulled out one of the earbuds.

"Yeah?"

"Hi. I'm Veronica. I was a friend of Scott Culverson's." I was breathless when I reached him.

"Oh, wow. I'm sorry."

"Did you know Scott well?"

The teen shrugged. "We'd shoot hoops once in a while." He nodded his head toward the basketball hoop at the head of the driveway. "Cool guy."

"He was. Were you at home Monday afternoon?"

"Nope. I stayed after school to watch a soccer game."

"What time did you get home?"

"Around six. My mom picked me up."

"Did you notice anything going on over at Scott's house? Any cars parked out front? Anyone walking around in the neighborhood you didn't recognize?"

The teen shook his head. "Nope. Not until later, when the cops came. Then it was crazy out here."

"I bet. And your mother? Did she notice anything before the police arrived?"

"Nope. And she would. She's the unofficial neighborhood watcher. She runs to the front window every time she hears a car door slam. She's really freaked out about this. She's talked Dad into going up to Lake Placid for the weekend to get away."

An SUV passed the house and turned around on the cul-de-sac, parking a few feet from Scott's driveway.

"Not a bad idea. Have fun. And thanks for your help."

"Sure thing."

The teen went into his house and I headed back to Scott's, watching the driver's side door of the SUV open from the corner of my eye. I prayed it wasn't an unmarked police vehicle.

"Is that you, Veronica?"

The deep voice eased my worry. Rob Burton slammed shut the car door and was standing beside his car, staring at me. "I didn't know you lived in this neighborhood," he said, giving me a puzzled look.

"Um, I don't. I was on my way home from an, uh, appointment, and my curiosity got the best of me." I walked over to the cul-de-sac, an abashed smile on my face.

Rob stared at me for an excruciatingly long moment. "You're playing sleuth again."

"Yeah."

"Sabrina told me you called yesterday with some questions about Vin Bradley."

"Yes. I did."

He opened the back passenger door and pulled out a large cardboard box. "Let me know if you have any more questions. The more brains that are trying to figure out who killed Scott, the better."

"Thank you for not reading me the riot act."

Rob started for the house. "I'm officially here to collect Scott's work product and bring it back to the office. But I'm going to do exactly what you're doing. Check out the crime scene for anything the police may have overlooked."

"I didn't see much through the kitchen window."

"Why don't you come inside? Maybe your objective eye will catch something."

A bracing chill punctuated the eerie feeling that struck me when we walked into the dimly lit house. The tiny entry foyer was bookended by the living room on the left and the dining room to the right. A staircase led to the second floor and a narrow hall led to the kitchen.

"I'm not going to bother pushing the heat up, unless you need it. We won't be here long." Rob flipped on the entry-hall light. "I'll be in Scott's office. Take a look around and give a shout if you need anything."

He headed down the hallway and turned left while I went into the living room. Arranged before the big-screen television were a brown leather couch and two brown recliners. Brass lamps stood on the two end tables. Scattered across the coffee table were several copies of *Sports Illustrated* and *Architectural Digest.*

I spent a few minutes looking at the photographs arranged on the mantel. There was one of Scott and Isabel, taken on one of the boats that make daily cruises around Lake George, and a second photo of the couple sitting at a table overlooking the lake, toasting each other with margaritas. I crossed the oatmeal-colored carpet and went into the dining room. I breezed by the table, the only furnishing in the room, and moved into the kitchen.

The clear-glass cabinet doors revealed shelves of cereal, canned soup, and bags of potato chips, pretzels, and Doritos. Two of the boxes of chocolates from All Things, the gold ribbon still tied around them, sat on the table in the breakfast nook. A quick look in the drawers revealed the usual kitchen items. There were no slips of paper with random notes scrawled across them; the habit of storing appointments, addresses, and reminders on tablets and iPhones stymied my search. I turned into the hallway and took a glance at the staircase. As the police would have gone through Scott's personal effects, I knew a search of his bedroom would be inappropriate.

I found Rob in a small room at the end of the hall. Scott's home office. Rob stood beside the drafting board positioned in front of the window. He was rolling a wide sheet of blueprints.

"Find anything?"

"No."

"Me, neither." Rob placed the paper roll in the cardboard box and closed the flaps. "I'm finished, too."

"How many architects work in your firm?" I followed Rob into the hallway.

"Two, now that Scott is gone. So much for expanding the business." Rob paused at the kitchen doorway and was silent. "None of this makes sense," he finally said. He turned and headed for the front door.

I held the storm door open for Rob. "Thank you for allowing me to look around the house."

"I appreciate the company. Sabrina offered to come, but I think that would have been too upsetting. She was very fond of Scott."

I walked with Rob to his car, chatting about his family while he put the box in the back of the SUV, and waited on the cul-de-sac until he drove away. As I turned to head for my car, I noticed a lump of silver among the leaves and grass that met the graveled edge.

A ladies' watch.

To avoid smearing any fingerprints on the watch, or adding my own, I pulled a tissue from my purse and held it between my fingers when I picked up the watch. Made by Fenton, a jewelry company famous for their luxury goods, the piece was gorgeous. Small diamonds encircled the oval face. The clasp was unlatched. I noted the watch showed the correct time and was in excellent condition. It hadn't been lying in the cul-de-sac for very long.

I wrapped the tissue around the watch, tucked it into my purse, and walked to my car. An intuition I could not shake told me it was evidence in the murder case.

CHAPTER FIFTEEN

Four officers were at work in the main room of the police station when I arrived. Relieved to find that Tracey was one of them, I nodded a greeting to the officer at the front desk and zoomed over to where she sat.

"You look intent on something," Tracey teased as I sat in the chair beside her desk.

"I think I found a piece of evidence in the Scott Culverson case," I whispered.

Tracey gave a quick nod as her face drew blank. "Why don't we go to the conference room." She opened her drawer and pulled out a pair of latex gloves.

I followed her through to the back hall, past Chief Price's closed office door, an interrogation room, and into the small conference room at the end of the hall. Tracey closed the door as I sat down at the table and took the tissue-swathed watch from my purse. Tracey sat at the head of the table, eyeing what I held in my hand as I unwrapped the watch.

Tracey slipped her hands into the gloves, took the watch, and examined it. "Where did you find this?"

"On the cul-de-sac next to Scott's house."

"And why were you there?" Tracey turned the watch in her hand. Her voice and expression held no clue as to whether she was angry or irritated by my response.

"Paying my respects."

"They have something for that. It's called a wake. And then

113

there's something known as a funeral—"

"All right. I wanted to take a look around." I dared not tell her I had also gone inside the house, though at Rob's invitation.

Tracey let out a chuckle. "You are funny, Veronica. I'll give you that. And why were you looking around?"

"Just to see what I could see."

Tracey's stern look lasted a good twenty seconds. "Well, you did the right thing bringing the watch to us. I'll show it to Chief Price and we'll catalog it."

"Thank you."

"And please, no more investigating, Veronica. We're hard at work on the case."

"I know you are. But you always ask for help from the public."

"But we don't ask the public to visit the crime scene."

"You won't tell Chief I'm the one who found the watch, will you? He's not as calm, patient, and understanding as you are, Tracey."

"You can be an anonymous source. How about that?"

"Thank you."

I followed Tracey from the room. I held my breath as we passed Chief Price's office, praying he wouldn't suddenly charge from the room and see his "anonymous source." I made it down the hall without incident.

"Good luck," I said when we reached Tracey's desk. "I hope the watch is a good lead."

As I left the station, I thought how ironic it was that I was thrilled to be an unnamed source after I had spent my career not wanting to be "anonymous." Hey—I'm an actor; I like attention. But I don't need credit in the catching of a killer.

"You survived," Claire trilled when I walked into All Things.

"And I didn't spill or break anything."

"Bravo!"

Tina appraised me from head to toe. "You wore *that* to Leona Kendall's?"

I was still in my jeans and boots. "No. I changed, afterwards. Obviously."

"You just missed a group of leaf lookers," Claire said.

It was that time of the year when buses filled with fall-foliage fans pulled into Barton a few times a week for an hour or two of shopping and eating. I always enjoyed meeting the people; they are enthusiastic and appreciative of the beauty of our little village.

"I'm sorry I missed them."

"A Charlie Gannon was here about fifteen minutes ago to see you."

"Why?"

"He didn't say. I told him you'd probably be back soon. He said he'd be over at the gallery for a while."

"Thanks."

I crossed Orchard and headed for the gallery. "Charlie wants to see me?"

"He just stepped over to the bank. He'll be back in a minute," Jamie said. "Let's wait for him outside."

We sat on a bench in front of the gallery's window. "Do you know why Charlie wants to see me?"

"Yes. He was hired to do a reproduction of *Orchard Street*. Charlie's done a sketch from the newspaper photo and would like your opinion of it before he starts on the painting. I can't help him since I never saw the piece, so I suggested he ask you. There he is now." She gave a wave as Charlie passed the pharmacy next door and ambled toward us. He held a large, manila envelope in his hand.

Jamie slid to the end of the bench and patted the space between us. "Sit down."

"A thorn between two roses." Charlie settled on the bench.

"Has Jamie told you of my request, Veronica?"

"Yes. I'd love to see your sketch. I have to tell you I only saw the painting for a minute or two at the flea market."

"That's more than anyone else, except for Scott Culverson and, I guess, his girlfriend. I obviously can't ask her for help. I sketched from the photograph in the newspaper. Not the best way to work. The photographer wouldn't give me a digital copy of the photo."

He pulled a sheet of heavy, white paper from the envelope. He flipped it over, revealing a colored-pencil sketch of George Bradshaw's *Orchard Street*.

"That's beautiful," I said.

Jamie said, "I told you Charlie has talent."

Charlie handed me the sketch. "How does this look to you, Veronica? Did I get close to the real thing?"

I studied the drawing for a minute or two as I recalled the original Bradshaw. "It's very close to what I remember. I do think the color of the sky was a shade deeper."

"All right," Charlie said.

"May I see your work when it's completed?" I handed Charlie the sketch and he slid it back in the envelope.

"Of course. Why don't you come over on Friday?"

"You'll be done by then?"

Charlie nodded. "I'm going to start on it this afternoon. The buyer called this morning and asked me to rush it. She wants to give it to her father for his birthday."

"That's sweet."

Charlie stood. "Thank you, Veronica. I appreciate your help with this."

"I'm happy to do it."

"I'll see you on Friday." Charlie gave me his address on Mountain Bluff Road, tipped his Yankees cap, and got in the navy SUV parked in front of the gallery.

"Does Leona Kendall have a husband?" I asked Jamie. The question had been in the back of my mind since lunch. The only male presence I had seen at Oli Hill was George Bradshaw's.

"Her husband died years ago," Jamie said. "In the late nineteen eighties, if I remember correctly. Theo and Natalie were kids. Poor man had a heart attack at a young age."

"When did Leona move into her father's house?"

"After her father died. Her mother didn't like being in the house alone. Olivia died five years ago."

"And Leona has never remarried?"

"I think she's too wrapped up in being George Bradshaw's daughter to be another man's wife."

"My impression, too," I said.

I said good-bye to Jamie and headed across Orchard Street. As I neared All Things, I saw Vin approach his truck and dump his toolbox in the bed. As he walked around the truck, he took his cell phone from the back pocket of his jeans and dialed a number.

"I've got some stuff for you. Can you meet now?" he asked as he climbed into the driver's seat. He slammed the door and started the engine, so I could hear no more.

My car was parked just feet away, in the alley behind All Things. I had my car keys and the instinct that Vin Bradley was up to something. Why was he leaving? It was nearing four o'clock and his crew was still in the corner house, making it amenable for blushing brides.

Vin did a U-turn on Sycamore just as I reached the alley. I hurried to my car and turned onto Sycamore just in time to see the truck cross Orchard and shoot by The Hearth.

My heart beat from the thrill of my sleuthing reaching a new level—trail and surveil.

CHAPTER SIXTEEN

Bradley sped along Sycamore, rolling through a stop sign as he made a right turn on Hill Road. I observed traffic rules, stopping for three seconds at the sign before continuing my pursuit onto Hill, and then making a left when Bradley turned onto Birchwood. I strained to get a look at what "stuff" he had in the bed of his truck, but I was too far behind and the back of the truck was too high for me to see the goods. A minute later, Bradley made a turn onto Brewery Road, and then a left onto Parson's Lane.

"What a coincidence," I murmured.

The dead-end street has just two buildings—the Methodist church and the parsonage. Built in the mid-nineteenth century, the parsonage had been vacant since the 1970s. A fifty-yard stretch of trees separated the parsonage from the church, making the historical site an overlooked relic of Barton's past.

Vin flew by the church and headed for the parsonage. I turned into the church parking lot. No way could I follow Bradley to the end of the road without him spotting my car. I sat for a minute, considering my next move, when I saw a second pickup truck pass by, also headed for the parsonage.

I pulled out of the church lot and drove down the street, slowing as I passed the parsonage. Neither pickup was visible. I continued several yards beyond the property and pulled off the road onto a patch of dirt and gravel. I got out and hurried back to the parsonage, thankful the soft grass of the neglected grounds muffled my footsteps.

The building didn't present itself well these days. A new roof was in order, as well as several coats of yellow paint (green for the shutters). The windows on the three-story house also needed restoration—more than a good washing of the filthy panes. The plant life around the foundation needed a date with a sharp pair of clippers. And I would not dare step a toe on the rotted porch boards, secured, more or less, by rusty nails. Staying close to the parsonage, I walked along the side toward the back where the barn was located. I heard the slam of a truck's door and Vin saying, "Hey, Chip."

A bush in desperate need of pruning provided me a hiding spot. I slid into a narrow space between the bush and the parsonage. A small gap between the bush and an adjacent rhododendron allowed me a view of the two men.

As they unloaded spools of copper wiring from Bradley's truck and hoisted the spools on the bed of the second truck, Chip asked, "How's the project going?"

"We're moving along. We'll be getting more lighting fixtures than we need next week."

"I always need lighting fixtures," Chip said with a chuckle.

"As long as you have the bucks."

Chip turned and gave the parsonage a sweeping look. I shrank against the building, hoping I blended in with the foliage. I glanced at the balcony two stories above my head, worried it was not of sound structure, and prayed Murphy's Law wasn't in effect.

Chip turned back to face Vin. "This renovation is some prize. Are you bidding?"

"Yeah."

"That little matter from a few months back won't hurt ya?"

"Nah."

Vin slammed shut his truck's tailgate while Chip dug his

hand in his back pocket and pulled out a wad of money. He counted out a few bills and handed them to Vin.

"It's always good doing business with you, Vin." Chip closed the back of his pickup.

"Same here. I'll call you about the fixtures."

The two got into their vehicles and pulled around the opposite side of the parsonage to where I was hidden. I waited a couple of minutes to make sure they were gone and then exited the bushes.

I hustled back to my car, mulling over this new information. Vin was up to his dirty contractor tricks. Rather than cheating customers by using cheaper materials than they had paid for, he was selling materials already purchased by clients.

What if Scott knew about Vin's dealings? He would be a certain impediment to Vin's chance of winning his bid for the renovation work. A renewed grudge spelled out an excellent motive for murder.

CHAPTER SEVENTEEN

Had I a mouthful of coffee, or any other beverage, I could have done a marvelous spit take. However, I didn't, so I had to contain my surprise to a "What a lovely tree, Dotsie!"

I was the first to arrive for the weekly canasta game. Dotsie was the week's hostess. I looked forward to cards at Dotsie's, for something unexpected always happened. At my first visit, Dotsie insisted I mount her horse, Moose, and take a ride around the backyard paddock. Dotsie and her deceased husband had kept horses for years. Dotsie continued their tradition of supplying horse rides at every Barton child's birthday party, upon request.

During the second visit, Dotsie served crème brûlée and set fire to the deck of cards when she attempted to caramelize Myrtle's serving with a blow torch.

On my third trip to Dotsie's, she switched the canasta game to a tarot card reading, bringing in a professional reader from Lake George. Ella wasn't happy about the maneuver. I wasn't amused either once the reader told me I would soon put my trust in the wrong person. Madeline feared that person was Mark; Sandy thought one of my employees would steal from All Things. I ended up in the kitchen, playing gin rummy with Ella.

The surprises weren't limited to Dotsie's house. During my first hosting gig, I stepped away for a moment to take a phone call. When I returned to the dining room where we were playing cards, I found Dotsie seated there with a toilet seat around her neck. I assumed she had removed the seat from my own bathroom and almost flipped out and quit the canasta club. I calmed down when Dotsie said she had purchased the seat at Home Depot for Ella and Madeline. I didn't ask why.

Since it was Halloween, I expected suitable decorations. Dotsie certainly did not disappoint, for spider, witch, bat, and ghost decals covered her windows. A three-foot, jointed, cardboard witch was taped to the front door. Pumpkins sat on each porch step and a life-sized Frankenstein doll rested in a rocking chair next to the door.

The time warp happened once I was inside and down the hall to her family room. I turned the corner and it was Christmas. A fully decorated artificial tree stood next to the fireplace and the coffee table was covered with boxes of Christmas cards.

"It's beautiful," I said, marveling at how Halloween had not even passed and she was already celebrating the Nativity. What happened to Thanksgiving?

"It's just one of the trees I put up," Dotsie explained. "I'll get a real one to put in my living room. Then I'll have a small one in the kitchen and two in the dining room."

"Wow. No wonder you got a head start." I walked over to the tree and admired the ornaments, many of which were equine related.

"Excuse me while I check on the sauerbraten."

"It smells delicious," I said of the aroma that permeated the house.

I went back to the living room while Dotsie tended her sauerbraten. Knowing it would give her a chuckle, I texted Carol about Dotsie's Christmas preparations. I noticed I had received a text from Pauline.

NAT K UPDATE. IN MTGS ALL DAY. SAID NADA.

Natalie was off my suspect radar, but I appreciated Pauline's effort to help. I replied with my thanks.

The doorbell rang a few moments later. I stepped into the hall as Dotsie greeted Sandy, Ella, and Madeline.

"You know where to put your coats," Dotsie said as she chugged past me into the kitchen.

Ella handed Sandy her coat as I helped Madeline ease out of hers. The sisters then headed into the living room, leaving Sandy and me to hang their coats.

"You should check out Dotsie's Christmas tree," I said. "It's in the family room."

Ella grunted and said, "We've seen it thirty times. Horses everywhere!"

"Well, I would like to see it," Madeline said. She headed down the hall as Ella resolutely took a seat on the sofa.

"Did you enjoy the Kendall lunch?" Sandy asked as she handed me a wooden coat hanger.

"For the most part. The food was delicious."

"Connie's a master. It's amazing that she nabbed Leona Kendall's business so fast. Though Leona does like to *discover* people."

"You sound like you know her well."

"No. I've just heard stories through the years from her housekeepers."

"There's a housekeepers' network?"

"Of sorts." Sandy shut the closet door. "What were you and Leona up to down in the studio?" Her eyes narrowed as she tilted her head.

"We'd all like to know what you and Leona were doing," Dotsie said. She was carrying a tray of highball glasses filled with Seven & Sevens. Madeline followed with a bowl filled with pretzels and a plate of cheese and crackers. The doorbell rang just as Dotsie reached us.

"That's surely Myrtle," Madeline said.

"Got it." Sandy reached for the doorknob.

Myrtle Evans, local insurance agent, hurried into the house as soon as Sandy opened the door.

"I hate winter," she proclaimed.

"We're not even halfway through autumn," Madeline said.

"Well it's beginning to feel like winter out there," Myrtle retorted. She pulled her coat lapels together, like she was bundling up, and then shrugged off the coat. She clenched an unopened pack of cigarettes.

"Still clinging to the security blanket, I see," Dotsie chortled as she walked into the living room and set the tray on the coffee table. We followed her in and took our seats. Me on the sofa with Ella, Madeline, and Sandy on the love seat, Dotsie and Myrtle in chairs.

"It's been months since you quit," Ella said. "And you're still buying cigarettes?"

"Oh, no. This is the last pack I bought."

"That's still sealed," Sandy said, pointing to the package. "What about those cigarettes we've seen you fingering for months?"

"Those were from the second to last pack I bought," Myrtle explained. "I decided on Saturday to take the next step and get rid of the loose ones."

"But you can't get rid of that pack?" I asked, taking a glass from the tray.

"I'm still addicted to the feel of it in my hand," Myrtle said from her wingback chair.

"I have a mind to snatch it right out of your hand and flush it down the toilet," Sandy said.

"Not my toilet!" Dotsie exclaimed. I had a sudden flashback to her sitting at my dining-room table, toilet-seat necklace prominently displayed. "How about we have Moose trample it?"

"I'd like to see that," Sandy said.

"I thank you all for your support," Myrtle said, her sarcasm obvious.

"You're just in time," Ella said. "Veronica was just about to tell us about her visit to Leona Kendall's."

They all turned to me, expectant. I finished the pretzel I was nibbling, washing it down with a large gulp of alcohol. I had reviewed the events of the day, heavily editing my story so as not to upset or enrage the Griffins. I set the glass down on a coaster and began.

"Leona admitted to having an ulterior motive for inviting me."

"Aha!" Dotsie smacked her palms together.

"She thought I could convince you to relinquish your claim to *Orchard Street.*"

"How like her to ask someone else to do her bidding," Ella said.

"I would not have agreed to it."

"Thank you," Madeline said.

Ella nodded. "Leona was probably stunned by your loyalty."

I shrugged. "She wasn't happy."

I didn't need to say more because Ella told the rest succinctly. "I suppose she will try to bully everyone to get her hands on that painting. And I'm sure she and her children have alibis."

"Leona said she did. But she didn't give me the details."

"Hmm," Sandy said.

"I think a syndicate of art thieves is involved," Dotsie proclaimed.

"Really, Dotsie? Here in Barton?" Myrtle asked.

"Why not? I'm not saying they're operating in Barton. They could be based in Albany. Or Saratoga Springs. Or Schenectady. News of the painting could have mobilized them into action."

"You would think professional thieves would know how to get in without breaking a window," Sandy said.

I agonized over what I should do. Should I tell them about the watch and ask if Regina had one and was still in possession of it? How much information did I owe Madeline and Ella, at this point? If I couldn't prove Regina's innocence, nothing I told them would allay their worries.

Myrtle had no such ethical dilemma. "The girlfriend left town fast."

"Where did she go?" Sandy asked.

"Her parents' house in Albany."

"So she goes home, ostensibly to grieve," Dotsie said, "and hides *Orchard Street* at their house! Under her childhood bed!"

"Or puts it in a safe deposit box!" Sandy said.

Ella said, "You're very quiet, Veronica."

"I don't want to slow down these three when they're on a roll. Isabel was with a colleague at the time."

"Lawyers lie," Myrtle said.

"So, what's her motive?" I asked.

"Money, money, money!" Dotsie sang.

"She didn't have to kill Scott for that," Sandy said. "Just had to get a ring on her finger."

"Which may not have been an easy thing to get. I heard the couple's been bickering lately," Myrtle said.

"Who told you that?" I asked.

"The receptionist at Franklin. She said Isabel's been griping lately about Scott working long hours."

"She did make a snippy remark Monday night, when he didn't show at the gallery. She assumed he got lost in his work again."

"Doesn't she understand he's establishing a career?" Sandy queried. "Doesn't she work long hours, too, in her law career?"

"Sure. But the biological clock is still tick-tocking," Myrtle said. "It's different for a girl."

"This girl doesn't pass the sniff test," Dotsie said. "I think he broke up with her and she snapped like a twig and took a parting gift."

"What else did you learn at Leona's?" Ella asked, ignoring Dotsie's latest conspiracy theory.

"You're right about Leona. She plans on throwing money at everyone from Scott's parents to Ned Fleming."

"But not us," Ella said. "She knows better."

"If she's willing to pay everyone off, why didn't she just offer Scott a sum for the painting?" Sandy asked.

"Leona would never buy her father's work," Ella replied. "It's beneath her. She'd rather pay people small sums to get out of her way."

"Maybe she'd have to sell one of Daddy's paintings to buy *Orchard Street*," Myrtle said.

"Did she say anything about Regina?" Madeline asked.

My silence served as an answer.

"The train is on the tracks and it's barreling toward Regina," Dotsie cried.

"We don't know that," I said.

"But you're not doing anything to help us," Ella said. "Veronica, you have no leads."

"I do have something," I blurted. "I went to Scott's house after the lunch and took a look around. I found a watch. Near Scott's property but—"

"Where is it? Produce this evidence." Dotsie leaned forward in her seat.

"I turned it in to the police," I said.

"You gave it to the police?" Ella asked.

"I would get into a lot of trouble for withholding evidence. And it might be the piece of evidence they need to find the killer. I did take photos of it before I gave it to Tracey Brody."

I went into the hall to get my purse. When I returned, Madeline had moved to sit next to Ella on the sofa. I pulled up the photos and handed my phone to her. Madeline leaned against Ella's shoulder as they scrutinized the photograph.

The sisters swapped glances, each surely trying hard to recall if she had ever seen such a watch on Regina's wrist.

"I think Regina's watch has a black band," Madeline said. Her face brightened.

"It's very fancy," Ella said. "It's beautiful. Regina wouldn't wear this except on a special occasion. I know my niece. I am certain it is not hers." She handed the phone to Myrtle.

"This is the kind of jewelry a man gives his girlfriend. It could belong to Isabel Fischer," Myrtle said.

"You really want to pin this on the gal pal," Sandy said, taking the phone from Myrtle.

"People are usually murdered by someone they know," Dotsie said. She stood and declared, "The sauerbraten's ready!"

Still clutching the package of cigarettes, Myrtle raised and dropped her arms in a show of bemusement. "I guess that's the end of this discussion."

Madeline placed her hand over mine. Her hand was cool; I took it in both of mine and gently rubbed it.

"You'll find out who is the watch's owner?" she whispered.

"I will. Let me tell you this, Madeline. You and Leona both have family portraits hanging in your homes. Leona's made me sad and slightly cold. Harvey Yount's depiction of your family was warm and welcoming. That will see you through."

Madeline withdrew her hand and patted my cheek. "You're a good woman, Veronica," she said.

She got up and with Ella and Myrtle followed Dotsie down the hall to the kitchen as Sandy and I brought up the rear. Sandy handed me my phone. With everything that had happened since Leona's luncheon—my visit to Scott's house, meeting with Charlie, and witnessing Vin's illegal sale—I had forgotten about Dusanka's parting words to me.

"I need to talk with Dusanka. Can you get in touch with her?"

"Yes. Why?"

"I want to ask her about the Kendalls' alibis."

"I'll call her tomorrow morning and get you two together."

"Thanks. How's your Czech?"

"What?" Sandy asked as she glanced into the family room, shaking her head. "Have you ever?"

"I bet you prefer it to Leona Kendall's."

Sandy grinned. "I do."

"After dinner I'll have you pick out your Christmas cards," Dotsie said, startling us as she came up behind us. "You can write out your name and I'll add the love later."

"Good idea," I said, turning to follow Dotsie.

"Actually, it is a good idea," Sandy said. "Very efficient."

"Don't start," I said as we headed for the kitchen. Knowing Sandy, she would take Dotsie's idea a step too far and have cards for not just Christmas, but Thanksgiving, Valentine's Day, Easter, our birthdays, and next year's Halloween set out for us to sign the next time we were at her house for canasta.

"What were you saying about my Czech?" Sandy asked, her eyebrows closely knit.

"When I left Bradshaw's studio today, Dusanka said something that sounded like 'onna lesi.' " I looked at the phone in my hand and blurted, "Google Translate!"

I thumbed my phonetic pronunciation of Dusanka's statement into the website. The English translation was the same spelling.

"Take one of the *n*s out," Sandy suggested.

I did and made progress to *She lesi*.

"Maybe it's a *z*," I muttered as I re-spelled *lesi* as *lezi*. Bingo.

I read the short but telling statement to Sandy.
"She lies."

CHAPTER EIGHTEEN

"You should not have followed Bradley. He might have hurt you if he had caught you."

"I can't go for a drive through my own town?"

"A drive, not a surveillance excursion."

"Well, I had a feeling Vin was up to no good. What if Scott found out he was double-dealing again? Vin wouldn't win the parsonage job."

"That's a plausible scenario. But I still can't decide if you were in the right place at the wrong time or the wrong place at the right time. Did that just make sense?"

"When in doubt, default right."

Mark and I were sitting at my kitchen table, he having a beer, I enjoying a mug of chamomile tea. Canasta had ended early that night, after just one game. Dotsie, as she promised, had pulled out her boxes of Christmas cards and insisted we go through them and pick out the greeting we wanted to receive in a few weeks. Madeline fussed over each of the five choices; I got the impression this signing was a yearly tradition and she was playing her part well. I chose one, wrote *'Dear Veronica, the most beautiful, talented, graceful woman in the world'* and then addressed the envelope. I left, praying that, by the next week's game, the murder would be resolved and Regina would still be the chef at The Hearth.

"Are you sure you correctly heard what the housekeeper said? You're not exactly fluent in Czech."

"It didn't translate to something outrageous, like 'Your hair is on fire' or 'You have a cat on your head.' It fits in the context of the situation."

"Just step carefully. You don't want to get the woman fired."

"If it comes to that, I'll hire her. And so will you."

"Our relationship has put a dent in my wallet."

"What do you think of this business over Judge Sorensen's will?"

"I agree with your new friend, Naomi. I think the judge's daughter is trying to make a power grab." Mark tapped his finger on my phone. "The watch was a good find."

"I'm thinking it could be Debbie Bradley's."

"So, you're suspicious of both husband and wife. Do they have any pets? Let's accuse the whole family." Mark leaned his chin against his palm as his lips curved upward. I loved to amuse him.

"Well, Debbie wasn't fond of Scott either. Maybe she was Vin's lookout."

Mark gave me a lingering kiss. "Tell me about the inside of Leona's house."

"It's gorgeous, but very proper. I was afraid to walk on the floor. I assume houses like that have one room that's an absolute mess, with pizza boxes everywhere and stains on every surface."

"I doubt Leona Kendall has such a room."

"Probably not. And there's a Bradshaw painting in every room. Except the powder room. There was a Monet print in there. Will you put a copy of your book in every room of your house?"

"I don't think so. But I expect you to."

"Of course I will. With a big spotlight trained on it twenty-four seven. I spoke with Alex today. He's prepping to play Van Buren."

"I'd pay to see that. I miss Alex."

"No, you don't."

"A little bit. Do you still want to go to the Halloween benefit on Friday?"

"Yeah. We need a fun night out."

"Do you really think people will know I'm F. Scott Fitzgerald? I don't want to have to tell people all night long who I am. Maybe I should wear a name tag."

"Did they have name tags in the nineteen twenties? You could tuck a copy of *The Great Gatsby* in your pocket. That would be a great identifier."

"Good idea. Thank goodness it's a short novel. I couldn't lug *Don Quixote* or *War and Peace* around in my pocket."

The comic relief was a wonderful distraction, but my thoughts returned to the case. "The receptionist at Isabel's law firm told Myrtle that Scott and Isabel had been going through a rough patch. They had been arguing a lot."

"Well, I guess the glow of the physical attraction was dimming and they were getting to really know each other."

"Myrtle suggested Isabel was involved in Scott's murder."

"But she was with Hillary."

"Yeah."

"What do you say we stop pointing fingers for the night?"

"It is exhausting." I remembered my lunch with Brenda Donovan the next day. "I'm not in the mood for lunch with Brenda tomorrow. I bet she's going to hit me up for money to help pay for the parsonage renovation. Has she asked you for a donation?"

Mark shook his head. "I give annually. Years ago I drew a line, making it clear that the yearly sum is all I will give. Otherwise, they'd hit me up for every project. Perhaps she wants to ask you to take part in some historical re-enactment."

"We could play the Griffins who opened the inn. Godfrey and wife."

"An actor I'm not."

"Do you think Eloise Griffin regretted not marrying Brad-shaw? What a secret she had, keeping his painting hidden all those years, probably sneaking looks at it when her husband wasn't around."

"I hope she had no regrets, because that would be a very sad way to live."

"It would be," I agreed, leaning in to give Mark a kiss. "I referred to you as my *companion* today."

"Because I'm such good company, I suppose."

"Exactly."

CHAPTER NINETEEN

Carol smeared cream cheese over her bagel and said, "Poor Madeline and Ella. They shouldn't have this stress at their age."

"It's not good at any age." I took a sip of coffee and a bite from my cherry danish.

The two of us were sitting on the bench in front of Rizzuto's bakery. It was our Bakery Thursday—every Thursday we met at the bakery and treated ourselves to one of their fresh-baked delights for breakfast. We sat outside when the weather was good, inside when inclement.

"I hope that watch is a lead for the police."

As I lifted my coffee cup for another sip, I spotted Isabel standing on the opposite corner, waiting for the light to change.

"There's Isabel," I whispered as she started across Orchard.

We watched as the lawyer, dressed entirely in black—pencil skirt, jacket buttoned to the collar, pumps, sunglasses—hurried across Orchard.

I shoved the danish into the bag. "Hi, Isabel," I said as she approached.

"Hi, Veronica."

I made the introductions. Isabel merely nodded at Carol, who said, "I'm very sorry about your boyfriend."

"Thank you." Isabel took a step toward the bakery. "I'm going to run inside and get some caffeine and sugar and get back to the office."

"You're back at work?"

135

Isabel nodded. "I have a big case starting next week. And I couldn't stay at my parents' house. I need something to do or I'll go crazy." She took another step toward the bakery door.

"I won't keep you. Take care, Isabel. And really, if I can do anything for you, call me at All Things."

"Thanks, Veronica. It was nice meeting you, Carol."

"Bye, Isabel," Carol said to Isabel's back.

We returned to the bench and finished our breakfast.

"One can only immerse oneself in work for so long," Carol said.

"Yeah. I wouldn't be surprised if she eventually left Barton, to get away from the bad memory." I gulped down the last two mouthfuls of coffee. "Time to get to work."

"Have a good day. We'll talk later."

Carol headed up and I down Orchard. I paused in front of the bookstore to tap on the window and wave hello to Mom before heading for another "show time" at All Things.

"Show time" happened without me.

I was in the store for twenty minutes and prepping the register when Tina charged in from the stock room, her coat still on and her purse dangling from her shoulder.

"The police just arrested Regina Quinn!" she shouted.

I practically tripped over my feet as I abruptly stopped and turned.

"What do you mean?" I asked.

"I just drove by the house and saw Tracey putting Regina in the back of her police car. And Ella was getting in the front seat."

CHAPTER TWENTY

Thanks to my lunch date with Brenda, I had decided to drive to All Things that morning. I arrived at the police station a few minutes after hearing Tina's news. I met my friend Tim Petersen, who is a lawyer, in the parking lot.

"Are you here for Regina?" I asked.

"I am." He held the door into the station open for me. "And why are you here?"

"I'm a friend of the family."

Tim followed me into the entry hall and stopped. "Friends of the family usually don't show up at the police station."

"This one does. Ella and Madeline need me." When Tim sighed and shook his head, I added, "I'll stay out of the way."

He flashed a grin. "Sure you will." Here was a man who understood irony.

We went into the main room of the station. Several officers worked at their desks. Tim nodded to the officer at the front desk, authoritatively said that I was with him, and strode confidently to the half-wall that separated the desk from the work area. Tim opened the door in the dividing wall and stepped aside so I could pass through. Once I did, I let him take the lead.

I followed him to the back hall. As we neared the chief's office, I heard Ella's stern voice chastising Price.

You go, girl, I silently cheered.

"This is outrageous. What evidence do you have to march my

niece out of her home, for all of Barton to see?"

I cringed, thinking of how I had learned the news. I should have warned the ladies at All Things to keep quiet.

"I'd like to know that myself," Tim said as he strode into the office. Chief Price sat behind his desk, with Ella and Madeline seated across from him.

"Thank goodness you're here, Tim," Madeline said, turning in her chair. "And Veronica!"

"Hi," I said.

"And why are you here, Ms. Walsh?" Chief Price asked.

"She is here as a friend of the Griffins," Tim answered.

"Then she can take them home. You two shouldn't have forced yourselves into the patrol car."

"We didn't force ourselves," Madeline said.

"I'm not going anywhere," Ella huffed. She shifted in her chair to reaffirm her commitment.

"Now, Miss Griffin." The chief's exasperation level was high for so early in the day. "You should heed your lawyer."

"Ella. Madeline. It would be best if you left. I will bring Regina home when we're done here," Tim said.

Ella let out a huff and stood. "You better not set one toe wrong, William."

The chief, chastened, nodded. "Miss Griffin, you should know we do everything by the book in this station."

Ella glared at him for a moment and then walked out of the office.

"I second my sister's words," Madeline said as she left.

As I turned to leave, Chief Price said, "Ms. Walsh, I certainly hope you are not playing amateur sleuth again."

"Of course not." I kept my eyes fixed on the chief's for a moment and then left.

Tim said, "Chief, I trust you haven't started questioning Miss Quinn."

Turning into the main room, I stole a glance and saw Tim and the chief entering the interrogation room. I said a quick prayer for Regina and shifted my path to pass Tracey's desk. Leaning over, I whispered, "Does this have anything to do with the watch?"

"No," she said in a hushed voice.

I relaxed, but just a bit.

"Why did they bring Regina in?" I asked Ella and Madeline as we walked down the sidewalk outside the station.

"Price wouldn't tell us," Ella griped. "I certainly hope it has nothing to do with that watch you gave them," she snapped.

A car's squeal interrupted my response. Sandy's minivan took a sharp turn into the lot. She slammed on the brakes at the foot of the sidewalk, which we had just reached.

"What's going on?" she asked. "Your neighbor told me Regina was arrested."

"They did *not* arrest her," Ella replied. "They are questioning her."

"Why?"

"Chief Price wouldn't tell us," Madeline said. "He sent us home."

"Outrageous," Ella said.

"Totally," said Sandy.

"Drive us home, Sandy," Ella said. "We'll see you there, Veronica."

"All right."

"Put the parking brake on, Sandy." Ella knew Sandy's fighter pilot tendencies behind the wheel as well as I did. When Sandy applied the brake, Ella stepped in front of the car and walked to the passenger door. Madeline and I followed.

I helped Madeline into the back seat and then headed to my

car as Sandy tore from the lot. I admired her nerve, flaunting the safe-driving laws right in front of the police station, but was also thankful that I wasn't one of the passengers.

Sandy stood on the Griffins' front porch, awaiting my arrival.

"I'm praying they didn't find Regina's prints on that watch," she said as I walked up the steps.

"This isn't about the watch." I walked up the steps. "I asked Tracey as we were leaving the station."

Sandy blessed herself and led me inside. I heard piano music as I crossed the threshold. I knew it was Madeline striking the chords; it took me a moment to identify the tune as "Moon River."

"Madeline's way of relaxing," Sandy explained.

We went into the parlor, where Ella sat in a chair beside the piano.

"Would you like a cup of coffee or tea, Veronica?" Sandy asked as a kettle whistled in the kitchen.

"No, thanks."

"I'll be right back. I have to make a call, too." Sandy gave me a suggestive look before leaving.

I sat on the sofa and listened as Madeline finished playing. I hoped the music soothed the two sisters as much as it comforted me.

"The police aren't questioning Regina because of the watch."

Madeline turned on the piano bench to face me. "Thank goodness."

"Tracey didn't say anything in the patrol car?"

"No," Ella said. "And for Price to think we forced ourselves into the car, huh! I wanted to make sure Regina didn't say anything."

"Smart move," I said with admiration.

Sandy came into the parlor carrying a tray with a carafe and four china cups. She set the tray on the table and filled two of the cups with coffee. Sandy sat down next to me after handing the cups to Ella and Madeline.

"The rendezvous is at sixteen hundred hours. Your place," she said to me.

"Huh?"

Sandy rolled her eyes. "Dusanka and I will be at your house at four o'clock."

"Oh. Okay."

"Who is Dusanka?" Ella asked.

"Leona's housekeeper," I said. "I think she overheard my conversation with Leona yesterday because, as I was leaving, Dusanka whispered to me that Leona was lying. I'm betting she has quite a bit of information on the Kendalls."

"She takes care of Leona's dirt in more ways than one," Sandy said.

Ella nodded. "Excellent. Let me know if you need a bit of cash to loosen her lips."

"Ella!" Madeline cried.

I was too shocked to react.

"It's the way of the world, Madeline."

The four of us sat for more than an hour, wondering and worrying over what was happening at the police station. When Ella griped all our fretting was giving her indigestion, Madeline went back to the piano and started in on tunes from *The Sound of Music*. She was halfway through "Climb Every Mountain" when the sound of the front door opening caused her to stop playing, and Sandy and me to momentarily cease breathing.

Sandy leapt to her feet. "Who is it?"

"Me."

Regina stepped into the parlor, followed by Tim, Chief Price, Tracey, police officer Ron Nicholstone, and a police officer I knew only by sight. The police officers carried latex gloves.

Ella quickly rose from her chair. "What's going on?"

"I have a confession to make," Regina said.

CHAPTER TWENTY-ONE

"You allowed that, Timothy?" Ella asked. Her ferociousness had returned.

"Yes. Regina will explain."

Regina took a few more steps into the parlor. Her poise impressed me. "I *did* go to Scott's house Monday evening."

My stomach twisted. Sandy groaned. Madeline let out a despairing cry.

Ella erupted. "You did what?"

"Scott *invited* me. He called me at The Hearth on Sunday afternoon and told me he would give me the letter. He really felt it belonged with us. He hated the idea of people reading over such an intimate letter. He thought it would be disrespectful to the memory of Bradshaw's wife. And Scott didn't like the idea of getting money for it. So we arranged that I would go to his house Monday to pick it up. We talked for a few minutes when I got there. Scott let me take a close look at *Orchard Street*. It's so beautiful. And he put out wine and cheese. He joked it was a private viewing party."

"Yeah, and the knife used to slice the cheese was used to kill him," the chief said with impatience.

"It was stuck in the cheese wedge when I left!"

"Why didn't you tell us, dear?" Madeline asked.

"Because Aunt Ella was angry about the letter. You said it was disrespectful to Great-Grandpa. And I thought, since I had established a friendly relationship with Scott, maybe I could

143

convince him to give you the painting. And then, of course, when I heard Scott had been murdered, I was afraid to say anything."

"I want to know what evidence you had for hauling Regina to the station this morning," Ella demanded, fixing her glare on Chief Price.

"Regina's fingerprints were found in Scott's home," Tim said.

"How would they know they were your fingerprints?" Madeline asked.

I knew the answer would be that Regina's fingerprints were in the police database. I braced for the explanation.

"I was arrested five years ago for DUI. I had one beer too many at a party." She cast a sorrowful look at Ella and Madeline. "I'm ashamed to tell this. I didn't want you to know. I'll never do it again. And I swear I only took two sips of wine at Scott's."

Ella and Madeline were quiet for several moments. Then Ella showed the compassion that had made me so quickly come to their aid at the start of this mess. "You learned from the experience and grew into the responsible, mature woman you are now. I'm proud of you, Regina."

"Ditto," Madeline said with a wink to her great-niece.

"Did you find her fingerprints on the knife?" I asked.

Chief Price avoided my stare. "No."

"So why are all of you here?" Sandy asked. "And what's with the latex gloves?"

"We have a warrant to search this house," Chief Price said.

"For what?" I asked. "Regina said she doesn't have the painting. And you just said her fingerprints weren't on the knife."

"Easily wiped off. We can't just take Ms. Quinn's word."

"I'm going to show them where the letter is," Regina said.

"This all sounds like circumstantial evidence to me," I said.

Chief Price flashed a fleeting yet withering glance at me.

"Let's get on with the search," he said.

"I am not amenable to this!" Ella said.

"You don't have a choice," the chief replied.

"I'm sorry, Aunt Ella. Aunt Madeline. My back's against the wall." Regina led Tracey, Ron, and the third officer into the hall.

Tim turned to the chief. "I'm sure the officers will be very respectful in their search."

Price cleared his throat. "Of course they will."

The two left the parlor. We heard their footsteps trailing the fading steps of Regina and the officers as they went up the long flight of stairs to the second floor.

Sandy, who always keeps things moving, said, "I'll make more coffee," as she dashed into the hall.

"We shouldn't provide beverages for the uninvited rogues going through our personal things!" Ella said. She tossed a scowl Sandy's way and then went into the hall.

"Not for them," Sandy bellowed from the kitchen.

I followed Ella into the hall and watched her head up the stairs. She was as spry as a woman half her age. Though angry over the search, I did feel a twinge of compassion for the three police officers. They would be doing their job under Ella's hot glare.

I hovered in the hall, waiting for the next crazy thing to happen. Going over everything Regina had said, I realized Scott did not walk in on his killer. The killer walked in on him.

Sandy returned. She nodded to the second floor and said, "They better be neat about this. I don't have the time to tidy up after their *unwarranted* search."

"I feel so much better now that everyone knows the truth," Regina said to Tim as they came down the stairs.

"Will you get my purse?" I whispered to Sandy.

She nodded and hurried to the parlor.

"I need to talk with you in private, Regina," Tim said when

he saw me at the foot of the stairs.

"May I speak with Regina for a moment?" When Tim hesitated, I said, "She needs a break. And I don't have a getaway car warming in the driveway."

Sandy returned with my purse. "And I don't have a cake with a file in the batter baking in the oven."

Tim relented. "All right. Just a minute."

"Thank you." I led Regina and Sandy into the dining room, to the far end of the table so no one would overhear us. I took my phone from my purse and pulled up a photo of the watch.

Sandy took both of Regina's hands in hers. "Are you okay?" she asked with maternal tenderness.

"Yeah. I'm relieved that everyone knows I was at Scott's Monday night."

I showed Regina one of the photos of the watch. "Is this yours?"

Regina took my phone. "Nope. Nice watch. Expensive. If you can't find the owner, I'll take it." She grinned and gave back my phone. "Why do you ask?"

"I found it near Scott's house yesterday. I have a nagging feeling that it's evidence in the case."

Regina's eyes widened. "What were you doing at Scott's house?"

"Veronica's good at finding killers," Sandy said.

"Well, I've only found one and that was sort of by accident."

"Fftt," Sandy muttered.

"Mark was there, too," I reminded Sandy. "Your aunts asked me to help the police on the investigation. Without the police knowing I'm helping them."

Sandy added, "Ella and Madeline are afraid the Kendalls are going to stick the blame on you, and the police will go along with it because the Kendalls are stinking rich."

"What time were you at Scott's?" I asked.

"I got there about five o'clock and left about fifteen, twenty minutes later."

"Did you see anyone out walking? Was anyone on the street?"

"No. This is so frustrating!"

"Don't worry. We're going to figure this mess out."

"Thanks for being on my side. Both of you."

We were in the middle of a group hug when Tracey interrupted us. She held a clear plastic bag containing what I assumed was Bradshaw's love letter to Eloise Griffin.

"Miss Quinn. Chief Price would like to speak with you."

"Thank you, Officer," Regina said. She gave Sandy and me a heartbreaking look of gratitude and walked out of the room. We waited one beat and then scurried into the front hall.

The scene had the appearance of a showdown. Tracey and Chief Price stood on one side of the hall. A few feet across from them Regina, Tim, Ella, and Madeline stood in a straight line. Neither Sandy nor I needed a moment to consider our places. We stepped behind Regina, straightening our shoulders, ready for a rumble.

Chief Price expressed his displeasure with a loud sigh. "What a group."

"A group that demands you exonerate my grandniece and find Mr. Culverson's killer," Ella said.

"We're not ready to do that, Miss Griffin. Even though Miss Quinn has *finally* been truthful about her visit to Mr. Culverson's Monday evening, we cannot assume she is being completely forthcoming."

"But I am!"

The chief ignored Regina. "You are not to leave Barton."

"I wasn't planning to," Regina answered with defiance. "False accusations aren't enough to drive me out of town. I have a great job, a supportive family, and wonderful new friends."

"That's right," Sandy said.

"You will need to surrender your passport."

"I don't have one."

"All right. We may call you in for more questioning."

"My story will be the same, no matter how many times you ask me to repeat it."

"Griffins do not lie," Ella said. "And I trust that neither you nor anyone in your department will discuss Regina's interrogation and this search of our home with the press."

"I can only promise that I will not discuss it."

"Nor will I," said Tracey.

"Hmm," Ella said. She gave Chief Price a withering stare and then went into the parlor. Madeline mimicked her sister's glare and followed.

"Regina, I need to talk with you in private," Tim said. "Let's go into the kitchen."

Regina followed him down the hall while Chief Price went to the front door.

"I'm going back to the station, Officer Brody."

"Yes, sir."

As soon as he was out the door, I asked Tracey, "Did you find out anything on the watch?"

"No."

"Did you dust it for fingerprints?"

"We will." Tracey started up the stairs.

"You haven't done it yet? It could be important!"

Tracey stopped and turned. "Veronica, don't tell us how to do our job. We *will* follow up on the watch. Thank you for bringing it to us. But right now, I need to do my job *here*." Tracey continued up the stairs.

"But I've given you something that could help you do your job!"

"I don't need your help to do my job, Veronica." Tracey took the stairs two at a time and rounded the turn on the landing.

My shoulders sagged with discouragement. I had given the police a clue and they were totally disregarding it!

Sandy came up behind me and said, "We need to get Regina out of this jam."

"Don't I know it."

I said good-bye to Ella and Madeline and headed out to my car. I was already exhausted and still had the lunch date with Brenda Donovan. But before I sat down with Brenda, I had another stop to make. If the police weren't going to make the watch a priority, I would.

CHAPTER TWENTY-TWO

"Everything's fine." I breezed across All Things's main floor and up the stairs to my office before any of the ladies could quiz me on Regina's encounter with the police.

I shut my office door and plopped into the desk chair. "Come on." I tapped my knuckles against the desk, impatient while my computer awakened and opened to Google. Within moments I pulled up Fenton's website and had their customer-service phone number. I took out my cell phone, zoomed in as much as I could on the photo of the back of the watch, and wrote down the numbers etched on the metal.

"Hello. I'm calling in regard to a watch I found. I'd like to track down the owner and thought if I give you the serial number on the back of the watch, you can tell me who that is."

"I'm sorry, ma'am, but I cannot give you that information." What kind of customer service is that?

"I'd really like to return the watch to its owner. It's a beautiful piece."

"Thank you, ma'am. But I can't give out personal information. You should bring the watch to your local police department and tell them to contact us. Thank you for calling us today. Is there anything else I can help you with?"

I breezed into Bern Jewelers, my cell phone in my hand. Dolores Bern, co-owner of the shop with her husband, greeted me.

"Good morning, Veronica." Dolores slipped a necklace

sparkling with sapphires into the display case.

"Hi, Dolores."

"What can I do for you? Shopping for a bauble to celebrate your new business?"

"I'm waiting for someone else to buy me that bauble. I only have some spare change left after buying All Things."

"I don't believe you."

"I hope you can help me find the owner of this watch." I held up my phone to show off one of the photos.

Dolores's eyeglasses dangled on a chain around her neck. She set the cat's eye–style glasses on her nose and picked up the phone.

"I took several photos."

"We don't sell Fenton watches," Dolores said after a minute of flipping through the photographs. "It's good you got a shot of the serial number on the back."

"I called Fenton's customer service and tried to give them that number. They said they couldn't give me the owner's name."

"No. Privacy reasons. But I can give the serial number to local jewelers. Perhaps one of them sold it."

"I would appreciate that, Dolores."

"Where did you find this? Where's the watch?" Dolores peered at me over the top of her eyeglasses.

"I found it near Scott Culverson's house and gave it to the police. But they're not moving too fast on it." I knew Dolores well enough to know she wouldn't share that information.

She absorbed the statement without reaction. "Email me the photos and I'll get to work on it."

Dolores wrote down her email address and had me write down my cell-phone number.

"You're worth more than all the jewels in this store, Dolores."

"Tell my husband that."

The bell announced my arrival at Emerson Florist. "I need a best-friend hug."

"What's happened?" Carol walked over from the refrigerator and gave me the requested embrace.

"The police brought Regina in for questioning, she admitted to being at Scott's house Monday night, he gave her the love letter, she was arrested a few years ago for DUI, the police are dragging their heels on the ladies' watch, and Madeline plays 'Moon River' to relax."

"I need to sit for this."

We went to the register, with Carol taking her seat on the stool behind the counter while I claimed the one reserved for customers. I told her everything that had happened in the time since our breakfast.

"Life can change in a moment," Carol said when I finished. She stared at a vase of dried flowers on the corner of the counter.

"What are you thinking about?" I asked after a moment.

"My daughter," Carol said, her voice catching. "Regina did nothing wrong. She got a bit angry and now she's a prime suspect. Innocent people are accused and convicted every day." She stopped, shaking her head as she pressed her hand over her eyes.

I slid off the stool and went over to a bucket of white roses standing on a nearby display table. I plucked one and brought it to Carol.

"Don't tell the florist."

"I say nothing."

Carol grinned and took the flower. I took my seat again and rested my hand lightly over Carol's. We sat like that for a few minutes, in silent, best-friend commiseration, until a customer entered the shop.

I left, my worries still heavy, but feeling lighter thanks to having a friend to help me carry them.

CHAPTER TWENTY-THREE

"How are you enjoying life as a business owner?" Brenda asked as she swirled a lemon slice in her glass of water.

"I'm enjoying it very much. I have to give most of the credit to the amazing staff."

Brenda and I were seated in the Farley Inn's elegant dining room. As usual, there was a full house for lunch, a mix of inn guests enjoying a leisurely meal and business folks having a working lunch.

"Yes. Claire Camden is a wonderful manager."

"That she is."

"I'm happy that All Things continues to be the success it was under Anna Langdon," Brenda said. "It's a very important business in Barton."

"Thank you." I glanced over Brenda's shoulder. Two tables away, Isabel dined with Aaron. Aaron met my glance and smiled. I acknowledged him with a nod and returned my attention to Brenda. "I appreciate that."

"And how long have you and Professor Burke been seeing each other?"

"About four months."

"Mark is a good man. And a wonderful patron of the historical society. Thank goodness he doesn't want my job, because he could have it in a heartbeat."

"He's too busy. Your job is secure."

As the hostess passed our table, a familiar voice said, "Fancy meeting you two here." Sabrina pressed her hand against my shoulder before shaking Brenda's hand.

"How are you, Sabrina? You must be having a difficult week." Brenda's expression was etched with concern. She wrapped her hand around Sabrina's wrist.

"It's getting better. I'm finding some comfort in taking over Scott's role with the parsonage project."

I maintained a calm expression while my pulse quickened. The odds of an encounter between Scott and Vin at the parsonage suddenly skyrocketed.

"I'm sorry for the reason you have to do that. But thankful you are. We'll be sure to put in a permanent tribute to Scott on completion."

"Thank you, Brenda. I'll let you ladies get back to your lunch. It was good to see you both."

"Sweet woman," Brenda said when Sabrina left.

We stopped talking for a moment as our waitress delivered our food. My gaze drifted to the nearby corner table. Theo Kendall sat there with an older gentleman.

The lunch was turning into a pleasant distraction, indeed.

"Scott is a great loss for the Burtons," Brenda said. "He showed such promise so early in his career. He was going to be a star."

"I heard yesterday about Judge Sorensen's role in the project. What a wonderful gift he gave to the historical society. Congratulations."

Brenda nodded as she swallowed a bite of food. "Thank you. Judge Sorensen was a very generous, kind man. And now the historical society is finally moving ahead with a long desired renovation of the parsonage and barn. It's a shame the two buildings have stood empty and unused all these years. But now we have an architect, and contractor bids will be due in three weeks. We want to open the parsonage for tours and use the barn for society events, as well as rent it out for weddings and other gatherings."

"That is a wonderful idea."

"I'm very proud of it. The parsonage is the reason I invited you to lunch, Veronica."

I braced myself for her money grab. "Oh?"

"You can imagine this renovation will cost a small fortune. We're relying on donors to help us with the financial burden on this ambitious project."

"It sounds grand."

"This project is of particular value. The parsonage is a vital part of Barton's past, as well as the county's history. It will be wonderful when it is restored to its former glory."

"I'm sure."

"You are an important part of this community, Veronica. You represented us well in your career and now that you have returned as a permanent resident and businesswoman, you have become a very integral part in the life of Barton."

"Thank you." Brenda had laid her spiel on so thickly, I thought she'd have to pry her tongue off the roof of her mouth.

"The society, and I personally, would value your contribution to the renovation fund. Your generosity would be perpetually appreciated."

"I will have to consider this. And discuss it with my accountant."

"By all means. It is a big investment. Of course, it will qualify as a tax deduction. And a plaque bearing donors' names will be placed at the parsonage's entry, in a place of prominence. Your role will forever be acknowledged."

"I'll keep that in mind."

"I'm giving a tour of the parsonage on Saturday to a few of the donors," Brenda said. "Sabrina will join us and talk about Scott's design for the renovation. Why don't you join us?"

"All right. I'd like to see the parsonage." I thought of my last visit there. I hadn't seen much of the place from my position of concealment behind the bush. I did notice the building was in desperate need of a paint job.

"Now that we've got the business talk out of the way, how are you enjoying your new role in Barton?"

There was no more talk of money. Instead, Brenda described her work as the historical society's director and she showed great interest in my career as a soap actress. By the end of the meal I was still noncommittal about becoming a benefactor, though I was relieved the meeting wasn't as dreadful as I had feared.

Brenda left after lunch and I went to the ladies' room to freshen my lipstick. I met Isabel by the vanity.

"We meet again," Isabel said.

"How's your day going?"

"Busy," Isabel replied. "I can't wait until this week is over. This month. The whole year."

We were quiet for a moment as she checked her makeup and I applied my lipstick. I glanced at Isabel just as she lifted her hand to push aside a strand of hair. The sleeve of her jacket slipped and I could see her wrist. She did not wear a watch.

I thought of Myrtle's skepticism over Isabel and the state of her relationship with Scott. "You didn't happen to lose your watch, Isabel?"

Isabel jerked her head. A nervous reaction? I wondered.

"Watch?" She turned away and shoved her brush into her purse.

"I found a watch on the sidewalk the other morning," I said. "Outside the gallery."

Isabel turned and stared at me for a long moment. "No, I didn't lose my watch," she finally said.

We met Aaron by the inn's front desk and together walked to the exit.

"Has Brenda Donovan gotten her hand in your wallet?" he asked, stepping aside to allow me through the door ahead of him.

"Not yet."

"Remember, a donation would be a tax write-off."

"Are you an accountant now, too?"

"No. A victim of the historical society's annual pledge drive." Aaron gave a meaningful look to Isabel. "The parsonage is a worthy cause. Not that I'm twisting your arm."

Once outside, Aaron and Isabel turned to the left. Theo, oblivious to my presence, rushed by as I walked to my car. His pace slowed when his phone rang, allowing me to get close enough to hear his conversation.

"I just got out of lunch . . . Excellent . . . Seven thirty is good. Yes, The Mountain Bear again . . . I'll see you then."

Theo pressed his car remote and unlocked the door of the silver BMW parked next to my car.

He got into his luxury ride and backed out without showing the courtesy of allowing me to get into my car first.

"Well," I said to myself as I opened my car door. "I wonder what a guy like Theo Kendall is doing going to a place like The Mountain Bear."

A roadside restaurant, The Mountain Bear is on Route Nine, about a mile south of Lake George Village. The menu is standard fare—hamburgers, spaghetti, chicken, steak. The restaurant is popular with vacationing families, particularly those with young children. The Mountain Bear's proprietors aren't put off by the squeals and cries little kids tend to emit. Theo Kendall struck me as the type who would take great offense at such noises. Perhaps, though, I was wrongly assuming he had the same intolerance to poor etiquette as his mother.

Theo's evening rendezvous intrigued me as I turned out of the inn's parking lot.

CHAPTER TWENTY-FOUR

As I drove up Orchard Street, I spotted my hairdresser, Andrea Garner, standing outside her shop. She was chatting on her phone as she paced the sidewalk. I pulled into an empty parking spot and got out of my car.

I hovered around a bench for a few moments as Andrea finished her call.

"Do we have an appointment?" Andrea lifted a strand of my hair and rubbed it between her fingers. "You don't really need a cut."

"I'm not here for a cut. I'd like to talk with you about something."

"What?"

I suddenly felt nervous, worried that Andrea, a rather outspoken woman, would blab my suspicions of Debbie Bradley up and down Orchard. She would definitely share all gossip about Debbie and would then tell everyone else.

"Can we keep this between us?" I asked. I feared Andrea repeating our conversation to all of her customers.

Andrea moved closer as her eyes lit up. "Sure."

"Did Debbie Bradley work Monday afternoon?"

"Yeah. Why?"

I pursed my lips, wondering how much to divulge. Andrea put the pieces together before I could answer.

"Are you investigating that guy's murder?"

"His name was Scott Culverson."

Andrea nodded. "Yeah. Debbie complained about him a few months ago. She said he caused some trouble for Vin on a job. I found out that Scott caught him cheating a client."

"I know."

"And Debbie started talking about it again on Monday. She was ticked off about this Scott guy finding the painting."

"Oh yeah?"

"Yeah." Apparently eager to share information, Andrea moved closer. "And you know, Debbie left the salon about five o'clock Monday afternoon. She said she was going to Vera Beecham's to do Vera's mother's weekly setting. But she usually goes to Vera's on Tuesdays!" Andrea's eyes flashed from the thrill of being an informant. "When I asked her why the change in days, Debbie said Mrs. Russo had a doctor's appointment on Tuesday."

"All right."

"But then Debbie went out on Tuesday, at the time she usually leaves for Vera's."

"Well, since she didn't have the appointment with Vera, maybe she was just going home."

Andrea shook her head in a know-it-all kind of way. "I didn't get that impression. I wouldn't be surprised if she's the killer. Debbie's got a mean streak and grudges stick to her like glue." Her eyes popped and she held one finger in the air. "I have an idea."

She hurried into the salon, leaving me on the sidewalk feeling bewildered. In a minute she came back out with a slip of paper in her hand.

"I'll call Vera!"

"I'm not—" I feared Andrea was about to become the proverbial bull in the china shop. Or salon.

"I'll be cool." Andrea punched Vera's phone number into her cell. She grinned at me as she waited a moment. "Vera, hello!

This is Andrea Garner. How are you today? . . . I'm great. I'm just calling to check if you need to reschedule your mother's appointment for next week . . ."

Andrea grabbed my arm and squeezed it rather hard. She stared at me, unblinking. "Oh, I'm sorry. It was my understanding that this week's date was changed because of a doctor's appointment. My mistake. It must have been for someone else. I'm glad your mother's well. Thanks, Vera!"

Andrea shoved her phone into her pocket. "Vera's mother didn't have a doctor's appointment Tuesday. The hair setting wasn't rescheduled. Debbie lied!"

"Not so loud," I hissed.

"Sorry," Andrea said. Then whispered, "Debbie lied!"

I nodded. "This is interesting. But it doesn't mean she was at Scott's."

"Well, she was up to something no good. I'm going to keep my eye on her."

"Just don't say anything. Or do anything. And please, don't repeat this to anyone."

"I won't, Veronica."

"There's one more thing." I showed her the photo of the watch. "Do you recognize this watch?"

Andrea closed her fingers around the phone. "It's probably Debbie's. She wears a lot of jewelry."

"But you're not *positive* it's hers?" I pressed Andrea to be honest rather than forcing the facts to fit her assumption.

"I couldn't positively identify any of her jewelry, because she wears so much of it."

I took my phone back. "Thanks, Andrea. I appreciate your help. And your discretion."

I returned to my car, drove the few yards along Orchard to All Things, and parked in the alley. Evan, the young guy from Vin's crew, stood on the opposite sidewalk. He took a chug from a can of Coke.

Seizing the opportunity to mine for information on Vin, I gave Evan a friendly wave.

"Hi there," I said as I crossed to his side of Sycamore.

"Hey," Evan said.

"Taking a break from the hard labor?"

Evan laughed. "Yeah. Vin lets us out once in a while for air."

"Well, he should. I'm sure he does the same."

"Yeah. He usually takes off for an hour or so in the afternoon to go back to the office or visit a supplier."

Or conduct a transaction behind the parsonage. "How's the renovation progressing?" I asked, nodding at the building behind us.

"We're getting there. I think we'll finish before the deadline."

"That would be great. Do you usually finish ahead of schedule?"

Evan nodded. "Usually. Vin's a great contractor. He gets things done on time and on budget."

"You like working for him?" I asked.

"Yeah. Vin's a good guy. He expects hard work, but he's fair. And he's good about showing his appreciation. He treats his crew right."

"How so?"

"He gets that we sometimes need to get away from the hammering and drilling for a few minutes." Evan lifted his soda can to emphasize his point. "And every Monday after work we have pizza at Martini's and go bowling. Vin buys the pizza and we all chip in on the drinks at the alley."

"Sounds like a good boss."

"He is. I hope you don't get the wrong idea about Vin because of his problem with Scott Culverson. Everyone seems to think Vin's a bad guy now."

"Who?" I asked with an air of innocence.

"Well, everyone seems to know that Scott found out Vin didn't follow a contract to the letter on a job a few months ago. Even the police checked Vin out to see where he was Monday. They checked his alibi with the whole crew."

"They did?"

"Sure did. We all went to Martini's straight from here. No doubt about it."

"Lucky for Vin you guys don't hang out on Tuesdays."

"Yeah. But that problem was a one-time thing. Vin's careful with business now."

A flashback to Vin's meeting behind the parsonage distracted me for a moment. Oh yeah, he's more careful. "Good."

"You and your crew should join us some Monday night."

"We'd kick your butts in bowling."

"We'll see about that."

I said good-bye to Evan and went back to my side of the street. One Bradley was off the suspect list, but one was most definitely still under consideration.

CHAPTER TWENTY-FIVE

I left All Things a few minutes before four o'clock for my rendezvous with Sandy and Dusanka. Sandy's minivan was parked at the top of my driveway when I arrived home. Sandy was standing behind the van, her arms crossed and her foot tapping. She shook her head when she saw me.

"Where's Dusanka?" I asked.

"Hush," Sandy snapped.

"Why?"

"You never know who is listening."

We reached my porch. "You did give Dusanka directions, right?" I asked.

"She's here," Sandy said. "I thought it best if we met in the Food Mart's parking lot and I drove here."

I unlocked the front door and let Sandy go in first. "Very stealthy," I said.

Sandy bounded down the hall. "Well, we couldn't risk Leona finding out. She's got spies all over the place."

"I suppose," I said. Sandy would be a fantastic soap writer, or C.I.A. agent, I thought as I followed her. She was an excellent plotter, had a taste for intrigue, and an eye for high drama.

I caught up with Sandy in the kitchen. She unlocked the back door, leaned out to the porch, and said, "Sorry about that." She pulled back and Dusanka stepped inside.

"Hello, Ms. Walsh," Dusanka said. She made a slight bow toward me.

"It's good to see you again, Dusanka. Thank you for coming."

"Sandy said you need my help. I will be happy to help the lady who taught me English."

I wanted to ask her if the six husbands I had on the soap also helped her learn English, but I'd leave that question for another day. Instead I asked, "Would you like a drink, Dusanka? I have soda, or I can make coffee or tea."

"No, thank you, Miss Walsh."

"Please, call me Veronica."

"You are a very nice lady, Veronica. And you are, too, Sandy."

"Thank you," I said. "Why don't we go sit in the living room?"

"I'll get us all some water," Sandy said, making herself comfortable in my kitchen.

Dusanka followed me into the hall.

"You have a lovely home," Dusanka said as we settled on the couch.

"Thank you. Where did you live in Czechoslovakia?"

"We are now the Czech Republic." The correction sounded a tad like a scold. "I am from Zlin."

Sandy came in carrying a tray holding three glasses filled with water, a plate of Lorna Doones, and a few paper napkins. She set the tray on the coffee table and handed a glass to Dusanka. She gave a glass to me, took the last glass, and sat in the chair across from us. She cleared her throat and gave me an impatient glance. "I mentioned to Dusanka that you want to ask her about the Kendalls."

"Yes." I turned to Dusanka. "I don't want you to get into trouble. We certainly will not repeat what you tell us."

Sandy said nothing as she crossed her heart and raised her right hand as if about to take an oath.

"Dusanka, a friend of ours has been accused of murdering Scott Culverson."

"Regina Quinn. Mrs. Kendall talked about her today. She said Miss Quinn stole her painting. She's angry the police let Miss Quinn go home."

"She said that to you?" Sandy asked.

Dusanka shook her head. "No. She was talking to her lawyer on the phone. Mrs. Kendall said Miss Quinn is guilty and she is going to sue her."

My heart sank. I had not anticipated Regina facing a lawsuit. I set aside that new worry. "Do you know where Leona and her children were Monday evening? Were they at Oli Hill?"

Dusanka shook her head. "No. They went to dinner at La Maison Berenice."

A fancy shmancy French restaurant in Bear Lake. And a very public alibi for the Kendalls. "Yesterday, when I was leaving Oli Hill, you said something that caught my attention."

Dusanka nodded. "I told you that Mrs. Kendall is a *lhá*. She did not tell you the truth."

"I thought that's what you said." I'd have to tell Mark to give me more credit for my Czech. "How, exactly, is Leona a liar?"

"I heard her tell you that she did not think it wise to meet with Mr. Culverson again after they went to the restaurant Saturday night. But Mrs. Kendall and Mr. Kendall did meet with Mr. Culverson. *Bh opatruj jeho duši.*" Dusanka slowly blessed herself as she said the words.

Dozens of English words rolled to the tip of my tongue. Just one slipped out. "When?"

"Sunday afternoon."

"Was Isabel Fischer with Scott?" Sandy asked.

"No. Only Mr. Culverson."

I doubted Dusanka was a witness to the conversation, but I had to ask. "Did you happen to hear anything that was said?"

Dusanka shook her head. "They were very pleasant when I was near. Mrs. Kendall thanked Mr. Culverson for meeting with her and her son. When I was bringing in the coffee, Mr. Kendall asked Mr. Culverson to keep the meeting confidential. Mr. Culverson said he would. He made a joke that his girlfriend would be very angry if she knew he came to Oli Hill without her."

"Oh, I'm sure Isabel would be upset about not seeing all the paintings," I dryly said.

"What else did you overhear?" Sandy asked.

"I did not hear anything more that was said with Mr. Culverson. But after he left Oli Hill, Mrs. Kendall called him a bastard."

"That's not good," I muttered.

"She said to her son that Mr. Culverson was a bastard who just wanted money." Dusanka's voice rose, her face contorted into a glower, and she raised her hand as if she were going to hit me. "She yelled at her son, 'How dare he say he is the painting's owner!' Mrs. Kendall was very angry that Mr. Culverson said that if he were to take less money than what the painting is worth, he would offer it to the Griffins or to the university that could benefit from it. She said he slapped her in the face."

"Figuratively, of course," I said.

"Mrs. Kendall told her son that he had a terrible idea to ask Mr. Culverson to her father's house. She said she was going to sue his bottom off."

I guessed Theo extended the invitation at The Hearth Saturday evening. He must have returned after we left and caught Scott alone at the table.

"What a bratty prima donna," Sandy said. "What was Theo's response?"

"He told his mother to calm down. He said he had someone who would help them get the painting back, because he didn't think a judge would give them the painting. After he left, Mrs.

Kendall said she would try a velvet glove and asked me to get her the phone number to your All Things shop."

I wondered if Theo's "someone" had succeeded where I had refused to tread. "Whose idea was it to go to La Maison Berenice?"

"Mr. Kendall invited his mother and sister."

"That was nice of him," I said. And a neat way to set up an alibi.

"I'm sure the police think this meeting very interesting," Sandy said.

"The police do not know about the meeting," Dusanka said in a quiet voice.

"Well, then you must tell them," Sandy said. "We will go right now to the station and talk to Tracey Brody."

"But, I've already talked with them! I lied to them!" Dusanka swiped the back of her hand across her eyes.

"Tell us what you told the police," I said.

"Mrs. Kendall did not want the police to know that Mr. Culverson came to Oli Hill on Sunday. She said they would not understand. She told me not to tell the police of Mr. Culverson's visit."

"Leona told you to lie to the police?" I was simultaneously incredulous and convinced that Leona would pull such a move.

"Yes. Mrs. Kendall told me to lie." Dusanka's face slackened and for the first time I saw vulnerability in her features. "Mrs. Kendall told me she would send me back to Zlin if I didn't tell her lie. *Fena!*" From her harsh tone, I guessed the last word wasn't a complimentary description of Leona.

"Leona threatened you, Dusanka? She told you to lie or face deportment?" I asked.

"Yes!"

"*Fena*," I muttered. I'd have to Google Translate it later. "And so you did not tell the police about the Sunday meeting."

"That is right. I love my home, but I don't want to go back there in shame."

I wished I knew more Czech curse words to call Leona. Ruing my choice of Latin for my foreign language studies in high school, I said, "Dusanka, you are not to blame. You are in a difficult position and Leona took advantage of that and threatened you." I placed my hand on her shoulder and lightly squeezed it.

Dusanka looked up; tears streamed down her cheeks. "I will go to the police and turn myself in. I will tell them the truth."

"No!" Sandy's exclamation startled Dusanka and me. "You will not sacrifice yourself. We'll figure this out." She gave me a stern glare, demanding confirmation.

"We will."

"Veronica will find out exactly what happened Monday night," Sandy said.

"The police lady was very nice. I'm disappointed in myself that I lied to her."

"Officer Brody?" I asked.

"Yes. I must apologize to her."

"Don't say anything now. You can apologize when this is all over. Tracey will understand. I haven't always been truthful with her and she's never thrown me in jail."

"You are good women."

"You've given us considerable help, Dusanka. Thank you."

Dusanka looked at her wristwatch. "It is getting late."

Sandy leapt to her feet. "Of course. I'll bring you back to your car so you can get back to Oli Hill before the wicked witch has a snit fit."

"Mrs. Kendall is not so mean," Dusanka said. "She's not usually a *fena*. She's . . . I don't know what you say? About chickens watching over their little ones?"

"A mother hen," I answered.

"Yes. A mother hen."

The description was apt. Not only was Leona protective of her children, she clucked about her father like there was no tomorrow.

"What is it like living among all those beautiful paintings at Oli Hill?" I asked as the three of us walked back to the kitchen.

"I am happy they are on the walls." Dusanka's expression was grave. "I could not move if there was a chance I make a spill or scratch on one of the paintings. Mrs. Kendall told me to never touch them. I can do that."

Knowing it would irk her, I said to Sandy, "You and Leona sound just like twins. Maybe you were separated at birth."

Sandy narrowed her eyes. *"Fena."*

After seeing Sandy and Dusanka off, I grabbed my cell phone to call Mark. I had dialed the first three digits of his number when I remembered he was busy that evening hosting a guest lecture on the U.S. in the post Korean War years. I called Carol instead.

"What are you doing tonight, pal?" I asked.

"Having dinner with my darling daughter," was Carol's delighted reply.

"Enjoy."

"What's up?"

"Oh, nothing."

"Be careful doing nothing."

"Yes, ma'am. I'll see you tomorrow. Give Bridget a hug from her favorite Aunt Veronica."

I considered my options for a moment and then picked up the phone and dialed a third number.

"What are you doing tonight?" I asked, aiming to turn a one-time murder suspect into my Doctor Watson.

CHAPTER TWENTY-SIX

After making the call, I trotted down my driveway to retrieve my mail. I was flipping through the envelopes, checking for bills, when a metallic-blue sedan stopped in front of the house next door.

Debbie Bradley slid from the car. "You're home early. Do you work banker's hours?"

"No."

Debbie went over to the For Sale sign Glen had stuck in the lawn. She studied it for a minute and then walked halfway up the lawn. She put her hands on her hips and swept her gaze across the Folk-Victorian home. "I've always liked this place."

I joined her. "Anna had great taste. She renovated the whole place a few years ago."

"It ticked me off when she didn't hire Vin to do that reno."

"Oh yeah?"

"Yeah." Debbie headed up the porch steps. "I really want to buy this house, but Vin doesn't want to move." She put her face near the living-room window and peered inside.

"Are you serious?" My stomach lurched. If Vin and Debbie moved in next door, I might have to move back in with my mother.

"Yep. Our house needs work. I'm trying to convince Vin that it would be easier to just move to a house that's already been remodeled. We can definitely afford it. Vin says he'll re-do our house, but I can't bear to lose my kitchen for months. And he doesn't have the time. He's busy with the bridal-shop project. And as soon as he's done with that, he'll have a project for the historical society." Debbie moved to the other side of the front door and glanced through the window into the room that served as Anna's office.

"The historical society? That sounds big."

"Well, Vin hasn't won the bid yet. But he will."

"Does he have inside information?" I said with a very light touch.

Debbie glared at me for an uncomfortable moment. "You think he's cheating?"

"No. Of course not."

Debbie gave me another piercing look and then sauntered over to the front door. "Are you a good neighbor?"

"The best." A few goose bumps went up my arm. I wanted Glen to sell the house, but not to the Bradleys. I didn't get a good vibe from them.

Debbie's eyes flitted over me. "Have you ever thought about highlighting your hair? You would look good with some streaks of gold."

"Um, no. I haven't."

"Give me a call if you do."

"Sure."

"You know, I've never been inside." Debbie gestured to the house with her thumb. "I wasn't exactly in Anna's inner circle."

"I'm sure you can get a Realtor to show it to you."

"You have a key, right? I heard about your exploits over the summer."

I did have a house key, only to be used in case of an emergency. A policy I was sticking to, thanks to my summer "exploits." I had gone into the home searching for clues to Anna's murder and ended up hiding under the table when unexpected "company" arrived.

"Well . . ."

"You can show me around right now."

"That's not a good idea. I wouldn't feel right about it."

"Oh, come on. Don't be a Girl Scout. No one will know."

"I'm going out in a few minutes. I have to change clothes."

Debbie let out an exaggerated sigh. "Okay. I have big plans for tonight, too. But I thought you'd be cool about it."

"I'm sorry. Call a Realtor."

"Yeah," Debbie said, clopping down the porch steps and across the lawn. "Bye." She got into her car and drove off.

I headed back to my house, thinking about all that Debbie had said. Why was she so sure Vin would get the parsonage job? Did she have a hand in helping him secure it? Debbie didn't have an alibi for Monday evening and she did just brag about being flush with cash. Money gained from the sale of *Orchard Street* would definitely cover the cost of the house. My cell rang in my pocket.

"So you've been caught in Brenda's web," Sabrina said when I answered. "I assume she asked you for a donation for the parsonage renovation."

"I haven't made a commitment yet. But I hope you're working on a really cheap, yet elegant, design," I replied.

"Now that I know you're involved in bankrolling the project, I was thinking of some minor tweaks to the blueprint. Gold-plated doorknobs. Crystal chandeliers. The very best of everything."

"But that wouldn't be authentic. I don't think they even had doorknobs back then. And they worked by the light of the sun and the flicker of candlelight."

"I'm not sure that's historically accurate, Veronica, but you do have an answer for everything."

"Yes, I do."

"I suppose I could cancel the bell I just ordered from Italy."

I plopped down on my top porch step. "You should buy American. Seriously, Sabrina, I'm happy SRB is working on the project."

"Thanks, Veronica. I hate why I had to take it over, but I'm going to put my whole heart into this renovation. In Scott's honor. He put all his energy into this project. He became so absorbed in renovating the parsonage, Isabel complained more than once that he'd show up late for a date because he lost track of time. I think he was headed there when he left the office on Monday. Scott had such a beautiful vision for the building. He must have spent hours at the site, taking photographs, sketching, going over every inch of the place. He wanted to restore the parsonage to its former glory."

"I'm so sorry that he won't see the result of his hard work."

"Me, too. I heard you were at Scott's yesterday. Still trying to help the Griffins?"

"Yes." Sabrina and I were quiet for a moment. "Will you decide on the winning contractor bid for the parsonage job?"

"No. Rob and I will go over the bids and make a recommendation to Brenda, but she will make the final decision."

"I see."

"I don't want to keep you, Veronica. I just wanted to add my own pitch for the parsonage. It is a very worthy project to support. Not that I'm twisting your arm."

"With your involvement, I'm more inclined to get behind it. I can't wait to hear your presentation on Saturday's tour."

"You'll be there? I'm so pleased."

"With American-made bells on my shoes."

Sabrina laughed. "I'd love to keep talking with you, but I have a meeting with a client. We really need to sit down for a proper conversation soon."

"We will. I'll see you on Saturday, Sabrina. And like I said, cheap is *in* now."

"It's my new mantra."

Sabrina's remark of how much time Scott spent at the parsonage solidified my theory that he had seen Vin there. I now had two solid suspects on my list. Theo, who had a very personal motive and Debbie, whose motive was based on pure greed with a smattering of revenge. Plus the nagging feeling I had about Isabel.

CHAPTER TWENTY-SEVEN

"I forgot to put on my beauty mark!" Claire said as she rummaged through her purse. "Here it is."

I glanced at her as she used an eyebrow pencil to apply a mole over her lip. "You're really getting into the part. Remember, we can't draw attention to ourselves."

"I know that. Have you decided on an alias?"

"I was thinking Rachel, for old-times' sake." Rachel was the name of the character I had portrayed on *Days and Nights*.

"You still miss her, don't you?"

"Sure. She was my bread and butter for decades. Rachel will always be close to my heart."

Claire pulled down the passenger sun visor, puckered her lips, and then blotted them with a tissue. "And I'm Scarlett. Or should I be Ruby?"

"Scarlett."

"All right." She adjusted her wig and then leaned over and tugged on the back of mine. "There you go."

"Thanks, Scarlett."

For our undercover surveillance of Theo and his mystery date, I wore the wig I would wear to the Halloween party. Claire, though she had never met Theo Kendall and therefore technically did not need a disguise, put on a hairpiece she had worn the previous Halloween as part of a mermaid outfit. The wig was a shoulder-length red piece that fell in loose curls around her face. Claire looked good and less conspicuous than she would have if she wore the platinum blonde wig that was part of the Marilyn Monroe costume she would wear to the party at The Hearth the next evening.

We arrived at the restaurant ten minutes before Theo's meeting time. I thought it wise that we be seated when Theo arrived, rather than risk meeting him at the door.

I guessed there were about thirty diners at the tables. Couples occupied a few tables, families with small children took up two, and in the center of the room a group of high school girls wearing track suits, accompanied by three adults, commanded five tables that had been pushed together. The hostess seated us in a booth along the wall opposite the entrance.

I surveyed the room, certain it was Theo's "hiding place." The dull hardwood floor and wall paneling didn't scream "fine dining." Leona would disown Theo if she knew he had eaten, or even just used the restroom, in an establishment where paintings of bears in rustic settings hung on the walls, I thought. That is if she survived the shock and scandal of the visit.

"This is perfect," Claire whispered with a gleeful sparkle in her eye. "We can see the entire room without looking nosy about it."

"It's excellent."

"May I ask something?"

"What?"

"Are you absolutely sure Regina is telling the truth? Do you one hundred percent believe Scott asked her to his house and gave her the letter?"

"I believe her."

"It's odd that Scott gave her the letter so quickly, don't you think?"

"Well, he knew the sentiments George Bradshaw expressed were very personal. And meant for Eloise Griffin. He didn't want the public poring over the letter."

"It just seems so convenient."

"I believe Regina."

Claire paused for a very long moment. "All right."

I watched the hostess seat a woman in a booth across the room from our table. The woman, a gal in her late twenties, had long, dark brown hair pulled back into a loose ponytail. Her ensemble was basic black: skirt, knee-high boots, leather jacket. She did wear a white blouse under the jacket, with the top two or three buttons undone. She was obviously dressed for a hot date. So what was she doing at The Mountain Bear?

I leaned over and discreetly nodded in the direction of the woman's booth. "That woman doesn't really fit in here."

"Hmm. We'll have to keep an eye on her." Claire gasped and lifted her hand to cover her face.

"What's wrong?"

"I know that waitress at the high school kids' table."

I looked over and noted the waitress refilling soda glasses. She was in her early twenties. Vivid pink strands streaked through her jet-black, pixie-styled hair.

"Oh, yeah?"

"She worked for Pauline for a few months."

"She can help us, you know."

"She can?"

"Yes. Maybe she can give us some information about Theo."

Claire dropped her hand and sat up straight. Her mouth formed an *O.* "You're good. But how do I explain the wig?"

"I'll handle it."

The waitress approached our table. "Welcome to The Mountain Bear. I'm Nickie. Would you like menus?"

"We're just having drinks," I said.

"All right. What would you like?"

"I'll have a Seven and Seven, please."

"And I'll have a rum and Coke." Claire turned fully to Nickie.

How quickly Claire had turned from a cowering spy to a bold redhead.

"Claire?" Nickie gave Claire a quizzical look.

"Hey, Nickie," Claire said.

"Wow, look at you. You look good as a redhead." Nickie eyed Claire's hair, nodding with approval.

"Thanks. It's a wig."

"Oh?"

"For Halloween." That's what I was going to say! "We're just getting accustomed to them. This is my friend Veronica."

"Nice to meet you, Veronica."

"Likewise," I said. "I like your hair."

"Thanks. It's not a wig."

"It looks better than that blue you used to have," Claire said.

"Thanks. Sorry I can't chat right now, but I'll be right back with your drinks."

Nickie hustled off toward the bar in the corner of the room.

"You handled that well," I said.

"But I wanted to be Scarlett," Claire said with a slight pout.

"Maybe you'll still get your chance."

Boisterous laughter came from the athletes' table. I glanced over just as Theo Kendall, led by the hostess, passed the celebrating teens.

"Theo is here!" A surge of adrenaline shot through me. "And he's going over to that woman's booth."

We watched as Theo, dressed in jeans and a navy sports coat, slid into the seat across from the lady in black. They shook hands across the table; it certainly was not the greeting of two people dating.

"He's very serious," Claire said. "And handsome."

"We're here on business."

She tossed me a sly glance and went back to studying Theo.

We observed Theo and the lady for a moment as they

exchanged words and nods. Nickie interrupted our spying by delivering our drinks and bowls of peanuts and pretzels.

"Can I get you ladies anything else?" Nickie asked.

"No thanks, Nickie," Claire said.

After Nickie left, Claire and I toasted each other and sipped our drinks. Claire's eyes shifted over to Theo's table.

"Theo's date slid something across the table," she whispered.

I shot Theo's table a glance, just in time to see Theo slipping something into the inside pocket of his jacket. He took an envelope from the jacket's pocket and pushed it across the table to the woman.

"I bet there's money in that envelope!"

As if he heard her, Theo looked away from his date, his eyes scanning the room. Claire and I turned toward the window.

"It's a beautiful evening, Rachel."

"That it is, Scarlett." Applause from the athletes' table provided me the opportunity to turn back to the room. Theo and the woman in black were still engaged in their conversation. I signaled to Nickie as she finished at the table next to ours.

"Nickie, that couple over there," I jutted my chin in the direction of Theo's table, "have they been here before?"

"Yeah. They were here Sunday night."

Claire and I exchanged conspiratorial nods. "Are they romantically involved?" Claire innocently inquired.

"Definitely not. The only touching I've seen between those two is a handshake."

"What's she like? Do you know her name?" I asked.

"She's nice. I never got her name. What's going on?"

"A friend of ours likes that guy," Claire answered.

"Did you follow him here?"

"No!" Claire said.

Nickie giggled. "Okay. I gotta get back to work. Any more questions?"

"No. Thanks, Nickie." I waited for her to be out of earshot. "I bet that woman is the person Theo said would *help* the family with their problem. He set the whole thing up right here on Sunday night." Claire and I sat in silence for a minute as we processed the new information.

"I have a guess as to what Theo's friend just gave him," I said.

"What?"

"A key to a safe deposit box. She stole the painting and put it in a box for him to later retrieve."

Claire sat back, her eyes and lips forming symmetrical wide circles. "Yes," she said in the same breathy voice as Marilyn Monroe.

"We should follow her. See where she lives."

"And then I can do a reverse address search online and find out her name!"

Great minds think alike. "Exactly. We should finish our drinks and get in position in the car."

After paying the check (and leaving a generous tip for Nickie) we hurried out of the restaurant. The hulking Hummer parked next to my car immediately caught my attention. I'm usually ticked when a mammoth vehicle casts its shadow on my car. The Hummer, however, provided us excellent cover—we could see the front door, but anyone looking out the window could not see us sitting in the front seat.

We settled into position and watched the restaurant door without talking for a few minutes, until my cell phone barked.

I pulled the phone from my purse. "Alex."

"Put him on speaker!"

I pressed the button and we both said, "Hi, Alex," though with quite different tones. Mine was a decidedly bland greeting, while Claire may as well have said, "Hey, big guy, come up and see me sometime."

"Ladies!" Alex had his speaker phone on as well. I heard motor sounds and guessed he was on some Los Angeles highway. "Are you still at All Things?"

"We just left a roadside restaurant," I said.

"Why?"

"Surveillance," Claire said in a kittenish voice.

I looked at her; she smiled at me like a woman who had received a huge diamond ring, fur coat, and gift certificate for unlimited cosmetic surgery.

"Explain," Alex said in his well-practiced suave manner.

I did so, with Claire interjecting a remark or two.

"And we're wearing wigs," Claire said when I finished.

"Send me pictures. I wish I was there with you, right in the backseat."

Claire giggled. "And where are you, actually?"

"I'm driving up Pacific Coast Highway."

"I can smell the ocean."

I gave Claire a glance that warned: This isn't a booty phone call. "We're on a stakeout!" I mouthed.

"Why isn't the professor with you?"

"He's at a lecture on the U.S. post–Korean War."

"Yawn."

Claire snapped from flirt mode. "There they are!"

I turned and saw Theo and his lady friend standing right outside the restaurant door. They talked for a few moments and then shook hands. The lady headed to a black Corolla on the opposite side of the lot. Theo, his head down, walked briskly toward our side. Claire and I slid down our seats.

"We have to go, Alex." I shut the phone and started the engine. I sat up in my seat, just enough to see Theo's BMW whiz by and turn onto Route Nine. Claire and I held our collective breaths as the black car backed from its spot and made a right turn onto the road. "Here we go." I pulled from the lot.

No vehicles separated my car from the woman's. I nervously gripped the steering wheel as I lightly pressed the gas pedal.

"Don't get too close," Claire said.

"I know that. I've done this before." I stayed three car lengths behind the Corolla. I checked my gas tank; I had more than a half tank of fuel left.

"Do you think she lives nearby?" Claire asked. "I hope we don't end up in Lake Placid. The village *or* the lake."

"I'm sure she's local," I said, tiring already of Claire's babbling.

A traffic light ahead turned to yellow and then red. I slowed and came to a stop half a car length behind the Corolla.

"Is Alex dating anyone?"

"Not that I know of."

"Hmmm."

I glanced at her; she had a faraway look in her eyes as she stared at the Corolla's bumper.

"Why do you ask?"

"No reason."

"You said back in the summer that he wasn't your type."

"He's not. But it is fun flirting with him. And we've been exchanging texts. And calls."

The light turned green; I followed the Corolla through the intersection, staying at a comfortable distance.

"That's a mixed message. Do you want to have a long-distance relationship with Alex?"

Claire sighed. "I'm a lonely woman, Veronica. Barton isn't exactly a hot singles scene. I like the attention Alex gives me, even though I know he's giving it to every woman."

I snorted in confirmation of that statement.

"I guess I like the fantasy of a relationship with Alex. It would be ruined if he's seeing someone out in L.A. But, on the other hand, if he is seeing someone, that would force me to face reality and stop eating my heart out over every text."

"I wish I could introduce you to someone. Maybe Mark knows some young professors."

"We could double-date," Claire said. "She's turning!"

The Corolla's right turn signal was indeed flashing. I waited a few seconds and then flipped my own blinker.

"Bloody Pond Road," Claire murmured as she read the road sign. "What a name."

"There was a massacre here in 1755," I explained. "The Colonials surprised a group of Canadian and Indian forces and killed more than two hundred."

"Is this knowledge one of the benefits of dating a history professor?"

"Yes."

"Then make mine an English professor. I'd rather be literary-minded than be able to spout every historic reference. No offense."

"None taken. I don't want you stepping on my limelight."

The black car turned into a driveway.

"Go slow, so I can get the house number."

I followed Claire's direction, driving by the property as slowly as I dared. The house was barely visible, thanks to the heavily wooded front yard.

"Did you get the number? I didn't see anything! Turn around."

"Okay. Calm down!"

I passed the neighbor's house and turned into the driveway of the next property. I backed up and proceeded to retrace the drive up Bloody Pond as I muttered under my breath, "Bloody surveillance."

"Is that a two or a seven on the box?" Claire asked as we

passed the house again. "Bloody darkness."

"I'm not turning around again. Someone will call the cops."

Claire let out a loud sigh. "Don't tell me we did this for nothing. We'll have to come back tomorrow during the day."

I checked my rearview mirror. Theo's friend had pulled out of the driveway and was behind us.

"She's following us." I gulped as I got a sour taste in my mouth.

"Bloody hell."

We approached Route Nine. "What do I do now?"

"Make a right and head for Lake George."

Since it wasn't the time for a snappy rejoinder about ending up *in* Lake George (with the way the evening was going, a soggy ending was a distinct possibility), I said nothing and did as Claire said.

We rode in tense silence, my heart in my throat and Claire wringing her hands. Every few seconds she would turn and peer around her seat to check the car behind us.

We passed Water Slide World and approached the heart of Lake George Village.

"Turn here." Claire pointed to a street on the right.

Without signaling, I turned onto Fort George Road. We drove toward the lake and soon reached Beach Road. I made a left turn and headed back toward Route Nine, which had become Canada Street. The lake was calm and its steamboats, The Minne-Ha-Ha, The Mohican, and The Lac du Saint Sacrement, stood beside the dock. I shivered when I saw the black water, knowing it was frigid, and was glad when we were past the lake. I had an image of the car, the two of us trapped inside, sinking to the bottom of Lake George. This is what happens when you put yourself in the middle of a murder investigation and start following suspects along dark roads.

We reached Canada Street. "Do you know where the police

station is?" I asked Claire.

"I think the sheriff is up the road a bit, toward Glens Falls."

That meant a few miles separated us from law enforcement. "Should we call nine one one?"

"Let's head toward the sheriff. Maybe she won't follow us."

I made a left onto Canada Street and checked the rearview mirror. The Corolla's headlights glared behind me. "She's still behind us."

"Hail Mary!" Claire screeched.

"Finding religion in the foxhole, I see."

We drove up Route Nine and soon passed The Mountain Bear.

"Want to pop in for another drink?" I asked with more than a tinge of sarcasm.

"When we get back to Barton," Claire retorted. "We'll need one."

We continued along the dark, twisting road as Theo's friend/ accomplice continued to trail us.

After a few minutes I said, "She would have run us off the road by now, if she meant to hurt us."

"Maybe she's waiting until we stop and then she'll shoot us." Claire was quiet for a moment. "We're two drama queens."

"This is a strange way to bond."

"The outlet shops!" Claire's arm shot up, her finger pointing at the windshield. The shopping center was just beyond the light, on the left. "It's busy. She won't dare do something to us in a crowded parking lot."

I kept my mouth shut, not wanting to agitate Claire even more by saying bad things happen in crowded parking lots all the time. I proceeded through the intersection and switched on my directional signal. As I made the turn into the lot, the black Corolla continued on Route Nine.

"She's gone." I pulled into the nearest empty parking space

and turned off the engine.

We leaned back in our seats. I felt as if we had just finished riding the roller coaster at the Great Escape a few miles farther up Route Nine. Claire covered her face and let out a muffled scream.

"That was exciting."

Claire pulled off her wig. "I lost about five years off my life." She scratched her scalp and fluffed her hair.

We were quiet for a minute. Then we turned to each other at the same moment and began laughing like fools.

"Do you want to come with me to Charlie Gannon's tomorrow to see his reproduction of *Orchard Street*?" I removed my wig.

"Bloody yeah."

CHAPTER TWENTY-EIGHT

Upon our arrival in Barton, Claire and I headed straight for the Farley Inn. We had a choice: drinks and chocolate cake at The Hearth or hot chocolate and warm apple pie at the inn. After considering the homemade vanilla ice cream that would accompany the pie, the decision was a no-brainer. We tossed our wigs in the back seat, checked our hair, and went into the inn.

We got an eyeful the moment we stepped into the dining room. Debbie Bradley and five friends sat at a table in the center of the room. Debbie appeared to be the hostess; she commanded everyone's attention and obviously controlled the bottle of champagne chilling in a bucket beside her place setting.

"What are they celebrating?" Claire whispered as we settled at a table by the fireplace. The crackling flames and smoky scent soothed my overworked nerves.

"I don't know," I said, "but Debbie's getting a big bill." The Farley is the crème-de-la-crème of fine dining in Barton; diners pay handsomely for the experience. "Debbie stopped by Anna's today."

"Why?"

"She said she's interested in buying the house. Her husband doesn't have time to renovate their home, so she wants to move."

"They can afford the asking price?" Claire's glance shifted to Debbie's table. She gave the hair stylist an assessing look.

I shared my suspicion of Debbie as Scott's murderer. Claire was already deep in this with me thanks to our Mountain Bear jaunt. She might as well know everything.

"I thought we were certain Theo's friend is the murderer?"

"I was eighty-nine percent sure you were a murderer just a few weeks ago."

"Right. It's good to have a backup killer," Claire said.

For the umpteenth time that day, I pulled out my phone and displayed the photo of the watch. "This was on the ground outside Scott's house," I whispered.

Claire leaned in and squinted at the phone's screen. She glanced at Debbie, whose shoulders were shaking with mirth as she drained her glass of champagne.

"What if you show it to Debbie and see how she reacts?"

I stole a glance at the hairdresser. "If she's guilty, she won't claim it."

"Sometimes you can trick someone into revealing the truth when you catch them off-guard. And she's been drinking. She's probably half in the bag."

"*In vino veritas.* Or, should I say, when champagne goes in, a confession comes out."

"Debbie doesn't know you're looking for Scott's killer and she might not know where she lost the watch. She wears so much hardware on her arm, how could she tell if one piece went missing? Don't show her the photo. See if she can describe it!"

"I'll do it." I slipped my phone in my purse. "Save my seat."

I walked over to Debbie's table. I intentionally didn't go to Debbie but stopped between the women sitting opposite her.

"Good evening, ladies."

"Want to join the party?" Debbie asked as the others gave their greetings.

"No, thank you, Debbie. I'm sorry to interrupt, but I found a woman's watch yesterday and wanted to know if it belongs to one of you ladies?"

"What's the make?" one of the women asked.

"Fenton." My gaze drifted around the table and landed on Debbie.

The women murmured in appreciation of an expensive piece of jewelry.

Debbie cocked her head. "Where did you find it?"

"In town." I waited a beat, wondering if I would have to confess to a priest the fibs I was telling about the watch. "If you hear of anyone who has lost a watch, please send them to All Things."

"We will. Thanks for letting us know," the woman next to me said.

"Enjoy the rest of your meal."

I headed back to our table. As I sat, I saw from the corner of my eye Debbie clambering to her feet. She took a few long strides, pulled a chair from the unoccupied table behind me, dragged it over, and plopped down beside me.

"Do you have the watch with you?"

"No."

"What does it look like?"

"It's silver. Did you lose your watch, Debbie?"

"No. But I'm thinking of getting one."

"You should go to Bern's. Dolores would be happy to assist you."

"I know she would. But I'm interested in the watch you found."

"The watch has an owner."

Debbie shook her head, frowning over my response. "What if no one claims it? You know, it could belong to a tourist who has already left town."

"That's a possibility." I played it cool as Debbie continued tugging on the lure I had tossed. "I suppose I should turn it over to the police," I said with nonchalance.

Debbie clicked her tongue. "You know Tracey Brody is just going to drop that watch in her pocket. If she doesn't take it, one of the other cops will."

I wanted to slap her for insinuating Tracey was a dirty cop. "Officer Brody does not steal."

"Of course she doesn't. Tracey is an honest cop," Claire said. Her attention moved from Debbie to me. The two of us locked into a stare as our waiter laid our pie and hot chocolate on the table.

"Hold on," Debbie said, jumping from her chair and hurrying to her table.

"She's nervous," Claire said.

I nodded. Excited, I forced myself to eat a forkful of pie and ice cream. "Oh, I'm glad we decided to come here and not The Hearth." The flaky, sweet dessert tickled every one of my taste buds.

Claire, her own mouth full of pie, nodded a vigorous agreement.

Debbie returned with her purse. She sat down, pulled out her wallet, and opened it to reveal a few hundred-dollar bills in the compartment.

"I'll give you a hundred for the watch." Debbie partially slid the top bill from the wallet, enough for me to see the top of Benjamin Franklin's head.

I acted as if I were giving serious consideration to her offer. "The watch is worth more than that." I bit my lip. "I really think it's best if I give it to the police. The owner may have already contacted the station."

"And what if they haven't? You found the watch; it's yours. Just like that painting belonged to Scott because he found it. You're a choir girl, Veronica. Get over your moral values and take the easy hundred." Debbie pulled the bill from her wallet and set it by my plate. Then she took out a second hundred-dollar bill and slapped that on top of the first. "I'll give you two."

"How about I wait a week?" I said, "And if the watch isn't claimed, I'll sell it to you?"

Debbie clenched her jaw and forced a huff of air through her nose. "Forget it."

As she stuffed the money back into her wallet, Claire asked, "Are you celebrating a special occasion tonight, Debbie?"

"Success," Debbie said with an air of superiority and entitlement.

"Fabulous," Claire said without a hint of genuine congratulation.

Debbie sprang from her seat. "I have to get back to my friends."

"Have a good evening," I said to her backside. "So, what did we prove? Debbie is either guilty and scared or innocent and greedy. In other words, we learned nothing from this exercise."

"It was entertaining. And helped us forget how we were hotly pursued through Lake George. It's good to be alive."

My cell phone rang. The call came from the Griffins' home. "Hello?"

"Veronica." It was a cheerless Ella.

Now what? "Good evening, Ella."

"I would like you to join us for breakfast tomorrow morning."

"Has something happened? Regina hasn't been—"

"No. There have been no developments. My sister Amelia and her son and daughter-in-law have arrived from Hartford. They would like to meet with you."

"All right. I would like to meet them, too."

"Please arrive promptly at eight thirty."

"I will."

"Is everything okay with Regina?" Claire asked after I set the phone on the table.

"She's fine. Her parents and grandmother are here. They must want to hear what I've been doing to prove Regina's innocence."

My phone beeped a text-message alert. A daily update from Pauline.

CALL ME FRI AM. HAVE TIDBIT ON NAT K.

"Huh."

"Something good?"

"Just a hello from Pauline." She was probably going to tell me about the Kendalls' dining experience at Maison Berenice. I added a reminder to my calendar to call her.

My cell rang again. This time the caller was Tim.

"Suddenly the whole village wants to talk with you," Claire quipped.

"I'm going to take this in the hall." I hustled from the dining room. "Hi, Tim."

"Veronica. I'm sorry to bother you."

"It's no bother. What's up?" I headed for a comfortable chair positioned outside the ladies' room.

"I understand you will be having breakfast with the Griffins tomorrow."

"Word travels fast. Ella just called with the invitation."

"I had dinner with the family. Madeline mentioned you're helping them."

I wish she hadn't said that in Tim's presence. Like the police, lawyers don't like amateurs involving themselves in criminal cases.

"You promised at the police station you'd stay out of the way."

"And I am."

"I hope you're not snooping around, Veronica."

"I'm supporting my friends."

"That's all well and good. As long as you are giving them emotional support and not trying to dig up evidence."

"You know Ella and Madeline are very worried Leona Kendall will use her power to get the police to do her bidding."

"They've expressed that concern, yes. Let me worry about it. I'm working hard to get Regina out of this mess."

"I know you are. You're the best, Tim. Regina is lucky to have you."

"Remember you're a potential witness, Veronica. You want to be a credible one for Regina."

"I suppose the Kendalls would be witnesses, too?" I asked.

"Yes."

"Good. Because they're keeping something from the police."

"How do you know that, Veronica?"

"I know someone."

"Who?"

"Someone."

"Veronica."

"I can't say. This person is frightened of the Kendall power, just as the Griffins are." I considered Dusanka's situation. I wanted to do more than give her the thrill of knowing an actress from her favorite soap opera. She put her neck on the line to help me and I wanted to return the gesture by helping her find a more nurturing work environment. "On second thought, you might be able to help each other. What's your schedule like tomorrow?"

Tim and I made an appointment for the next afternoon. I then made a call to the number I had programmed into my phone just a few hours earlier.

"Dusanka," I said when the unmistakable voice answered. "It's Veronica." After Dusanka rattled off a greeting, I asked, "Do you trust me?"

"Celým svým srdcem."

That sounded like a yes. I'd look it up later.

CHAPTER TWENTY-NINE

I love having a professor as my whatever you call him. Mark is smart, handsome, witty, and sweet. He also has a large white board in his home office, which he uses to gather his thoughts for lectures and his Martin Van Buren book.

After I dropped Claire off at her car behind All Things, I scooted over to Mark's. I had called him from the Farley Inn to make sure he was home. "I bet my night was more exciting than yours."

"Says you," Mark cracked.

It took me five minutes to cover the white board with a blue-ink summary as I narrated my eventful day for Mark.

"I should have asked for the abridged version." Mark scratched his chin and took a few steps back from the board. "You have enough on here for at least three months' worth of soap scripts."

I beamed. "Maybe that should be my second career." I dropped the lighthearted tone. "Now that we know that Scott was home, we know the person went there to kill him."

"Not necessarily. The killer could have gone there to try to persuade Scott to hand over the painting. The conversation could have escalated to murder." He picked up the eraser and wiped clear my hard work.

"Hey! That was an excellent paragraph on my Farley Inn encounter with Debbie!"

"And you get an A for it. But let's condense your day into

who is a suspect and who isn't."

Once the board was clean, Mark wrote across the top: *Who Wanted The Painting* and *Who Wanted Scott Dead.*

"Interesting headers," I said.

"Thank you." He wrote Ned's, Ella's, Madeline's, Regina's, and the three Kendalls' names in the first column. He wrote *Alibi* next to the appropriate names. He wrote *Lady in Black* at the bottom of the list. "Theo may have sent his lady friend to have a chat with Scott and when he didn't comply—"

"She moved to Plan B. The cheese knife."

Mark wrote *Theo Kendall* in the *Who Wanted Scott Dead* column.

"You know, Dotsie thinks an art syndicate is involved."

Mark let out an amused huff and then added *Art Syndicate* to the first column. "So who else might have wanted Scott dead?"

I did not hesitate to answer. "Vin and Debbie Bradley."

Mark wrote the couple's names in the column. "And then there's our old friend, the wildcard."

The wildcard was Mark's term for a suspect we did not know, someone who had not revealed a motive for the crime. He first used the term over the summer when we were investigating Anna's murder. As it turned out, a wildcard had killed my neighbor.

"I have a niggling suspicion about Isabel."

"Still?"

"Hillary wore a cocktail dress to the gallery. And evening eye makeup. So she must have gone home to change and then gone to Isabel's."

"Good observation."

"That means Isabel was alone for a part of the afternoon."

"She doesn't fit in either column. She didn't want the painting and she didn't want Scott dead."

"They've been arguing."

"Well, it wouldn't be the first time a lover's quarrel led to murder." Mark wrote Isabel's name in a white space between the two columns. "So, *if* the Kendalls are involved, how does the stolen painting end up at the Bradshaw House?"

We were silent for a minute as we contemplated the puzzle.

A theory suddenly took form in my mind. "Art laundering."

"Explain."

"Theo hired the woman he met at The Mountain Bear to kill Scott and steal *Orchard Street.* Forget about her having a *friendly* chat with Scott. Theo enlists a friend or two or three from the art world to help him launder," I paused to wiggle my fingers into air quotes, "the painting. He holds the painting for a year or so, has his dealer friends write up some fake sales receipts to make it look as if the painting has passed through a few hands, and then one of his friends steps forward with the painting and a *legitimate* bill of sale. Leona then goes forward with her plan to take advantage of the Culversons and get the painting back."

"That sounds like one of your soap plots."

"Well, on *Days* it involved jewels, not artwork. My maid, Francine, stole a few of my—I mean Rachel's—expensive pieces, had a buddy create fakes, and then slipped the fakes into Rachel's safe. Francine sold the real jewels and got away with it for a while until the diamond necklace Rachel's third husband gave her showed up in town around the neck of a Greek heiress."

"Wow. And Rachel figured out Francine's involvement?"

"Yep."

"What happened to Francine?"

"She locked Rachel in Herbert's wine cellar and stole off to Argentina."

"How long did it take Rachel to get out of the wine cellar?"

"In soap time, three days. In real time, it was two-and-a-half weeks' worth of episodes."

"It's funny that a maid is involved in each plot."

"Life imitating art. Though Dusanka is exposing the plot in real life, not engineering it."

"Mm-hmm. Be careful with her."

"Why?"

"You don't really know her motives. You hardly know her at all. And you don't want to get caught up in an international incident."

"I trust Dusanka."

"All right." Mark's gaze lingered on me for a moment before sliding back to the white board. "Art laundering does make sense if Theo hired a professional to kill Scott and not simply have a *friendly* chat. They would need Scott out of the way so he couldn't make a claim when the painting resurfaced. Theo could have instructed the woman to make it look like an amateur committed the crime."

"Like Regina. This gives me the chills."

Mark tapped his finger on the words *Art Syndicate*. "If Theo's plan involves the art laundering, Dotsie's supposition would be correct."

"She'll be impossible to deal with."

"It's also possible that Debbie killed Scott. Scott was her husband's nemesis. Maybe Scott knew about Vin's latest dealing and Debbie went to plead with Scott not to report her husband. Scott refused, so she stabbed him and took *Orchard Street*. It's a simpler theory than one involving hit women and art laundering. With or without an art syndicate."

"But I like my theory. If you're correct about Debbie, I did U-turns in the dark on Bloody Pond Road for nothing."

"What if Theo's meeting at The Mountain Bear was just a meeting?"

"I stand by my incredulity at Theo Kendall stepping foot in The Mountain Bear for an innocent, legitimate meeting. He's established himself, along with his alibi, as a La Maison Berenice kind of guy."

"Maybe he's having an affair with the woman and knows his mother would not approve."

I thought of the Lady in Black's sexy outfit. "But there was absolutely no affection between the two."

"Some people are very shy about that kind of thing."

"I don't know." After a minute's pause, I asked, "And what did she slide across the table to Theo, and what was in the envelope he gave her?"

Mark shrugged. "It could be anything."

"Maybe she's a matchmaker and he's embarrassed about needing one."

A laugh rumbled through Mark. He put his arm around my shoulder and awarded me a long kiss on the cheek. "I love your wild imagination."

"It's served me well."

"Here's another question. What if the watch is just a watch, and not a piece of evidence?"

"Don't go all Freudian on me."

CHAPTER THIRTY

I awoke Friday with a "too much drama" hangover. My muscles ached and I felt, after eight hours of sleep, that I needed eight more. I rolled out of bed, did a combo stagger/limp to the bathroom, and stood in the shower for fifteen minutes until the warm water massaged me into an alert state of consciousness. That and a large serving of black coffee helped put the memory of being followed by a possible murderer in a quiet corner of my brain.

Regina was sitting on the top porch step when I arrived at the Griffins'. She appeared as if she, too, had had a rough evening, which was understandable in light of her interrogation twenty-four hours earlier. Her hair was pulled back in a messy bun and she wore a gray sweatshirt and faded jeans. She clutched a mug of coffee between her hands as if it were a life raft.

"Hi," Regina said as I sat beside her.

"How are you doing?"

"Still freaked out."

"It must be comforting to have your parents and grandmother here."

"I feel awful about putting them through this," she said.

"It's not your doing." I put my hand on her shoulder. "It will be resolved soon."

Regina nodded. "I hope so." She wiped her face. "I'm so grateful for your help and support, Veronica."

"It's my pleasure, though not really. If you get what I mean. I wish you didn't need it." I waited a beat and then asked, "When you were at Scott's, did he happen to mention if anyone else was coming over?"

Regina shook her head. "No. But Scott was distracted. Something seemed to be on his mind. Maybe he was just thinking about the showing at the gallery."

"Hmm."

"He was very kind." Regina blinked back tears. "He didn't have to give me the love letter. Especially after the way I behaved at the flea market and Hearth."

The front door swung open and a stern voice interrupted our moment of silence for Scott.

"What are you two doing sitting out here?"

I turned; a woman with a strong facial resemblance to Ella, a head of hair dyed strawberry-red, and eyeglasses with lenses wide enough to serve as dinner plates stood on the threshold.

"We're coming, Grandma."

I walked over to Amelia, my hand extended in welcome. "I'm Veronica Walsh, Mrs. Quinn."

"Yes. I figured that out," Amelia said. She regarded my hand and turned her back on me. Obviously, I was dealing with Ella, Part Two.

Regina shrugged her shoulders and pushed me into the house.

"Good morning, Veronica," Madeline greeted from the parlor. A man seated on the couch rose as I entered.

I gave Madeline a warm embrace, thankful someone in the family was happy to see me.

"This is my nephew, Don."

"Thank you for coming, Veronica," Don said. "And this is my wife, Joyce."

I turned to greet the woman who had just walked into the parlor. I immediately recognized where Regina got her beauty;

both mother and daughter had chestnut-colored hair, clear hazel eyes, and beautiful smiles.

"Hello." When Joyce moved closer, I noticed the weariness in her eyes. I immediately felt protective of Regina's worried mother.

"I hear you've been a good friend to Regina," Joyce said.

"Regina is a wonderful young woman. We're happy to have her here in Barton. And I'm proud to know her."

Joyce gave me a nod of gratitude as Ella called from the dining room.

"Breakfast is ready."

Joyce and I crossed the hall together. "I'm anxious to hear what you have learned about the case," she said.

I gave a weak smile and said nothing.

In the dining room, serving dishes and carafes filled with coffee and orange juice stood on the sideboard. We had our choice of scrambled eggs, sausages, pancakes, and mixed fruit.

We chatted politely for a few minutes about the weather and Barton.

Finally, Amelia turned the conversation to the investigation. "Veronica, tell me what qualifies you to conduct a murder investigation?"

"Grandma, stop. We discussed this last night."

"This is a serious matter, my dear. We need a person with excellent credentials working for us."

"Veronica is well-qualified," Madeline retorted.

Ella set her fork on her plate. "Veronica has had access to information that a professional investigator would not have. She was invited into Leona Kendall's home and gained important knowledge while she was there."

"And what is that knowledge?" Amelia directed her piercing gaze at me.

"I'm not at liberty to say," I said. "I must protect a source."

I caught Ella and Madeline exchanging smug looks. They were pleased that they knew who my source was and Amelia did not. Ah, sibling rivalry. A phenomenon I never experienced in my real or soap worlds.

"I don't think the First Amendment rights granted journalists extend to actresses turned amateur detective."

"Mom, Veronica is *helping* this family. Stop deriding her."

I sent a grateful nod across to Don.

"Mind your manners, Amelia," Madeline said.

"I apologize. My only granddaughter is precious to me and I'm desperate for someone who will guarantee her exoneration. I do appreciate whatever assistance you can give, Veronica. It certainly can't hurt. Please, tell us what you have learned."

Recalling the scenes I played on the soap in which my character led important business meetings, I summoned a confident dose of authority. "What I tell you cannot leave this room."

"Of course," Don said as Joyce murmured, "Absolutely."

Amelia leaned forward. "What do you know?"

I put my fork on my plate. "Theo and Leona met with Scott Culverson Sunday afternoon at Oli Hill. The meeting did not go well. I don't know what exactly was said, but I know Leona called Scott a greedy bastard after he left. I also know they did not tell the police about the meeting."

"Because it makes them look guilty as sin," Amelia said.

"I also know Theo told his mother he knows someone who can help them. I think he hired someone to steal *Orchard Street.*"

Amelia nodded. "Didn't want to get his hands dirty."

Ella slapped her hands against the table. "I knew that family was involved!"

"But do you have anything to support this theory?" Don asked.

"I followed Theo to a restaurant last night. It was a place a guy like him wouldn't frequent. He met a woman there. She slipped Theo something small and he gave her an envelope."

"That contained payment for the nefarious deed!" For a moment I thought Dotsie was in the room and had possessed Amelia's body.

"Perhaps the watch you found belongs to this woman he met," Madeline said.

"You found a watch?" Joyce asked.

I explained to her, Don, and Amelia my visit to Scott's house. "The watch might belong to Theo's mystery woman. There's also another woman on my radar."

Madeline said, "Oh?"

"I know someone who had a grudge against Scott. Let's just say she's been behaving in a way that has raised my suspicions."

"Excellent," Amelia said.

"It's wonderful that you have gathered this evidence, but what about hard and fast proof that my daughter did not commit this crime?" Don asked.

"I asked our local jeweler about the watch. Dolores did not sell it, but she's making inquiries of other local jewelers. I'm hopeful one of them will provide us with helpful information."

Amelia gave me a brisk nod of approval. "Very good work, Veronica."

"Thank you, Mrs. Quinn."

Madeline beamed and threw me a wink of approval. I glanced to the head of the table; Ella gave me a solemn nod. I resumed eating, suddenly ravenous. With the approval of all three Griffin sisters, I felt I had received a blessing from the pope.

I called Pauline on my walk to All Things.

"This is probably more 'It's a small world' stuff than anything important. But I went into Natalie's office yesterday to give her the mail and she was on the phone with Theo. So I shamelessly stood in the hall and listened. I pretended to be sorting through the other mail."

"Ingenuous." What have I wrought?

"Natalie told Theo that 'the hearing for the judge's will is delayed because of Scott Culverson's girlfriend.' She said Bianca, she's Natalie's best friend, just called her."

Holy smokes. "What else did she say?"

"Natalie explained that Scott's girlfriend was supposed to testify on Monday but can't because his funeral is that morning. Theo must have already known about it, because Natalie snapped at him for not telling her. Do you know anything about a hearing?"

"I've heard about the case."

"Does this help?"

"I don't know. But thank you for letting me know, Pauline."

"My pleasure. I'll call if Natalie spills any more beans."

I tried to fit this new information into the puzzle. What was Isabel's role in the will contestation? I'd put the question to Tim that afternoon.

CHAPTER THIRTY-ONE

Charlie Gannon's house was set back from the road and well-hidden by a dense patch of trees. The sprawl of the log house was so impressive it could easily be mistaken for a ski lodge.

"Art reproduction must pay well," Claire said.

We walked up the gravel driveway and were about to head up the wide steps to the front door when a voice beckoned us from the red barn on the other side of the driveway. Charlie stood in the open entry to the barn. His Yankees cap shaded his face.

Claire and I followed him into the barn. The hunter-green stalls that formerly housed horses remained along the right side of the airy barn. Linoleum rather than hay covered the floor.

I peeped into one of the ample-sized stalls and found one reproduction each of the *Mona Lisa, Starry Night, Sunflowers,* and *American Gothic* leaning against the walls.

The next stall was occupied by animal portraits. The presentation of dogs, cats, and horses delighted me.

"My bread and butter," Charlie explained.

"And here are my meat and potatoes." Charlie led us to the next stall.

There he had stored formal and informal wedding and family portraits. There were also canvases depicting people in candid moments.

"Do you work from photographs?" I asked.

"Yes."

"How long have you been doing this?" Claire asked.

"Professionally, four years. In my previous life I was an art director on Madison Avenue. I lost my job in 2008 and decided to make my beautiful Barton vacation house my permanent home."

"Do you do original work, too?"

Charlie's chin took a modest dip in response to Claire's question. "I do." He gestured to the end of the row. As we walked down the aisle, he said, "You might think I was tired of painting after doing the job all day, but it inspires me to push harder on my own vision."

He stopped in front of the last stall and pointed at the canvases propped against its walls. Claire cooed with delight at the several landscape paintings on display.

"Does Jamie show them at her gallery?" I asked. "I'll give her a good scolding if she doesn't."

"She does. She's even sold a few."

"That's no surprise. You are very talented."

Charlie's pale cheeks reddened. "Enough about me. Let me show you the Bradshaw."

He led us to the open area behind the stalls. Three large windows in the back wall and two skylights provided ample natural light, with three overhead fixtures available for enhanced brightness. Three easels held Charlie's works in progress and the finished 1920s depiction of Orchard Street.

"Remarkable," I murmured.

Claire stepped aside so I could get a better view of the painting. Charlie had the blue of the sky right. A perfect azure. The sun glistened off the Griffins' inn just as it did in the original *Orchard Street* and the Model-T was right where Bradshaw had parked it.

"Charlie?" a voice called from the front of the barn.

"Back here." Charlie moved up the aisle to greet the caller. "Hi, Julie."

Claire and I turned to see the newcomer. Claire took in a sharp, nearly inaudible breath and I bit my lower lip to keep from gaping. The woman walking toward us was the person who had followed us up Route Nine the previous evening.

Theo's Lady in Black.

CHAPTER THIRTY-TWO

"Is the painting ready?" Julie shot a curious look at Claire and me.

"Yes. I was just showing it to my friends, Veronica Walsh and Claire Camden. This is Julie Norton."

"Hello," Julie coolly said. Her black eyes studied me.

"I asked Veronica for assistance with the painting. She saw *Orchard Street* when it was discovered at the flea market. Veronica kindly confirmed that I got the details right."

"Thanks." Julie stared at me for a long moment before moving to the easel.

"Charlie did a masterful job," I said. "I bet if it were lined up next to the original it would be difficult to tell the difference between the two."

I observed Julie's reaction as she studied the painting. Her cheeks took on a soft pink hue and she pursed her lips.

"Well done, Charlie. May I take it now?"

"Of course." Charlie removed the painting off the easel. "I'll wrap it up for you."

We followed him back to the front. As Julie preceded us along the aisle, Claire and I communicated our astonishment via raised eyebrows.

"Thanks for showing us your work, Charlie," I said when we reached the open door.

Julie kept an eye on me as she pulled her wallet from her bag.

"My pleasure. And thank you, once more, for your help, Veronica."

"I hope the original is found soon so you can finally get to see it."

"It was nice meeting you," Claire said to Julie.

"Yes. It was," Julie replied.

Claire and I walked to my car in silence. A jolt of adrenaline shot up my arms as we passed the black Corolla.

"This is what I'm thinking," I said once we were in the car, with our seat belts buckled, doors locked, and windows securely shut. Claire started punching her index finger on the screen of her cell phone. "What are you doing?"

"Googling Julie Norton. I want to see what I can find out about her."

"Excellent idea."

"So what are you thinking?" Claire asked as she continued her Internet search.

I started, punctuating my theory with flourishing hand gestures. "I told you the art-laundering idea I came up with last night. Theo hired Julie to kill Scott and steal *Orchard Street*. Julie put the painting in a safe-deposit box that both she and Theo have keys to open. The key is the thing she slid across the table last night. Theo thinks the painting will sit in the safe-deposit box for a year or so—what's a year or two more when it was in Eloise Griffin's letter box for decades—but Julie goes rogue and hires Charlie to make her a replica of *Orchard Street*. She's going to put that in the safe-deposit box, take off with the original, and sell it."

Claire dropped her hands into her lap. "What about George Bradshaw's signature? It obviously isn't on Charlie's painting."

"She knows someone who can forge it. Or maybe she can do it herself."

Claire nodded. "Okay. That works." She resumed her one-finger typing.

"Have you found anything?"

"There are a lot of Julie Nortons out there." Claire lowered the phone. "It could be an alias."

I leaned against the headrest. "It probably is." We were quiet for a minute. "Do you think she recognized us? She gave me a few strange looks."

Claire swallowed hard. "We *were* in disguise last night."

"True. And it was dark. But her staring spooked me."

"You're scaring me. I'm going to have to sleep with my eyes open and a baseball bat at my side."

I started the engine. "We better go before Julie comes out and thinks we're spying on her."

"She might follow us again."

"How about we take a ride to the Bradshaw House? I'd like to drop Julie's name and see Theo's reaction."

"Sure. I'll call the shop and let them know."

Claire and I arrived at the Bradshaw House twenty minutes later. Only two cars were parked in the tiny lot alongside the house.

"Looks like we'll have the place to ourselves," Claire said.

Once through the front door of the farmhouse where George Bradshaw spent his childhood, we stepped into a narrow foyer, stopping to appreciate the setting. The gleaming hardwood floors, soft lighting emitted from the frosted-glass wall sconces, and white walls modernized the late 1800's structure. A woman seated in the small office to the left of the front door rose when she saw us enter.

"Welcome to the Bradshaw House."

"I was at the flea market when George Bradshaw's long-lost painting was found. It sparked my interest in Mr. Bradshaw's other work."

The woman's smile faded. "We've had a number of visitors this week who have said the very same thing. It's very bittersweet. We welcome all, but wish we had his *Orchard Street* to show them."

The woman extended her arm, guiding us to a room down the hall. "We have a number of Mr. Bradshaw's early paintings in here," she said. "As well as the work of a few of his contemporaries."

"Sheila." A voice I recognized as Theo Kendall's beckoned from an office at the end of the hall.

"Excuse me."

As Sheila hastened down the hall, Claire and I stepped into the gallery and soaked in the glories of the products of Bradshaw's talent. After about ten minutes, a soft cough broke the quiet. Theo stood in the doorway.

"Hello, Ms. Walsh," he said very formally.

"Mr. Kendall. This is Claire Camden."

Theo moved to Claire and shook her hand. "What brings you ladies here?"

"A luncheon at Oli Hill inspired me to see more of your grandfather's work," I said.

"One of Mom's luncheons," Theo said with a chuckle. "You're welcome any time."

"You put on special exhibits here, too, I understand," Claire said.

"Yes. We are committed to supporting working artists."

"Have you ever shown Charlie Gannon's work?"

"I don't believe I know him."

"He's a Barton neighbor," I said. "Charlie does portraits and art reproduction. Claire and I were there this morning to see a reproduction of *Orchard Street* Charlie has just completed. A young woman commissioned it as a gift for her father. Her name is Julie Norton."

I fixed my gaze on Theo and I knew Claire was doing the same.

Theo gave us only a very slight quizzical knit of the brow. "The name doesn't ring a bell," he said.

"Oh? I thought perhaps she and her father were patrons of the Bradshaw House. To act so quickly to acquire a copy of *Orchard Street* indicates the Nortons are great fans of your grandfather's work."

"My grandfather continues to have very loyal admirers. My family appreciates their support very much. But I don't recognize the Nortons as being on our membership list. Perhaps I will have the opportunity to meet Mr. Norton and his daughter one day."

"Are you going to the Halloween party at The Barton Hearth tonight?" Claire asked, adroitly changing the subject.

"Uh, no."

"It's a fund-raiser for the Red Cross."

"Yes, I know. But wearing a costume isn't really my thing." Theo blushed.

"No? You get to be someone else for a while. It's fun."

"I'm sure it is."

What I defined as a glimmer of sadness crossed Theo's face and quickly disappeared. My heart ached a bit for the young man as I realized he had never been allowed to be anything other than George Bradshaw's grandson. Leona's iron fist apparently had never permitted silliness or playfulness. The top button must always be fastened.

"I should get back to my work," Theo said. "I hope you ladies enjoy your visit." He nodded, his eyes lingering on Claire for a moment before he returned to his office.

"He's cute," Claire whispered as she nudged me with her elbow. "Did you see that look he gave me?"

"I hope you're not disappointed if it's proven he's involved in theft and murder."

"I can bake him cakes with files," Claire said.

"We learned nothing here. Can we make a fast getaway?"

"We did confirm Julie Norton is probably an alias."

"True. Let's go."

I fished a twenty-dollar bill from my wallet to cover the cost of admission and dropped it on Sheila's desk as we left.

"Please come back soon, ladies."

"We will," Claire said as I pushed her toward the door. "I may even become a member." She threw a longing glance toward the office at the end of the hall.

"If you're going to be a sleuth, you can't flirt with suspects," I said as we walked to the car. "You have to be objective."

"All right." Claire opened the passenger door. "But I reserve the right to objectively flirt."

"Whatever that means," I grumbled. As I climbed into the driver's seat, I caught a glimpse of Theo standing at one of the windows, watching us. My thoughts first went to every scary movie I had ever seen in which a dark and mysterious figure loomed in a window frame. Or did he look more like the kid who wanted to come out and play but his mother wouldn't let him because he might get his clothes dirty or scrape a knee or be stricken with a full-body case of poison-ivy rash?

"Objectivity," I reminded myself as I slid the key into the ignition.

Chapter Thirty-Three

Dusanka had not yet arrived when I got to Tim's office at two p.m. that afternoon. Tim and I sat in his office, chatting over cups of coffee.

I finished telling Tim about the transaction I saw Vin Bradley conduct behind the parsonage. I didn't tell him I had followed Bradley there; I explained that I was checking out the parsonage after Brenda asked me to help finance the renovation. So what if I was at the site twenty-four hours before Brenda made her pitch? Tim didn't need to know the exact timeline.

"You didn't see Bradley take the materials from the job site, put them in his truck, and sell them to the man he met at the parsonage, did you?"

"Not exactly," I said. "But where else would he have gotten that wiring? And he told the guy that next week he'd get in more lighting fixtures than he needed. That sounds like he intentionally ordered more fixtures with the purpose of selling the extras and pocketing the money. And Bradley has already been caught overcharging a client."

Tim leaned back in his chair and rolled his pen between his fingers for a moment. "I'll call a friend I have on the licensing board."

"Thanks, Tim."

"Do you have any other mischief to report? You're really taking advantage of free legal advice."

"Have you heard about the case concerning Judge Sorensen's will?"

"I've heard whispers. How do you know about that?"

"I've heard whispers, too. Ginnie Pinkerly mentioned it to me at a lunch at Leona Kendall's home Wednesday."

"I didn't know you had become a society lady."

"Bite your tongue."

"So that's how you met her housekeeper."

"Yes. About Judge Sorensen's will. I heard Scott Culverson's girlfriend is a witness in the case. She works for the judge's lawyer, Aaron Franklin."

"That's interesting."

"Does this mean Isabel wrote the codicil bequeathing three hundred thousand to the historical society?"

"That, or she witnessed the signing of it."

"So if Isabel witnessed the signing, and the judge wasn't of sound mind, would she get into trouble?"

"Well, she's not a doctor, so she couldn't render a medical diagnosis. She could testify that he appeared confused, but there would be no consequence for her."

"What if she wrote the codicil?"

"That depends. If she drafted it, she might have simply made a mistake. If she knowingly altered the judge's intention, and that was proven, she would definitely be in trouble. But let's not jump to conclusions."

"I'm not. Just curious. She's going through such a difficult time now, I'm sorry she has to deal with testifying, too. That adds to her stress. I suppose you knew Judge Sorensen?"

"I did. He was a gentleman and a brilliant legal scholar. He's sorely missed." Tim checked his watch for the time.

"So do you think you can help Dusanka with her situation? She needs to get out of Leona's house. Pronto."

"I'll know more after I've met with her."

"Hello?" a voice called from Tim's reception area. With Tim's secretary, Helen, gone for the day, Dusanka was left to announce herself.

An unrecognizable person watched as I walked down the hall from Tim's office to reception. Dusanka, wearing a black newsboy cap, wide sunglasses, a stylish black trench coat belted tight at her waist, and gray wool pants, stood beside Helen's desk. As I drew near I noticed she had tucked her long braid under the cap. Though I knew her disguise was prompted by fear of Leona, I couldn't stop the grin that curled on my lips.

She whipped off her sunglasses and beamed. "Hello, Veronica." Heat rose to my cheeks as she wrapped me in a fierce embrace. "I am grateful," she said.

"Dusanka, this is my old friend Tim Petersen. Tim, this is my new friend Dusanka Moravek."

Dusanka stuck her hand out and shook Tim's, her eyes fixed on his face the whole time. Her poise impressed me.

"Thank you for seeing me, Mr. Petersen."

"It's my pleasure, Miss Moravek. Why don't we go back to my office and talk?"

"Why not. But you call me Dusanka."

Tim smiled. "All right, Dusanka." He turned to me. "It would be better if Dusanka and I talk alone, Veronica."

"Okay." I respected lawyer-client privilege. "I'll meet you at Rizzuto's Bakery when you finish. I'll buy you a hot chocolate," I said to Dusanka. "It's down one street, on the corner."

Jack was seated at a window table at Rizzuto's. Dressed in tan pants, a dark jacket, white shirt, and loosened navy tie, he looked like one of his prep school students.

"T.G.I.F.," he said, holding up a cupcake slathered with chocolate frosting. It wouldn't help his cholesterol, but all that sugar would boost his emotional health. "Join me."

"I'll take a seat but will skip the treat."

"Are you still standing by Regina Quinn?" Jack's tone was ominous.

"Yes."

"I heard she was at Scott's house Monday afternoon. Scott actually served her wine and cheese."

"Who told you?"

"I talk with Scott's parents every day. They share the updates the police give them."

"Well, Scott gave Regina the letter Bradshaw wrote her great-grandmother. It was a congenial visit."

"Sure."

We sat in silence for a minute while Jack munched on the cupcake and drank a tall cup of coffee. "How well do you know Isabel?" I finally asked. "You made a remark Saturday night about being a stranger since she and Scott started dating."

"Do you suspect Isabel now? Are you going to use my words to convict her?"

"No. I've heard they had been arguing lately."

Jack put the cupcake on his plate and wiped his fingers and mouth with a paper napkin. "They'd had some arguments about living together. Isabel wanted to move in with Scott, but he wasn't in a rush. He was enjoying dating and didn't want to move into a pseudo-marriage after only a few months."

"But you think Scott and Isabel were a solid couple?"

"Yes. Veronica, place your suspicion elsewhere. If you had seen Isabel's reaction Monday night, you'd know she's innocent."

"Okay. What did you find when you got to Scott's. I mean, besides . . ."

"Everything was pretty much in place. A bottle of wine was spilled across the counter. And the kitchen window had been broken. The cheese board was on the floor."

"I'm so sorry to ask. You've had to recount this already for the police."

"I've reviewed it in my mind dozens of times. The first few seconds, I didn't know what had happened. Scott lay on the floor. There was blood, but I couldn't figure out why."

"Wasn't the knife—"

"There was no knife. The police told Mr. and Mrs. Culverson that the knife was found in the woods behind Scott's house."

No wonder the police weren't moving on the watch; they thought the killer parked on Hill Road and traveled through the woods to and from Scott's house.

"I can't imagine what Isabel is going through," Jack continued. "She found him. When we pulled up I noticed the bedroom and bathroom lights were on, so I was on my way up the stairs to see if Scott was there, maybe in the shower. Isabel's scream was unreal. I ran into the kitchen and hustled her outside. The next hour is one long blur. The street was filled with police cars, an ambulance, a couple of paramedics' SUV's. All the flashing lights made me dizzy. Isabel was hysterical. We had to practically carry her halfway up the street to Hillary's car. Thank God for Hillary. They sat in Hillary's car for a good half-hour before Isabel calmed down and was able to talk with the police."

Did they also have a lawyer-client conversation? I wondered.

Jack picked up his cupcake. "You're ruining T.G.I.F."

I laughed. "Sorry. Could you give me Isabel's address? I'd like to send her flowers."

Jack gave me the address and then we talked about the classes he was teaching that semester until he finished his coffee. After Jack left, I said to Anita Rizzuto, "If a Czech in a trench coat comes in looking for me, tell her I'll be right back."

I rounded the corner of Orchard and Maple and trotted into Yau's. The Chinese restaurant's owner, Henry Yau, stood at the register. Just the man I needed. Henry or his wife had taken every takeout order since the restaurant's opening in 1987.

"Here for a late lunch, Veronica? Or an early dinner? You didn't place an order?" He rustled through the stack of menus on the counter.

"I'm here to talk, Henry. Though the aroma coming from your kitchen is whetting my appetite."

"Okay, let's talk."

"Did Isabel Fischer place an order Monday evening? The delivery address would have been Seven B in Treetop Condominiums."

"No delivery was sent to that address Monday night."

"What about Hillary Simmons?"

Henry's face brightened. "Yes, Hillary called in an order and picked it up."

"Do you remember at what time?"

"Six thirty. The news was just starting." Henry pointed to the small television on the shelf behind the register.

So that gave Isabel more than an hour of alone time. "Great. Thanks, Henry."

"Would you like something to go?"

As a thanks offering, I paid for an egg roll and asked for two fortune cookies.

Dusanka was waiting for me in front of Rizzuto's.

"Have a fortune cookie." I handed her a cellophane-wrapped cookie.

"I thought we were getting hot chocolate?"

"And we shall. How did everything go with Tim?"

"I don't need a fortune to know my future is bright, thanks to you and Mr. Petersen."

Dusanka put her arms around me and gave me a hug. As I struggled for breath, I spotted in the bakery's window the reflection of a patrol car cruising up Orchard Street.

CHAPTER THIRTY-FOUR

A delightful wave of nostalgia hit me when Mark and I walked into The Hearth's main dining room, triggering a rush of flashbacks to the soap's many Halloween galas. Every year the show would stage an elaborate ball. The actors wore fabulous costumes and the set decoration, so detailed and expertly designed, made us feel as if we were at a party rather than working our tails off late into the night. The Halloween Ball, which would take place over several episodes, would invariably provide a stunning plot twist: a murder committed or a killer revealed; an affair discovered or ended (sometimes the end of the affair would prompt the murder); a presumed dead character returned, his or her face hidden by a mask until the last second of the Friday episode. I loved participating in those shows and was thrilled this charity event, though decidedly less dramatic than the *Days and Nights* balls, filled the void.

Though The Hearth didn't spend as much on decorations as did the soap's producers, they did a great job transforming the dining room into a festive party locale. Fake spider webs dangled from the ceiling corners. Glowing jack o' lanterns jazzed up the buffet table. A scarecrow, propped on a stack of hay bales, observed the party from a corner.

I watched Mark as he headed to the bar in the adjoining room. He was very handsome in his suit and bow tie. His resemblance to F. Scott Fitzgerald was tenuous; I hoped he wouldn't have to spend the evening explaining his choice of costume.

"Veronica!"

Dotsie called me from a table in the far corner. I took in the group seated there as I made my way around the clusters of revelers gathered by tables, joking and comparing their costumes.

As a film buff, I did not need to see a nametag to identify Dotsie's persona for the evening. She was outfitted in a black top hat and tails over a white shirt and bow tie, with a large white pom-pom pinned to her label. Dotsie held an unlit cigarette in a silver holder. On the table sat a martini glass brimming with ginger ale and probably a shot of rye whiskey.

"Good evening, Ms. Dietrich."

"Call me Marlene." Dotsie stuck the cigarette holder in her mouth and toasted me with the "martini."

Madeline, in a Mary Poppins outfit, sat on Dotsie's right. The pink flower dangling from her black hat bobbed as she waved hello. To Dotsie's left sat a generic witch, otherwise known as Ella. Next to Madeline was Myrtle. All I saw of her costume was a black shawl and blouse. She had two props in front of her—a skein of gray yarn and a pair of knitting needles. Her husband, Merv, was in a more cheerful, and identifiable, costume. The genial Merv wore a white cowboy hat, jeans, and a red and blue plaid shirt.

Completing the group were Amelia, Don, and Joyce. Amelia wore a lovely royal blue, wool pantsuit. Don and Joyce dressed down in jeans and Arden sweatshirts.

"You are more beautiful than usual, Veronica," Merv said.

I gave him a peck on the cheek and twitched his hat. "Thank you, Merv. I always knew you were one of the good guys."

Myrtle rubbed the material of my pale-gold flapper dress between her fingers. "Is this a vintage dress?"

"Sadly, no. The soap's costume department made it for one of the show's Halloween Balls."

"It's very flattering," Joyce said. She sighed and added, "If only I had known we would be here, I would have come up with something better than an Arden supporter."

"My date is a professor at Arden. I'm a big fan of the college."

I spotted Claire slipping through the crowd. Her costume matched Marilyn Monroe's iconic white halter dress. We traded waves and smiles.

I turned to Myrtle. "I need some help on your costume, Myrtle." I pointed at the yarn and knitting needles.

"Madame DeFarge," Myrtle replied with asperity. She was obviously already tired of explaining her attire.

"Of course," I said. "I haven't read Dickens in a while. I hope you're not knitting my name into a shroud."

"Of course not."

"Do you have anything to report on the watch?" Joyce asked, her eyes betraying her desperation for good news.

"No, I'm sorry, Joyce," I said. "Soon, I'm sure."

Mark returned to the dining room. I caught his eye; he lifted our drinks and gestured to a table on the other side of the room where Carol and Patrick sat.

"Have a fun evening, everyone."

"A difficult task," Amelia said with a snort, "while my granddaughter is suspected of murder."

"We agreed to put that out of our minds for the night," Don said. "We're here to support Regina."

"Which reminds me. I must thank her boss for standing by Regina," Amelia said. "Most employers would suspend a staff member in Regina's circumstance, if not terminate employment."

"I'm sure Dan will appreciate hearing that," I said before

turning on my heels to make a dash to a more cheerful group.

Sandy darted in front of me. "Are you some version of a French maid?"

Carrying a pink feather duster, she wore a black dress with three-quarter sleeves and a white bib apron over the dress. On her head was a large, black hat with yellow daisy petals decorating the wide, upturned brim.

"I'm Amelia Bedelia!"

"Opposites attract," I dryly said.

"I thought I'd try viewing housekeeping through her eyes. Just for one night. You look great."

"Thanks."

Brenda latched her arm through mine as I made my way across the room. I couldn't quite put my finger on what historical person she portrayed. She wore a floor-length, white, off-the-shoulder dress. Lace encircled the top and the skirt had a rose print with a polka dot background. Brenda's wig was a black bun on which she had pinned a band of fresh, white roses. She really went all out on the costume.

Her glance moved from my shoulders to my feet as she studied my costume. "Look at you."

"And you."

"I'm Mary Todd Lincoln."

I guessed a pre-assassination Mary, based on the white dress and cheerful flowers. Though didn't Mary go a bit bonkers after her husband's death?

I mustered suitable enthusiasm. "That's very original."

"The old gal has gotten a bum rap. I wanted to show her off a bit."

"Good. The poor woman's suffered enough."

"If only I had your legs, I wouldn't be hiding them under this big skirt!"

"Don't be so modest."

Brenda touched her white-gloved fingers against my arm. "I really enjoyed our lunch."

"So did I."

"Wonderful. That's all the business I'll talk tonight. It's a party!"

"Happy Halloween," I said.

"Trick or treat." Brenda turned away, laughing.

I put my head down and made a beeline for the table.

"Did Brenda Donovan make another fund-raising pitch?" Patrick asked as I flopped onto the empty chair between Carol and Mark.

"No. You're not your usual self." I assessed Patrick's lime-colored golf shirt and baseball cap that had the trademark Swoosh logo. "What happened to the Yankee uniform? You're suddenly a golfer?"

"You two inspired me to change," Patrick said.

"Some change," Carol said, shaking her head.

I patted Carol's arm. "Baby steps, pal." I glanced over her sage jacket, curly, blonde wig, and zirconia-studded eyeglasses. "Hello, Rita. You're quite fetching tonight."

"Thanks," Carol said. A green peacock feather that served as a quill rested on the table. She picked it up and waved the feather with a flourish. "Do you have any good gossip for me?"

"Brenda Donovan is doing image rehab on Mary Todd Lincoln."

Mark chuckled and took a sip from his glass. "Good luck with that."

My mother soared in, dressed as a nun in a white habit that stopped above her ankles and a cornette people of my generation identified with Sally Field when she starred in the television show *The Flying Nun*. Mom carried a glass filled with wine.

"Mrs. Walsh," Carol said with wonder at the sight of Mom as a member of the clergy.

"Tonight, I'm Sister Nancy, Ms. Skeeter." Mom pulled out the chair next to Mark's and sat.

"Is that altar wine?" I asked.

"What an impertinent question, Veronica Anne."

"Sorry, Mother. I mean Sister."

"Regina Quinn just gave me a big hug and told me I have an amazing daughter."

"And you disagree?"

"She said you're helping her clear the Griffin family name. Your nose is in the murder investigation, isn't it?"

"Ella and Madeline asked me for help."

"I wish I had a ruler. I'd rap your knuckles."

I folded my hands in my lap and looked appropriately chagrined.

"So what's the latest on the case?" Carol asked. "You didn't pay your daily visit to me to stop and smell the roses."

"Remember when Hillary Simmons came into your shop on Tuesday to order flowers for Isabel? She said she was with Isabel at Isabel's condo before the gallery party."

"Yeah."

"Well, Hillary didn't get to Isabel's condo until after she picked up their dinner at Yau's at six-thirty. So Isabel was alone between the time she left the law office and the time Hillary arrived at the condo."

"Why would Isabel kill her boyfriend?" Mom asked.

"Scott's friend Jack told me Isabel wanted to move in with Scott, but he didn't want to live together. They could have had another argument that got out of control. She might have gotten upset because Scott gave Regina the letter Bradshaw wrote Eloise Griffin. Regina said she thought she might be able to convince Scott to give the Griffins the painting, too. Maybe Scott decided to do that, and Isabel freaked. And, get this, Isabel's testifying in the contestation case of Judge Sorensen's will."

"How did you learn all that?" Mom asked.

I gave Mom a full summary of the week's events, *sans* my post–Mountain Bear drive through the village of Lake George.

"With what Jack said about the knife being found in the woods," I concluded, "I wonder about the watch. Maybe it has nothing to do with the case, like you said last night, Mark."

"The killer could have tossed it in the woods, as an attempt to trick the police in the same way he, or she, might have broken the kitchen window to make it look like a random break-in."

The president of the local Red Cross stepped in front of the arrangement of hay bales, calling for everyone's attention. While he welcomed the crowd and described the items up for raffle, Mom put an end to our grim discussion.

"Let's have fun tonight and forget all our worries, and everyone else's, too."

And we did. We ate, laughed over the costumed revelers traipsing by our table, and debated whether F. Scott Fitzgerald would be a Harry Potter fan.

If only I had let Mark go to the bar to refresh my drink, the evening would have been perfect.

Chapter Thirty-Five

Instead, I took myself to the bar for a ginger ale. I met Hillary en route. She was dressed in a black pantsuit and a light pink, silk blouse. The jacket's lapel partially covered a white nametag.

She laughed at my quizzical glance over her attire and pointed at the tag. It read *Secretary of State Clinton.*

"Clever," I said, grinning.

"And easy. I didn't feel up to coming, but Aaron wants his people to make an appearance at these charity things."

We proceeded to the bar, where Debbie sat on a corner stool, gaining a wide clearance for her wild mess of hair. She apparently had used mega-volume shampoo and then a hair dryer and snow-removing car brush to give her mane a wingspan of two or three feet. Debbie swiveled on the stool when she heard me place my drink order. I had a good view of the tight, black, leather pants Debbie wore to accompany her very snug white tee shirt. Vin sat beside her; his hair was also a mess and he wore an everyday flannel work shirt over a white tee shirt.

"Hi, Debbie. Hi, Vin."

"Hey," Vin grunted as he tipped his bottle of beer toward his mouth.

"Hey, Veronica," Debbie said as she finished off a bottle of beer. "You look pretty."

"Thanks." I struggled for a return compliment. "Is that your real hair?"

"Yep," she said, fluffing the end of her mane with her

fingertips. "I went overboard on the hair products, but why not?"

"Why not? Halloween comes just once a year," I said. Hillary let out a quiet snort behind me.

"I'm not interested in Anna's house anymore," Debbie said. "I talked with Vin about it and he doesn't want to live so close to Orchard Street."

"Oh, well," I said, conveying disappointment while my soul breathed a sigh of relief.

"Have you found the owner of the Fenton watch?"

"Not yet. I'm going to wait the weekend and if the owner doesn't turn up, give it to the police on Monday."

"You do that. It's funny how you just found it *in town*," Debbie said.

"Not really," I said.

"You're being very mysterious about it. Why not be specific about where you found it? You're not snooping around Culverson's murder, are you, Veronica?"

"Why would I do that, Debbie?"

Debbie shrugged. "You just better not be trying to point a finger at me."

"And why would I ever suspect you, Debbie?"

Regina, carrying a large serving dish loaded with chicken wings, pushed through the kitchen door. She re-directed her path to the dining room when she spotted me.

"Can you meet me outside in about five minutes?" she asked in a hushed voice.

"Sure."

"I remembered something about Monday night," she said. "Meet me by the back door to the kitchen."

Debbie and Vin followed Regina with their eyes until Regina turned the corner into the dining room. "She's in a heap of trouble."

I detected a hint of glee in her voice. "Regina will be proven innocent very soon," I said.

"Sure she will," Debbie said, making no attempt to stifle an evil grin.

I took two gulps of my soda and set the half-full glass on the bar. "Thank you," I said to the bartender. I walked through the bar and into the hall. After the high school girl working the coat check handed me my coat, I stepped out the front door and onto Orchard Street. My breath quickly formed a white cloud visible in the street lamp's circle of light. I slipped my arms into my coat and pulled it around me.

After a minute or two of watching a few cars pass, I headed around to the back of the restaurant to meet Regina. The silence of the parking lot and the eeriness of the moon glow through the branches of trees behind the restaurant spooked me a bit.

A bang and the crunch of something sliding across gravel came from the area of the Dumpster standing along the lot's left border. My heart thudded against my ribs as I contemplated how fast I could run in my heels. A woman's giddy laughter eased my fear.

"Who knew you were so naughty?! You are such a stallion, Mr. President."

I immediately identified the speaker. Brenda Donovan.

"Take that beard off!" she said.

A man's muffled laugh reached my ears and then a long moment of quiet ensued. I colored it in with my soap-opera thinking: A passionate kiss with some adult touching was taking place behind the Dumpster.

As I considered what would happen if Brenda and her paramour stepped around the Dumpster and saw me, the kitchen door swung open. Regina, wearing no coat over her chef's smock, stepped outside.

"Hey, Veronica." The door behind me shut with a bang and

Regina stepped to my side.

I jerked my head and spoke in a hushed voice. "Let's walk around to the front."

Regina gave me a querulous look. "All right."

When we turned the corner and I was sure we were out of earshot of the Dumpster, I said, "A couple was having a romantic liaison behind the Dumpster."

"Ha!"

We arrived at Orchard and Sycamore. "So what do you want to tell me?"

"It may mean nothing. But when I left Scott's, I noticed a dark car parked on the cul-de-sac next to his house."

"That's where I found that watch."

"Oh," Regina said, as if the wind had just been sucked from her lungs.

We stared at each other for a few beats as the two puzzle pieces locked together in our minds.

"Did you recognize the car model? Or see its license plate?" I thought of Debbie Bradley's blue car and Julie Norton's black Corolla.

Regina shook her head. "Nope. I thought nothing of it at the time."

"You need to tell this to the police."

"They'll think I'm just making it up." Regina rubbed her hands over her arms to warm them.

"Tell them anyway."

"I will."

We didn't say anything for a minute. Regina stared across Orchard to the future home of the bridal shop. Her forlorn expression saddened me.

"I really love it here in Barton. I don't want to leave."

"Stop thinking you're off to prison."

"I'm not thinking of prison. What if I'm no longer welcome here?"

"No one is going to run you out of town. Everyone I know believes you are innocent."

"The Kendalls—"

"The Kendalls don't live in Barton." I watched as a car pulled up in front of the bridal shop.

Regina grinned and we were quiet for a moment. Then she said, "This needs to be resolved soon. I'm losing my mind living under the same roof with my grandmother and Aunt Ella."

"You have my deepest sympathies."

Isabel got out of the car and crossed Orchard. She was dressed in jeans and a bulky, turtleneck sweater. I thought of the previous Saturday, when I met her and thought she looked like a carefree young woman. What a difference a few days made.

"Oh, no," Regina said under her breath as Isabel reached our corner.

"Hi, Isabel." I tried to defuse the scene before it escalated to anger and shouting.

"I'm so sorry—"

Isabel interrupted Regina. "Don't even say it. You murdered Scott."

"No, I did not. I swear to you I did not kill Scott."

"Why should I believe you? You were *there*!"

"Someone else was there after me."

"Who? Everyone else has an alibi!"

"I . . ." Regina started. She stood with her mouth open, her pleading expression focused on Isabel.

"You're already a proven liar. Telling the police you were taking a nap. What a laugh. Until evidence proved otherwise."

Regina stiffened and challenged Isabel. "And what's your alibi? Where were you?"

"Your insinuation is offensive," Isabel said.

"The accusation that I murdered someone is even more offensive."

"Go inside." I gave Regina a firm push with both hands.

"Yes! Why don't you," Isabel said, "while you still have a job."

Regina took a step toward Isabel. I grabbed the tail of her smock with one hand and her elbow with my other hand. "Go inside."

"All right." Regina gave Isabel one last narrow-eyed glance and went into the restaurant.

"I can't believe she's allowed to roam free. I hate the law. All these guilty people walking around free."

I knew defending Regina would only further inflame Isabel's anger. I aimed to calm her by asking, "How are you?"

"Fine. I'm tired of everyone asking me that." After a moment of uncomfortable silence, she said, "I'm sorry. I shouldn't snap at you. You've been very kind, Veronica. I'm angry and exhausted from not sleeping and drowning myself in work to forget everything."

"You need to give yourself a break, Isabel. Physically and mentally. Maybe you should take a leave of absence at work. Go back to your parents' house for a while."

"I'm on my way there now, but not for a break. I have Scott's wake and funeral this weekend." Isabel gave me a half-smile, as if I had made an absurd suggestion. The smile faded. "I feel so guilty. I had pestered Scott to spend more time with me and less time on his work. And what was I doing Monday night before the party? Work." She glanced at the restaurant's front window. "Scott and I were supposed to come to this party." Isabel hugged herself and pursed her lips. "I've got to go. Bye, Veronica."

"Take care, Isabel."

I watched her cross the street and get into her car. Was that all a genuine display of emotion, or a brilliant courtroom summation designed to manipulate the jury?

Regina was waiting for me in The Hearth's entry hall. "Did you notice the color of her car? Dark green. What do you think of that?"

I patted Regina's arm. "Let's forget this for tonight, what do you say?"

Regina hesitated before nodding. "Okay."

She returned to the kitchen while I checked my coat and headed for the ladies' room. I met Lois Franklin, Aaron's wife, as she was exiting the bathroom. She wore a shimmering gold gown with a plunging neckline. She accented her costume with large teardrop earrings of glittering gold.

"Hello, Veronica." Lois pointed at my dress. "We're both in gold tonight."

"You're much more glamorous."

"I'm Meryl Streep, the night she won the Oscar for *The Iron Lady*," Lois explained.

"Very original."

"Thank you. You look terrific."

That was the end of our conversation. I freshened up in the bathroom and started back for the dining room by way of the bar. I met Brenda there, her face radiating a healthy flush. She held a fresh glass of bourbon.

"Having a good time?" I asked.

"Marvelous."

Only I knew how "marvelous" her evening was. What Brenda did behind the Dumpster was her business, but, damn, I wanted to know the identity of her "stallion."

I followed Brenda to the dining room, stopping at the threshold as she blended into the crowd.

As I was about to head to my table, a voice behind me said, "Good evening, Veronica."

I turned and found Aaron behind me. He wore a black frock

coat and pants over a white shirt. He held a black hat. Was he the Monopoly man?

He offered his hand. "You're looking quite lovely."

His cold palm startled me. "Thank you. May I ask, who are you supposed to be?"

He laughed. When he lifted the hat to his head, I realized it was a stovepipe hat. Aaron reached into his pocket to pull out a false beard. "I started the evening as Abraham Lincoln. My beard stopped cooperating."

So Brenda's Mary Todd was not yet a widow.

"Oh dear. Use stronger glue next time."

My eyes swept across the party, stopping for a moment on Brenda, who was chatting with Sabrina and Hillary, before moving to my table, where I met Carol's gaze fixed on me.

"I think next Halloween I'll just wear a Knicks tee shirt and sweatpants and be done with it."

"Your glamorous wife might not like that."

"Lois and I tend to go our separate ways on Halloween." He tipped his hat and returned to the party.

"I'll say you go your separate ways, Mr. President," I muttered.

I headed straight for my table and took my seat next to Carol.

"Everything all right?" Carol asked.

"Sure." I picked up her quill and tickled her cheek with its tip. "This party turned out to be soapier than any Halloween Ball *Days and Nights* ever produced."

CHAPTER THIRTY-SIX

I quietly shared the events of the last fifteen minutes.

"They were behind the Dumpster?" Carol asked, dumbfounded and peeved. "His wife is here!"

"I guess they didn't think she'd have any garbage to throw out," Patrick said.

"She should throw her husband out!" Mom said.

"Frances Wells has a very good reason to contest her father's will," I said. "I wonder if her lawyer knows about the affair."

"But you're not absolutely certain that was Aaron with Brenda," Mark said.

"They came dressed as the Lincolns! She called him *Mr. President!*"

"Circumstantial evidence, like what the police have on Regina."

"At least Frances's lawyer can put Brenda on the stand and ask if she has a relationship with Aaron. I wonder if Ginnie would have Frances's phone number."

"Perhaps you shouldn't get into the middle of it," Mom said.

Carol agreed. "You're already caught up in the murder investigation. Leave well enough alone."

The president of the local Red Cross called for the crowd's attention. He would be drawing the winning raffle tickets in a moment.

"I hope we win the weekend in Lake Placid," Patrick said.

"Excuse me, Mark." Mom leaned toward me, her cornette

forcing Mark to push his chair back to avoid a poke in the eye. "Veronica. What if Scott caught Aaron and Brenda having a liaison at the parsonage Monday afternoon? Scott would question the validity of the codicil and discuss it with Isabel. What if she knows about the fraud, maybe even helped perpetrate it, and killed Scott to keep him from exposing the truth?"

Mom's hypothesis made sense. Isabel's remark about too many guilty people roaming free repeated in my mind. Did she include herself in that group?

"By George Bradshaw, I think Sister Nancy might have it!"

CHAPTER THIRTY-SEVEN

"You won't give Brenda any strange looks during the tour to make her suspicious?" Mark asked me the next morning over breakfast at Herman's.

"I'm an actress," I said with indignation.

"But you couldn't keep a straight face about it last night."

"I'm in full control of my expressions now." I suppressed a yawn. I had tossed and turned in my bed for a long while before falling asleep. Thoughts of Isabel, Brenda, Aaron, and Judge Sorensen's will kept me awake.

"Why don't you take the day off from all these worries, enjoy the parsonage tour, and meet me for dinner later."

"Sounds like a perfect day."

After breakfast Mark left to pick up Patrick and head over to Arden for a twelve-thirty football game. I popped into the bookstore, visited with Mom for a few minutes, and then went into All Things to check in with the weekend staff and do a bit of work. When I left a half hour later, I met Tracey Brody. She was carrying a coffee cup from Rizzuto's and heading to her patrol car on the corner.

"Are you ever off-duty, Tracey?"

"Once in a while."

"Any news on the watch?"

"We didn't come up with a match on the prints. And the chief doesn't think it has anything to do with the case. It wasn't found on Scott's property."

I stopped myself from blurting out what Jack had told me about where the knife was found and the danger of making assumptions. "What? It was pretty darn close to his driveway."

"Chief thinks it belongs to someone from the media. A number of reporters covered the story and parked on the cul-de-sac. And then there are the folks minding their own business, walking their dogs or doing their cardiovascular workout."

"While wearing a diamond-encrusted watch?"

"I don't have the time now to track down the owner, Veronica. I'll get to it once the Culverson case is solved."

"I showed Dolores Bern photos of the watch. She's helping me find the owner. I'll let you know what she tells me."

"Don't act on the information."

"Of course not," I said, irritated. "But perhaps I should be reimbursed for the freelance work I'm doing for the Barton P.D."

"Sure. Just submit your invoice straight to Chief Price."

"Maybe I'll just consider it volunteer work. Regina told me last night that when she left Scott's house, she saw a dark car parked on the cul-de-sac."

"She didn't tell us that."

"She only remembered it yesterday."

"That doesn't give us much to go on. I assume she didn't get a license-plate number?"

"No. But put that information together with the watch, and the person in that car might be the killer."

"Perhaps. I saw you in front of Rizzuto's yesterday afternoon. Leona Kendall's housekeeper was hugging the stuffing out of you."

Oops. "She was happy to see me."

"So you know Dusanka Moravek?"

"Yes." I would remain noncommittal as long as I could.

"How did you meet Leona Kendall's housekeeper, Veronica?"

"At Leona's house. I was there for lunch on Wednesday."

"And now the two of you are friends?"

"Yes."

"I know you're an inclusive sort of person, Veronica, but this seems a bit odd. And sudden."

I pulled out my fame card. "Dusanka mentioned at the lunch how she was influenced by my soap opera. She told me my character helped her learn English. Isn't that cool?"

"It is. What a bonding experience." I detected a trace of facetiousness in Tracey's response. "So you're best buddies now?"

"Dusanka isn't very happy in her present place of employment. I'm helping her get another situation."

"That's kind of you."

"I like her."

"You're not pumping Miss Moravek for information on the Kendalls, are you, Veronica?"

"Of course not. That's your job." I made a quick move to change the conversation. "Do you happen to know a woman named Julie Norton?"

Tracey's eyes narrowed. "Why, *Veronica*?"

"Nothing. Just wondering."

A commotion a few shops down Orchard ended our conversation. Two women had burst from Andrea's hair salon and stood on the sidewalk, screaming bloody murder at each other. A squint of my eyes focused my vision. The women were Andrea and Debbie.

Tracey tossed her cup in a nearby trashcan and hustled across Sycamore. After waiting for two passing cars, I followed.

"What a slithering, low-life, greedy, ungrateful creep you are!" Andrea swung her arm in a wide swipe at Debbie, missing Debbie's scowling jaw by inches.

"I owe you nothing!" Debbie hurled a few words unfit for

print at Andrea.

Tracey forced her body between the feuding hairstylists, placing a hand against each of their chests. "Ladies! Back it up!"

I joined the group of slack-jawed bystanders gawking at the pair. Several more onlookers stood inside the salon, watching through the window. One woman had foil wrapped around strands of her hair. Another was blotting her wet scalp with a towel. Several clutched at the plastic capes draped over their shoulders.

"I want this woman arrested!" Wide circles of purple blotch colored Andrea's cheeks. Three women stood behind her, their hands on their hips and their chins nodding support for Andrea.

"Don't have a stroke." The bracelets on Debbie's arm clattered as she shook her fist at Andrea.

"What's going on, ladies?" Tracey maintained her strong-armed stance.

"This cobra stole customers from my shop!" Andrea's declaration sent gasps through the crowd.

"I didn't steal customers. I gave people unhappy with your service a choice." Debbie reached into the sleeve of her leather jacket and pulled up her bra strap. That she wore a bra surprised me.

"You're fired."

"I quit!"

"Good luck starting your own business. I hope a pipe bursts in your basement . . . I mean *salon.*" Andrea's eyes popped as she spewed her sarcasm.

Debbie literally spat at Andrea's feet and stomped down the street. No one uttered a syllable until she had disappeared around the corner.

The crowd dispersed, returning to their Saturday-morning errands. Andrea hugged herself, her breathing quick and her mouth still fixed in a pout.

"Are you all right?" Tracey asked.

"I'd like to beat the crap out of that—"

Tracey raised her palm. "Don't say it."

Andrea nodded.

Tracey switched from police officer to regular gal mode. "You're better off without Debbie. I think her customers will tire of having their hair done in a basement and will come back to your hip salon soon enough."

The words had a soothing, confidence-raising effect on Andrea. "Thanks, Tracey."

The hair-stylist whisperer smiled and headed for her patrol car.

"If soap operas weren't dying, you'd be a daytime star. What started that?" I asked Andrea.

"One of my girls, Elisa, met a customer at the deli this morning and noticed her hair looked like it had just been done. And Elisa hadn't seen the lady in a month. So Elisa acted all innocent and asked her when she would be in for an appointment. She shamed the woman into admitting she had gone to Debbie."

"Wow."

"Elisa stormed into the salon ten minutes ago and confronted Debbie about it. Scared the bejeebs out of Debbie's customer."

"I'm sure, with all those razors, scissors, and bleach you have just lying around."

Andrea gave me a doleful look. "Debbie has an alibi for Monday afternoon. You don't know how sorry I am she's not guilty of murder. I'd love to see her ass in prison."

"Andrea . . ."

"All right. I don't mean it. Debbie admitted to lying about changing Vera Beecham's mother's appointment so she could accommodate an emergency request for coloring. She did the job at her house."

"Thanks for telling me."

"I'm going to get those customers back. Every single one of them."

"I believe you will. Just do it in a legal, nonviolent manner."

"I will. I don't want to be a suspect in one of your future investigations."

"So there goes Debbie off the list," I muttered as I walked to the corner.

Rather than turning on Sycamore to go home, I hurried across Orchard and dashed up the block, heading for Bern Jewelers. Stanley Bern manned the gem case.

"Is Dolores here?"

"She won't be in until one, Veronica. What can I do for you?"

Stanley disappointed me with a shake of his head when I explained about the watch. "I don't know anything about it. I'll have Dolores call you."

Stanley was right: Dolores did call me. At the wrong place and the wrong time.

CHAPTER THIRTY-EIGHT

I paid a visit to Carol in her shop and then grabbed lunch at home before heading to the parsonage for my tour. My phone rang just as I turned onto the property. Though it was ten minutes to two, I was surprised to be the first person to arrive. I parked on the grass and pulled my phone from my bag.

"Veronica. It's Dolores Bern."

A charge of adrenaline went up my arms. "Hi, Dolores."

"I've got some information for you about that watch," Dolores said.

"Great. Did you find the owner?" I pulled the key from the ignition.

"Yep."

My hand dropped into my lap when Dolores gave me the name. "Huh."

"It was purchased in a boutique in Albany."

"Interesting."

We were silent for a minute. "You'll pass the information on to the police?" Dolores finally asked. "I'll assist them in any way I can."

"I'll tell them. Thank you for your help, Dolores."

I dug into my purse for my phone to call Tracey. "Myrtle was ri—" A tap on the driver's window startled me.

"Brenda!"

"I didn't mean to scare you." Brenda opened the car door.

"That's all right. Where is everyone?" I slid from the seat.

"You're the first to arrive." Before I could make an excuse for needing to make a phone call, Brenda linked her arm through mine and started for the parsonage. "There are exposed roots along here," she said as we headed for the side of the building. "I don't want you to trip, Veronica."

"Thank you. Did you enjoy the party?" I tried to keep an image of Brenda, her hoop skirt, and Aaron from my mind.

"Oh, yes. Very much."

We walked around the back of the parsonage to the barn. I decided my call to Tracey wasn't urgent; I figured the matter could wait another thirty minutes until I had heard Brenda's sales pitch.

I reconsidered my assumption when I spotted Vin Bradley's pickup parked in front of the barn, beside a black Sonata. "I thought you said we were the first ones here?"

"Not quite," a female voice said. I looked toward the barn's open door as Hillary and Vin emerged. Hillary wore jeans and a zipped fleece jacket. Vin had a black leather jacket on over a flannel shirt and ripped jeans.

"Hi, Veronica." Hillary's hands were shoved into her jacket's pockets.

"Hello." I pulled away from Brenda, who still had her arm entwined with mine. I suddenly regretted not insisting on making my call to Tracey.

"It will just be us four for the tour," Brenda said.

"Why is that?" I asked.

"I canceled the tour. I decided in light of Scott's death, a gathering seemed a bit insensitive. But I thought it would be nice to give you a private showing. Isn't it wonderful Hillary and Vin could join us?"

"Sure. But I was looking forward to hearing about Sabrina's design, or I should say Scott's, for the renovation. Maybe we should wait until Sabrina and the other donors can join us. I don't mind."

Brenda's chilly smile faded. "But we're here now. The most important people. You don't want to inconvenience us, do you, Veronica?"

"Well—" I turned and made a move to pass her.

It took Vin two long strides to reach and grab my arm, knocking my purse from my hand. He said, "You're not going anywhere."

Hillary pulled a handgun from her jacket pocket and pointed it at me.

As I was thinking, before Brenda interrupted me: Myrtle was right. Lawyers lie.

"All right, I'll take the tour." I forced my tone to be light and carefree. "You don't need to force me at gunpoint."

"Very funny, Veronica," Hillary said.

Since the act was up, I asked, "Is that gun a new purchase, or did you not have it on you Monday afternoon?"

"You're so witty, Veronica," Hillary said.

"Here's some more wit. If you'd like your watch back, you can claim it at the police station. I'm sure they'll want to question you about it any time now."

"Well, it will be simply explained. As Scott's friend, I've been to his house numerous times. They'll accept my response as I am a longtime, respected member of the community. I'm not some newcomer like the Quinn girl. And how convenient that she was at Scott's house when I arrived. She looks guilty as sin."

"But at The Hearth, you said you only saw Isabel at work since she started dating Scott. You were never at his house."

"An offhand comment only you would remember."

I wasn't going to mention Mark and his impeccable memory.

I tried to wriggle from Vin's grasp; he tightened his hold on my arm. I kicked him in the shins. He responded with a stinging slap to my cheek.

"So how does this all work out? How did the three of you entangle yourselves and what did Scott know that forced you to murder him, Hillary? Let me guess; it has to do with this money pit." I pointed my thumb at the building. "And Judge Sorensen's will."

Brenda exploded in anger. "This parsonage is *my* legacy! Not Damon Sorensen's. Not *Frances Wells's*. Mine! I have been working for years to secure this building for the historical society. I finally convinced the judge to help me. And then his daughter took all the credit and now wants to control every piece of the project."

"Did the judge honestly give the historical society the three hundred grand, or did Aaron forge the codicil for you?" My question left Brenda speechless. "If you want to keep your affairs secret, don't conduct them behind Dumpsters. Though I find it difficult to believe Aaron would put his career on the line by defrauding a client, particularly a prestigious client like Judge Sorensen. You did it, didn't you, Hillary?"

"I worked on the deal for the judge to donate the parsonage to the historical society. The judge wanted to leave the money to the historical society, in a trust with Frances as its sole trustee. Frances was an absolute bitch while we were working on the deal. She drove Brenda and me crazy. So we reminded the judge, several times, of how patient we were with his daughter's micromanaging and thunder-stealing. We coaxed him into giving the money outright to the society. He had dementia. It was easy."

"Of course it was easy. But that coaxing was actually coercion. It's called undue influence and it's illegal. Was the plan for Brenda to *mishandle* the money? Were you two going to take a nice cut from the thousands?"

"Yes," Vin said.

"No!" Brenda's face took on a brilliant shade of scarlet. "We weren't going to take a dime. It was simply so I could manage this project without Frances breathing down my neck. But this guy had to get involved." She pointed at Vin with a stabbing motion.

"How?"

"He found out about Aaron and me and decided he'd blackmail his way to the winning bid," Brenda gave Vin a bitter glance.

"And you were going to take a cut," Vin said. "You were happy to give me information on the job, overestimate the cost, and then skim some off for yourselves."

"Scott saw you here Monday afternoon, didn't he? Two of you? Three of you? Who?"

"The three of us," Hillary answered.

I shook my head in disgust. "You knew Scott would tell Isabel, and the dominoes would fall. And so you murdered Scott and took the painting to make it look like a burglary gone wrong. Now there's some *legacy*."

"I had to do it," Hillary said. "Yes, Scott would tell Isabel, who would go straight to Aaron. She clings to her law school idealism of truth, justice, and the American way. And Ms. Donovan here would tell her paramour she was being blackmailed and insist the bequest was my idea, and Mr. Bradley would divulge everything to save his own neck. I'm close to making partner at the firm."

"Yet you had no problem using Isabel as an alibi."

"Isabel asked me to cover for her. She had a videoconference with Sotheby's that afternoon. She didn't want people thinking she's a gold digger. Which she—"

"Shut up," I said.

"Yes, let's," Brenda said. "Now you know the truth, Veronica. Too bad you'll have to die for knowing it. I'll be absolutely devastated when you accidentally fall off the third-floor balcony. I'll tell everyone how I couldn't get in touch with you to tell you of the tour cancellation. And you must have decided to give yourself a tour. How torn apart I will be by my carelessness in leaving the back door unlocked."

I struggled against Vin's vise-like hold. If only I could break free and make a weaving run through the woods to the church parking lot. Of course, screaming my lungs out as I ran while praying Hillary couldn't hit a target zigzagging around the trees.

"So where's the Bradshaw painting? Which one of you has it?"

"I have it," Hillary said.

"It's time," Vin said.

I pulled away from him and was momentarily free from his grasp, until Hillary shouted, "Don't even think about it!" and took a few steps toward me, pointing the gun at my chest. Vin began dragging me toward the parsonage.

Brenda pulled a keychain from her jeans pocket and walked ahead of Vin and me. I twisted and flailed my arms, hoping to wrench myself from Vin's clutches a second time. I would definitely make a run for the woods if I did.

Brenda opened the back door and stepped aside to allow Vin to pull me into the dim, dank kitchen. Hillary followed.

We went along a narrow hall to the front of the house, took a turn, and started up a steep, creaking staircase. Vin maintained his bruising grip on my arm.

"This is a very disappointing tour." I twisted around to give Brenda and Hillary a withering glare. I clenched my hand into a fist and swung my arm with a fervent hope of connecting with Hillary's face, but my forward momentum thanks to Vin's caveman drag spared her dental work.

We turned on the landing and headed up a second staircase to the third floor. "Nobody is going to believe this was an accident. No one will believe the door was unlocked and I just walked in."

"Sure they will," Brenda said. "You have a history of walking into other people's homes, even when the door is locked." As we reached the third floor, she said, "It's the room at the top of the stairs."

Vin kicked open the door and pushed me into a tiny room. A battered desk and chair stood in one corner. A French-paned door led to the balcony of my doom.

"Any last words?" Vin asked me.

"You'll never get away with this."

Brenda shoved me toward the balcony door. "Did you ever play Juliet, Veronica? Too bad there's no Romeo waiting for you below."

Vin tugged on the doorknob. The door must have been warped; it took three pulls before the door gave way.

"After you."

With Hillary pointing the gun at me, Brenda jostled me again and I stumbled over the threshold and onto a small balcony, just wide enough for three people to stand side-by-side.

Another last word came to my mind. "Help!"

Hillary pressed the gun in my back. "Quiet!"

Vin tested the railing. My heart sank as I saw the decaying wood wobble. He turned to me just as Hillary put her hands on my shoulders. Her fingernails dug into my skin. They'd leave a mark; everyone would know my death was not an accident. Small consolation.

"Let's get this over with," Vin said as he wrapped his hand around my wrist. His grip was so tight I thought he would break the bone.

"Yes, let's," a voice behind me said. It wasn't Brenda who spoke; from her I heard a yelp.

I heard a click as Vin's expression changed from smug to

disbelief. His grip on my arm slackened. I used the surprise to pull away from his grasp and turned around.

Julie Norton stood there, one hand gripping Brenda's arm, the other holding a gun trained on Hillary and Vin.

CHAPTER THIRTY-NINE

"Who the hell are you?" Vin asked.

"That's really none of your concern. Put the gun down." Hillary, after a beat, set the gun on the balcony floor. "Now put your hands up."

Hillary and I immediately obeyed her; it took Vin a few seconds more to surrender.

"You can put your hands down, Veronica," Julie said. "Give me that gun."

"Thank you, Julie." I lowered my trembling hands. I picked up the gun and handed it to Julie, who shoved it into her pocket.

Julie shoved Brenda toward the wall, pulled Hillary back into the room, and waved Vin inside, saying, "Hands in the air and face the wall. Get in here, *sir.*"

I stepped aside as Vin slowly followed her command. I glanced at the railing and to the ground below it.

"Thank you," I repeated, hoping I conveyed in those two words my profound gratitude.

"Do you have a cell phone on you?"

"It's outside."

"Go call the police."

I took one look at the three lined up against the wall before rushing down the two flights of stairs, through the house, and out the back door. I stumbled across the yard to where my purse lay on the ground. I grabbed my phone and dialed 911.

When I finished the call, I walked around to the front and

paced across the grass, waiting for the police.

The beautiful sound of wailing sirens finally broke the silence. Two police cruisers soon turned off Parson's Lane and onto the grassy lawn. Tracey and Ron Nicholstone jumped from the lead vehicle.

"They're in a room on the third floor."

Ron led the two male officers who got out of the second car into the house.

"Are you all right?" Tracey asked me.

"Yes. I found the watch's owner." I gave the words some bite. If the police had been more thorough in investigating the evidence, maybe I wouldn't have ended up on that balcony with Vin and Brenda and Hillary and a gun in my back!

"Tell me exactly what happened."

I did as we walked around the house. I emphasized I wasn't snooping; I simply showed up for a Society tour.

"Still. This is becoming a habit for you, Veronica."

"Something doesn't become a habit until it's been done eighteen times," I replied.

"So let's hope you're two cats in one with nine lives each."

"I've always been a dog person."

Tracey sniggered and lifted her gaze to the third floor just as Julie stepped onto the balcony. When I saw she was about to touch the railing, I shouted, "That railing isn't stable!"

Julie waved and yelled down, "Thanks!"

"It's the least I could do!"

Tracey headed into the parsonage as Julie ducked back into the tiny, third-floor room. I paced around in front of the barn for a few minutes until Julie emerged from the house. We met halfway between the house and the barn.

"That was like in the movies." She seemed delighted.

"Not quite," I said. "I haven't been in the movies, but I've been in the soaps and my heart never pounded like this. Though maybe because I'm not much of a method actor."

"If you say so."

"Thank you again, Julie. You saved my life."

"This is probably a good time to tell you my name isn't Julie Norton." I took the hand she extended as she said, "Hi. I'm Kit Harper. I'm a private investigator."

My hand went limp in hers and dropped to my side.

"You're a P.I.?"

Her smile indicated many before me had been surprised by her occupation and that she enjoyed being the source of astonishment.

"Yeah. Theo Kendall hired me to investigate Brenda and Aaron Franklin."

"Because of the money Judge Sorensen left the historical society?"

Kit nodded. "Theo's a friend to Judge Sorensen's family. Months ago he spotted Franklin and Donovan having a cozy dinner at The Sagamore. When Frances Wells decided to challenge her father's will, Theo took it upon himself to gather evidence for her case. So he hired me to tail Ms. Donovan and get photographic proof of the two lovebirds."

"Is that what you slid across the table to Theo Thursday night, at the Mountain Bear? Photos of Aaron and Brenda?" I glanced at the parsonage just as the police led out Hillary, Brenda, and Vin, all in handcuffs.

"No. It was a flash drive. Theo gave me a second assignment last Sunday. He asked me to do background checks on everyone interested in the Bradshaw painting. Ned Fleming, Regina Quinn, even the elderly Griffins. He wanted to know everything about everyone. He wanted me to focus on Isabel Fischer in particular. Theo suspected she was involved with the will fraud. He thought if I could catch her in something, he could use it to get the painting from Scott."

So that was the "help" Dusanka overheard Theo promising Leona. I explained what I thought was going on, emphasizing Claire's supporting part. I wasn't going to look like a fool alone.

Kit laughed. "Now I understand why you followed me after I left the restaurant."

"You know that was me at the restaurant?" I turned and peered into the barn as a surge of embarrassment colored my cheeks. "Sorry. You scared the pants off me when you started following us."

"I first thought you were a P.I. hired by one of the people I've been hired to investigate. When you turned into the outlet parking lot, I figured you were simply lost. I had a source at the DMV run your license plate info anyway. My curiosity was raised when I found out you were a famous actress."

"Not so famous these days."

"And then my curiosity grew when we met at Charlie Gannon's. What are the odds a person who followed me the night before would be at that barn the same moment I was?"

"Small world. Is the painting really for your father?" With a large measure of embarrassment, I told her my theory of what she was going to do with the copy of *Orchard Street.*

"Yes, it really is for my father. Dad won an art prize when he was in grammar school. George Bradshaw presented him with the ribbon. Dad has a photo from the ceremony in a frame with the ribbon. He still talks about that day."

"That's sweet. So what made you come here today?"

"I followed you." She laughed at my dumbfounded silence. "I called Theo after meeting you at Charlie's. I wanted to give him a heads up because I had a feeling you were investigating Scott Culverson's murder. I read about your work on your neighbor's murder case. I thought Theo should know. And then forty-five minutes later he called and told me you had shown up at the Bradshaw House. He wanted me to keep an eye on you. He also wanted to know who Julie Norton is." She paused and let out a snort/laugh. "So I've been trailing you for the last couple of days. I'm sorry I didn't get here earlier. My mother called."

"Always take Mom's call," I said. I'd have to call my mother soon so she didn't hear about my latest misadventure through the Orchard Street grapevine. "I hope Theo is paying you well for all these assignments. You're really good at your job."

"Thank you. I got some great pictures of you and Leona Kendall's housekeeper walking along Orchard."

"You didn't tell Theo—"

"I did."

"Please don't get Dusanka in trouble."

"I won't. I'll delete the photos from my camera. Theo will be relieved this has been resolved. He likes Dusanka, too."

Tracey interrupted our conversation. "We'll need statements from both of you. Veronica, are you up to coming to the station now?"

"I sure am."

"My afternoon is clear." Kit flashed a grin. "I just closed a case."

"Great," Tracey said. "I'll meet you at the station in fifteen minutes."

"So why did you tell Charlie Gannon your name was Julie Norton?" I asked Kit as we walked through the parsonage's side yard.

"In light of the situation with the painting, I used an alias in case he called the cops. Chief Price isn't my biggest fan."

"Mine, neither."

CHAPTER FORTY

"So the woman you saw with Theo Kendall at The Mountain Bear is a private investigator?" Regina asked.

"Yes."

"And she was at the parsonage today?" asked Ella.

"Yes. It's a long story."

"Huh," Madeline said.

"I feel terrible I thought she was going to kill us," Claire said.

We were all gathered in the Griffins' parlor—Mark, Ella, Madeline, Regina, Sandy, Dotsie, Myrtle, Amelia, Don, and Joyce. And Claire, whom I had called from the station to tell her our surveillance days were over. After giving my statement to the police, I met Mark at my house and together we went to the Griffins' to share the news that Regina was finally exonerated.

"And the police have the painting?" Amelia asked.

I nodded. "Yes. One of the officers brought it in just before we left the station. Hillary had it in her home safe."

There was silence for a moment as the Griffins swapped glances.

"I'm sure Scott's parents will make the appropriate choice," Ella said.

"It should be in a museum," Madeline said.

Ella and Amelia nodded in agreement.

"What about the letter Bradshaw wrote to your mother?" Myrtle asked.

"I want to keep the letter," Regina said. "If that's all right with everyone. And if Scott's family okays it. Scott was right; it would be disrespectful to Bradshaw's wife to make it public. More than it already has."

"Olivia Bradshaw was a lovely woman," Madeline said.

"You are right, Regina," Amelia said. "This letter shouldn't be gawked over."

Sandy dashed into the hall at the chime of the doorbell. "I'll get it."

We waited, drinking the wine we had used to toast Regina's innocence, and listening as Sandy greeted the visitor.

Sandy returned to the parlor. "Charlotte Farrell from the *Chronicle* would like to speak with the family."

"We'll sit with her in the dining room. You go ahead," Ella said to Amelia, Don, Joyce, and Regina.

"We'll be there in a moment," Madeline said.

Regina came over and conveyed her gratitude with a breathtaking hug. I looked over her shoulder and spied Joyce, her wet cheeks glistening, beaming with relief.

"Dinner's on me at The Hearth tonight." She flashed a relieved smile and led her parents from the room.

Ella crossed the room to where I stood by the fireplace. "Thank you, Veronica, for what you've done for Regina and our family."

"You're very welcome."

Madeline came behind Ella. "We can't repay you for what you've done."

"I don't expect payment. We're friends."

Madeline beamed as Ella regarded me for a moment. I'm sure I saw a tear in one eye. And then she smiled.

"That's exactly right. We are friends."

She took a step forward and did the unthinkable—she hugged me.

"Thank you," I whispered.

Madeline embraced me. "I know how we can repay you! Piano lessons! You never did master the ivories."

Ella groaned and returned to her grumpy self. "Wait until I get a set of earplugs."

"You don't have to do that, Madeline. *Really.*"

"I want to, dear."

To avoid a back and forth, I said, "You should get to the dining room. The press awaits."

"We're not finished discussing this."

"Oh, yes we are," I mumbled.

"Looks like the tarot-card reader was correct," Dotsie said. "She said you would trust the wrong person. And look, you trusted two people you shouldn't have. I'll have to have Esme back for another reading the next time I host canasta."

"Don't even think about it!" Ella blurted. Dotsie cackled.

Mark put his arm around my shoulder and pulled me close as Ella and Madeline went across the hall.

I looked into his handsome green eyes. "Last night, when they were dirtying it up behind the Dumpster, Brenda called Aaron her stallion. Maybe that's how I should introduce you."

"Would that make you my little pony?"

"I think we're fine just the way we are. Whoever we are."

He kissed me hard on my lips. "I agree. There was a fake, just like on your soap."

"Yes, there was. But instead of Herbert's wine cellar, I almost ended up going over the parson's balcony."

"When does the Greek heiress show up?"

"What do you want with a Greek heiress?"

"I'd like to discuss the centuries of rich Greek history."

"Charlotte would like to talk with you, Veronica." Regina stood in the entry to the parlor. For the first time in days she looked like the carefree young woman she was when she moved to Barton.

I kissed Mark. "We'll talk more about your sudden interest in Greek history later."

EPILOGUE

On the Monday before Thanksgiving, George Bradshaw's *Orchard Street* was placed in its permanent home. Mark and I joined a sizable group at Arden's Daley Gallery and listened as the college's president introduced Scott's parents and his two sisters.

"This is a bittersweet moment," the president said, "for the Culversons and Scott's Arden family. Scott made a wonderful contribution to the college as a student and we proudly watched as his career as an architect soared."

The audience formed a semi-circle around the president, the Culversons, Isabel, and the gallery's curator. *Orchard Street* hung on the wall behind the group, guarded by a red velvet rope. Mark and I stood on the end of one tail of the semicircle, with the entire Griffin family, Jack, Sandy, Dotsie, Myrtle, Jamie, and Charlie Gannon. The Kendalls stood opposite us and were joined by Frances and Bianca. Mingled through the crowd were Sabrina and Rob, Ginnie, and the other women from Leona's luncheon.

"On behalf of the Arden community, Susan and I thank Christopher and Greta for their gracious donation to the Daley Gallery. George Bradshaw's depiction of Barton's Orchard Street beautifully evokes an era of local history. It is a treasure of national significance and we promise to be its faithful caretakers."

As the audience applauded, I studied Leona's expression.

Pinched would be the word for it. Despite her manipulations and entitlement complex, I sympathized with Leona. She was the keeper of her father's legacy and I understood her duty, no matter how obnoxious she was in carrying it out, to protect and preserve his work.

"Without further ado," the curator said, "let us enjoy this newfound masterpiece, *Orchard Street.*"

Mark and I stood back as the audience eagerly stepped toward the painting.

"The best possible outcome," Mark said.

Regina, appearing bashful, approached Isabel, saying a few words and extending her hand in peace. I held my breath as Isabel regarded Regina's gesture and then exhaled with joy when Isabel embraced Regina.

"That picture is even prettier than the painting," I said to Mark.

Arden's president came over, greeted me, and asked Mark for a quick word.

"Back in a moment," he said. He stepped away to confer with the president.

I observed the crowd for a moment, enjoying their excitement over the painting's unveiling. A gentle touch on my shoulder brought me eye-to-tear-filled-eye with Isabel. She threw her arms around me.

"I'm moving to Manhattan! I got a job in the legal department of Habacker Publishing."

"Congratulations. A fresh start. You deserve it, Isabel."

"Thank you, Veronica. I'm sorry for all the trouble my colleague put you through."

"That's an understatement. But I'm fine now."

Isabel gave me another hug and went off to join her parents. I stood alone for a few minutes, until I spotted Kit weaving her way toward me. I gave her a cheerful wave.

"Hello, Veronica," she said. Kit wore the black outfit she had on at The Mountain Bear.

"Kit, I'm glad you're here. It's appropriate. You played an important role in the painting's recovery."

"I'm glad it all worked out." We silently observed the gathering for a moment. "I noticed you standing with that handsome man over there. You're a good-looking couple," Kit said, nodding toward Mark.

The remark caught me off guard, but when one receives such a compliment, recovery is quick.

"Thanks."

"How long have you been together?"

"Four months."

"Really? You look like you've been together much longer."

"There's a look for that?"

Kit grinned. "Yeah. You just fit."

The warm spot I had in my heart for Kit grew to Grand Canyon-esque size.

Mark returned and I made the introductions, simply using their job titles. Mark gave me the sly grin he had been giving me for months over our joint identity crisis.

I laughed and said, "No reason to state the obvious."

ABOUT THE AUTHOR

Jeanne Quigley grew up reading mysteries, watching soap operas, and vacationing in the Adirondacks. These interests inspired *All Things Murder*, Jeanne's well-received debut cozy mystery. Her love of characters—real and fictional—led Jeanne to study Sociology and English at the University of Notre Dame. She has worked in the music industry and for an education publisher. Jeanne resides in Rockland County, New York, and is a member of the Sisters in Crime.